CW01391078

REVENGE
FROM THE
INSIDE

RICHARD C
MORGAN

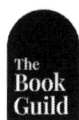

The
Book
Guild

First published in Great Britain in 2025 by
The Book Guild Ltd
Unit E2 Airfield Business Park,
Harrison Road, Market Harborough,
Leicestershire. LE16 7UL
Tel: 0116 2792299
www.bookguild.co.uk
Email: info@bookguild.co.uk
X: @bookguild

The manufacturer's authorised representative in the EU
for product safety is Authorised Rep Compliance Ltd,
71 Lower Baggot Street, Dublin D02 P593 Ireland (www.arccompliance.com)

This work is entirely fictitious and bears no resemblance to any persons living or dead.

Typeset in 11pt Minion Pro

Printed and bound in Great Britain by CMP UK

ISBN 978 1835742 136

British Library Cataloguing in Publication Data.
A catalogue record for this book is available from the British Library.

For Dave, never forgotten.

ONE

1997

At 7:45am on 23rd September, the international press gathered outside the impressive medieval court building of the Old Bailey, between Holborn Circus and St Paul's Cathedral, in chaotic Central London. Passers-by on their way to work stopped to catch a glimpse of the scene as the sun speckled brilliantly on the passing cars; the weather was much cooler than in recent weeks, as the summer of 1997 was finally ending. For hundreds of years, the Old Bailey has dealt with the UK's most shocking crimes, often becoming the centre of attention for the press eagerly awaiting the outcomes of major trials. The last four weeks had been no different for this historic landmark.

The Central Criminal Court had become the focal point for journalists, news reporters, and cameramen and women reporting every twist and turn in the murder trial of Charlotte Louise Reade, who was brutally stabbed to death in her home at the age of thirty-three. A schoolteacher since graduating, Charlotte grew up in a small Welsh village on the outskirts of Cardiff. As an only child, she tragically lost both parents in a car crash at a young age and was raised by her grandmother Linda, who had succumbed to cancer several years ago. Fiercely independent, Charlotte had a large group of friends and lived as a loving wife to her husband Patrick and mother to her only child Jacob.

The media frenzy surrounding this case was built on seemingly clear facts, as the prosecution argued. Charlotte had been stabbed twelve times in a frenzied attack in the small kitchen of her London home with a ten-inch knife previously used to prepare dinner. She was found clothed, lying on her back with her legs crumpled to the right and her long, light-brown hair strewn across her face, partially hiding her gentle features. But the scene was far from gentle; she was surrounded by a large pool of blood, which the coroner's office calculated had seeped from her body in less than ten minutes due to her horrendous neck wounds, taking her life with it. Many signs of a struggle and severe lacerations on both arms indicated she had fought a valiant, yet clearly one-sided, battle for survival against the razor-sharp knife lying just inches from her lifeless body.

The prosecution portrayed Charlotte's carefree existence, making this atrocious crime difficult to piece together in the eyes of her friends, colleagues, and the twelve jurors. The jury, composed of eight men and four women from a mixed demographic, was frequently left in shock upon hearing each gruesome detail.

Signs of a violent scuffle were evident, with many smashed items scattered across the light-brown laminate kitchen flooring, a damaged cupboard door hanging by one hinge, and the round kitchen table overturned with the remains of a glass fruit bowl shattered nearby. Three untouched plastic shopping bags near the front door indicated that Charlotte had just returned from shopping when she was attacked.

However, not everything was as it seemed. There were no signs of forced entry, leaving the jury to ponder whether Charlotte knew the killer and willingly let them in, or if the attacker had slipped in through the open door as she unloaded her shopping from the car parked out front.

The prosecution repeatedly emphasised the lack of forced entry, which led them to believe the killer was someone Charlotte knew, putting her husband Patrick, the only other keyholder, at a disadvantage. The prosecution revealed that the murder weapon held Patrick's fingerprints, their main focus during the trial. Clear prints, mostly in Charlotte's blood, were found on the knife, along with his blood-covered shirt, which he claimed resulted from his desperate attempt to resuscitate her upon finding her already dying. Despite his claims of innocence, Patrick sensed his already shattered life slipping further into misery.

Patrick explained that upon finding Charlotte's body, he removed the blade from her shoulder while desperately trying to stem the bleeding from two main wounds, one in her groin and the other in her neck. Under later questioning, he admitted he couldn't remember how his shirt had ripped but insisted it was intact when he entered the house. On the evening of 16th February, 1997, Patrick called the police himself. The tape played in court on the fourth day of the trial revealed his desperate plea for an ambulance and police, with two-year-old Jacob crying hysterically in the background. The tape's haunting playback left jurors and reporters squirming in their seats, some reduced to tears, including Patrick, who sat slumped in his chair, shaking, and rubbing the back of his neck vigorously.

When police arrived, Patrick was covered in Charlotte's blood, along with the phone he had used and the back of Jacob's T-shirt and trousers, which he explained was due to moving Jacob to another room to watch television, away from the destruction in the kitchen. One of the first officers on the scene, just twenty-three years old, later took a leave of absence to reconsider his future, opting for police counselling. A police spokesman described the home as "one of the grisliest crime scenes they had seen in years", made even more disturbing by the presence of a young child, although kept far from the shocking sights in the kitchen. Upon the police's arrival, Patrick immediately claimed he hadn't been home during the murder and had returned with Jacob to discover his wife's tangled remains.

Patrick's sobbing was so intense that it made his nose run into his mouth, causing him to spit while talking to the police, who tried to get him to sit down and keep still as he paced around the house, throwing his hands over his head in absolute despair. The police took five days to process the crime scene after removing the body, which lay in situ late into the night, covered by a white sheet occasionally lifted as new forensic teams arrived. Day after day, they took sketches, photographs, fingerprints, measurements, and tested every speck of blood, which was all Charlotte's. They collected every item of clothing from the crime scene, including those worn by Patrick and Jacob, as well as a full laundry basket from the master bedroom. All knives were removed from the drawers, bank statements from the kitchen windowsill, and the phone book on the hall table.

Every window and door of the house was sealed with yellow police tape, and a large white tent covered the front door to provide privacy from neighbours and the gathering press as six forensic technicians worked tirelessly to gather evidence. Every square inch of the house, garden, and both cars was scoured hour after hour, day after day, looking for any shred of evidence to lead them to another suspect or help convict their prime suspect.

As more police and forensic experts flooded the house, taking extensive notes, they took care not to disturb Charlotte's body before she was eventually moved to the mortuary, where a forensic pathologist would conduct an autopsy. One forensic expert commented on how light she was, as they lifted her onto the gurney. Another expert, holding her legs at the ankle, stated she never stood a chance, regardless of her attacker's physical size or gender. Before allowing Patrick and Jacob to leave the scene, they were photographed extensively before being taken away in separate cars to a nearby police station.

Later, distressing photographs shown in court revealed blood splatters from the hallway into the kitchen, with what appeared to be streaks, or maybe even handprints, of yet more blood on the walls. Patrick was photographed with a bright light shining in his face, covered in blood, and there was a harrowing picture of little Jacob watching television in the sitting room, his back to the camera. Patrick was questioned about his whereabouts during the attack and subjected to a range of personal and detailed questions as detectives probed for more information, seemingly convinced this was a case of domestic violence.

"Had Charlotte been acting differently in the weeks leading up to her murder?"

"No," Patrick replied.

"Did Charlotte have any enemies who would want her dead?"

"No, don't be ridiculous," he snapped.

"Had there been any arguments prior to her death?"

"No."

"With friends, work colleagues, neighbours?"

"No," Patrick shouted, before staring at the floor between his legs.

"Between you or anyone else?"

"No, I told you no." Patrick exhaled, shuffling uncomfortably in his cold court seat.

"Were there any money worries in the household?"

"Nothing we couldn't cope with."

"How was your sex life?"

"Normal."

"Had there been any suspicious behaviour, like telephone calls in the middle of the night or people hanging up on answering?"

"No, don't be so stupid." Patrick gasped under his breath, continuing to not make eye contact.

The questions were relentless and repetitive. After each ninety-minute session, the police, convinced they had their man, would break for fifteen minutes to give Patrick time to rest before resuming the onslaught. During each break, they reviewed his answers, searching for inconsistencies or clues to his guilt, but nothing stood out. As the time edged closer to charge or release him, the police, with no other evidence or active lines of inquiry, pressed ahead and charged Patrick with the murder of his wife.

Little Jacob, with his mop of near-white hair and round green eyes, was cared for by close friends and neighbours Greg and Isabelle DeWitt, after spending two days being checked over by police doctors and specially trained psychiatrists. Chosen by Patrick as the most suitable guardians, the surroundings of their home next door were familiar and wouldn't be upsetting to such a small child who wouldn't recall what had gone on in his family home. Jacob played almost daily with their son Matthew after school, so this was the perfect temporary home for him while Patrick tried to clear his name.

Patrick endured the indignity of a physical examination by three male forensic doctors, one of whom only took notes, and he remained in custody without bail for nearly seven months while the Crown Prosecution Service built their case against him. Throughout this time, Patrick continually pleaded his innocence to his legal team, shedding a lifetime of tears for his wife, whom he claimed to love so deeply. At six feet one inch tall, he was elegant and slim, some would say well built, and always prided himself on his tailored look, from his polished shoes to his neatly combed dark-brown hair.

During his torturous wait for trial, Patrick was kept on near-constant suicide watch and ate very little, struggling to come to terms with what had happened, and being persistently denied a visit from his son drove him into deep despair. He hardly spoke unless spoken to and was only visited on a handful of occasions by a few close people, including his estranged brother Lucas, who made the long journey back from New Zealand for the first time in nine years at the insistence of his wife Anna. His closest friend was Greg DeWitt, who was allowed brief visits to discuss Jacob's well-being and details of how the trial was likely to play out. Jacob, at two and a half, was oblivious to the events, except for the occasional call for Mummy and Daddy. The only other visitor during this time was his defence lawyer Marcus Leybourne, who desperately tried to piece together a plausible case to keep Patrick out of a life sentence.

Marcus oversaw a conversation between Patrick and Greg, where they agreed that, with no family in the UK, he and Isabelle would adopt Jacob if Patrick was convicted. Both men agreed that Jacob needed stability and long-term care, and without any plausible alibi and incriminating himself by touching the knife, the evidence against Patrick certainly suggested it was strong enough to lead to a conviction.

"If I were on the jury, I would be sending me to jail for a long time," Patrick said in a woeful demonstration of self-pity, tears rolling down his pale face during his first meeting with Greg. They clutched hands across the cold prison service table as Greg desperately tried to reassure and comfort his friend.

Greg helped Patrick with the mortgage payments to prevent him from losing the house while he pursued a sale, and it was agreed that any remaining monies would be put into a trust fund for when Jacob was twenty-one. He did everything a good friend would do in such times, always claiming he believed Patrick to be innocent, which provided little solace. Patrick assured Greg he didn't kill Charlotte, believing he was driving through traffic back home during the attack. However, his defence lawyer prepared him for the worst, which both men struggled to accept.

Patrick's once impeccable grooming had deserted him: his hair was dank and longer than he had ever kept it in his life, and his shaving skills seemed to be that of a teenager, patchy at best. Day after day, his lawyer Marcus questioned him for a plausible set of events, something to build a defence on, while the police pressed him hard for a confession. After six weeks of hell, as Patrick called it, his unkempt hair mixed with grey locks made an unsightly mat atop his head, suiting his blood-red eyes and dark bags. He had lost over twenty pounds, as light, if not lighter, than he was at seventeen. His appearance grew less pleasant by the day.

Patrick knew the prosecution was building him up as a murderer, keeping him constantly on edge. *How can this be happening?* he continually asked himself. He felt his freedom slipping away like water from his twice-weekly shower, and the thought of playing with little Jacob in the park seemed a million miles away. His moods shifted daily from relentless sobbing to uncontrollable anger, back to a defeatism that made his stomach feel like it had shrunk to the size of a pea. Considering a long prison sentence, the anxiety felt forced down his throat as he tossed and turned on his uncomfortable bed every night, crying himself into a light sleep. He longed to wake from this nightmare, for Charlotte to be alive, for Jacob to be in his arms and for life to be normal, but this was just the beginning of a long, wretched journey.

Patrick wasn't permitted to attend Charlotte's funeral, nor was he welcome, compounding his pain and leading him to shut himself off from everything and everyone around him while the suicide watch checks intensified. The guards wouldn't allow him an escape from this terrifying life.

He often thought about Jacob's confusion, suddenly losing both parents and thrust into a new life with a new family. In those early days of prison, it would have been easy to end his misery, but he never seriously contemplated suicide for one reason: his son, whom he absolutely adored.

TWO

With no signs of a break-in, no footprints, and no witnesses on either side, the prosecution team expected a quick trial. Yet, almost four weeks later, commentators continued to speculate why the trial had dragged on, despite the seemingly obvious outcome.

"Reade was there: his fingerprints on the knife, his shirt covered in blood, and no sightings of anyone else in the vicinity on the day of the murder. What more forensic evidence was needed?" reported one daily news bulletin on BBC World News.

The only notable delay came when a juror, Mrs Judith White, aged sixty-seven, almost fainted upon seeing the first pictures of Charlotte's body lying on the kitchen floor. Despite this, the trial proceeded at a steady pace. There was ample evidence, but without a confession from Patrick, the case was more complex than it could have been.

During the trial, Patrick pleaded his innocence repeatedly but struggled to answer a series of questions about his lack of an alibi posed by the prosecution's main litigator, Mr Oscar Tait.

"If you didn't kill Charlotte, how did the killer gain entry to your house?"

"If you didn't kill her, why were your fingerprints all over the knife, and why was your shirt ripped and covered in Charlotte's blood?"

"Why were you covered in her blood?" was asked about ten times in quick succession.

Each time, Patrick responded, "I told you; I was trying to save her."

"But this doesn't explain the rip in your shirt, which you openly admitted was not there the morning of the murder," the prosecutor retorted gleefully.

The questions boomed through the courtroom. Although Patrick had plausible answers, they were obvious ones. The jury and the packed gallery were not convinced by his mumbled responses, nor by the hours of police interview tapes in which he repeatedly expressed his love for his wife and his deep regret at picking up the knife in shock.

Patrick wished Jacob was older and could tell the police the truth about the drive home and his parents not being involved in such violence but on the other hand took some comfort in knowing Jacob was too young to remember or understand what had happened on that fateful day.

On the final day of the trial, most of the press were kept outside the courthouse, jostling for position, while those permitted into the Grand Hall made their way through the main entrance past the baying press photographers, news station reporters, and a smattering of the public seeking scandal.

Patrick's journey to the courthouse was the same every day, taking an average of twenty-three minutes from his holding cell at Brick Lane station to the back of the Old Bailey. Prisoners on remand would usually be held together, but with this being such a high-profile case, it was deemed best to keep him alone and close to the courthouse. At 8:44am, the police van, with blacked-out windows preventing the press from getting a shot, sped down the lane behind the Old Bailey, stopping sharply at the back entrance.

The tall, grey, historical building, a site of countless dramatic trials, fizzed with anticipation as Patrick arrived for the last time, the jury having reached a decision the previous night. Before leaving the van, he insisted on a navy-blue blanket over his head as the guards marched him into the building. A proud man who maintained his innocence, he didn't want a single picture hitting the press during the worst time of his life.

"So, this is it," one of the guards commented, handing Patrick a black coffee from a nearby vending machine, trying to show some compassion.

Patrick remained motionless and sat in the corner of the holding cell, hands cuffed in front of him, clutching the coffee. He looked pale and withdrawn, his eyes red from sleepless nights. His blotchy skin and unkempt hair made him look like a man who had given up on life as he contemplated the worst possible outcome.

The same poor coffee, the same wretched-smelling

cell, and the same dreadfully long wait had been his life for over sixteen days of interrogation. He just wanted to get it over with and move on, whatever the future held. Passionately maintaining his innocence hadn't convinced anyone, and even his defence team tried to persuade him to give a different plea to reduce his seemingly inevitable sentence, which he refused.

He walked into the courtroom to a chorus of boos and cries from the public, packed tight with some of Charlotte's closest friends, who had attended the entire trial. Everyone stood as Judge Ronald Lewis QC entered the Grand Hall, before shuffling back into their seats, ready for the drama to unfold.

"Patrick James Reade, please stand," said the court announcer.

Patrick, assisted by Marcus from his defence team, stood up. He could hear his heart pounding and felt his clammy fists clench as his fate was dealt in one cold breath.

"We, the jury, find the defendant Patrick James Reade guilty of first-degree murder," the male representative for the juror stated loudly, looking directly at Patrick as he read the verdict.

Patrick's chin fell to his chest, his head spinning as he was helped to stay on his feet. "Shit." He exhaled loudly.

His body oozed cold sweat, flinching, and tingling with numbness as his knees gave way, prompting him to collapse into the chair. The courtroom erupted with shouts from the packed gallery.

"Evil son of a bitch!" someone shouted from the back of the court.

"Silence in court!" the judge ordered, smashing the gavel as he prepared to address the room.

"Mr Reade, you have been found guilty of the murder of Charlotte Louise Reade and have wasted enough of the court's time, so you will be sentenced immediately."

Everyone held their breath at this unusual turn of events. The court was silent as the judge considered the verdict. Within minutes, the hall went crazy as the judge bellowed, "It is fixed by law, life, with a minimum of eighteen years in jail."

"Life should mean life!" one spectator screamed in disgust.

"Rot in hell, you bastard!" came another from the gallery near to where Charlotte's closest friends and colleagues supported each other with tissues and hugs in the front rows, within touching distance of the now guilty Patrick.

Confusion ensued as Patrick found himself pushed through the narrow, brightly lit back corridors to the detention centre behind the courthouse, ready for processing. His soul destroyed, he could no longer muster a single word or tear as his lawyer spoke about appeals and retrials, none of which sank into his numb brain.

"Patrick, listen to me," Marcus implored, crouched on his knees in front of him, "I've seen this judge sentence someone immediately on a couple of occasions, and we managed to get a retrial; keep the faith."

"Faith means nothing to me anymore. What the hell is going on? Nobody understands how much I loved Charlotte," Patrick replied, placing his hand on Marcus' right shoulder.

"This was never going to be an easy trial, but I will work on an appeal straight away," he assured Patrick.

Awaiting the transfer to jail, Patrick felt more scared and lonelier than ever. Convicted as a killer without so much as a parking ticket before Charlotte's death, he retched in the corner of the holding cell, his whole body shivering. The apprehension of his impending trip and the sheer distress of his life crashing to a halt took a steely grip on his stomach like something he had never felt before.

Unfortunately for Patrick, that feeling would last for several days, and he wouldn't have to wait much longer for the next chapter of his life to begin as the secure prison van backed through the twelve-feet-high gates at the back of the court.

THREE

Pentonville Prison in Islington, North London, was the first modern prison of its kind when it opened in 1816, initially intended to house 860 prisoners. It would soon become home for Patrick, along with over twelve hundred other inmates – a thought that had often filled him with dread. The prison was overpopulated, notorious for its crackdown on drugs, both dealing and using, and continually looking for ways of increasing the number of physical activities available to prisoners in a bid to reduce violence caused by stress, restlessness, and frustration. Patrick would eventually come to appreciate every second of activity outside his cell once he became less anxious about the company he was forced to keep.

Pentonville was known for its overcrowding, giving it a more threatening and intimidating feel than some smaller prisons. This made Patrick and other less hardened inmates feel sick with nerves during their first few months. Fighting, rape, attempted suicide, and mental breakdowns were frequent, and many who knew Patrick, as well as Patrick himself, wondered how he would last a week, let alone the next eighteen years.

On arrival, Patrick was taken to a cold holding room with a tatty metal desk and chair in the centre, holding a series of official transfer forms from the police transportation team to Her Majesty's Prison Service. He stood in front of the desk, staring blankly at the prison officer taking his photo before being handed his prison uniform: two pairs of grey trousers, four grey shirts, and two grey sweatshirts, all stamped with the letters HMP to brand each inmate.

"Patrick James Reade, date of birth 28th January 1958, age thirty-nine, sentence eighteen years minimum for the murder of your wife," barked the overweight prison guard, followed by a long, sarcastic whistle. "Looks like you'll be here for a long time, eh?" he mused.

Patrick declined to join in the chit-chat and just stared at the cracking light-blue paint on the wall behind the cumbersome frame in front of him.

"Patrick James Reade?" The guard's voice snapped him back to reality. Patrick looked straight at the warden, unsure of the protocol. "Say yes, Reade," the guard continued.

"Yes," Patrick muttered.

"Killing your wife, eh?" The guard's tone was mocking.

Patrick thought about pleading his innocence, but he was too tired and saw little point in wasting his breath on a lowly prison officer who couldn't change his wrongful life sentence. He remained quiet.

"You are no longer Pat, Patrick, or Mr Reade; you are inmate HMP046782. Got that?"

"Yes," Patrick said again.

"These are your cell basics; if you lose them or abuse them, you will go without. Sign here."

He looked down at the white printed page titled "Pentonville Prison – Her Majesty's Service". The list read:

Two white sheets
One white pillow
One blue blanket
One blue toothbrush
One white towel
One white flannel

The list continued with the clothes he had just received.

He signed in silence on the inmate line and collected his new belongings from the edge of the cold metal table before being shoved through the open gate at the far end of the room into a white-walled corridor. Carrying his large array of prison wear, he entered the long labyrinth of brightly light corridors and locked doors for the first time. There was no fresh air to flush out the stench of body odour and cleaning fluids hanging in the stale air. The slightest noise echoed far into the distance, and Patrick noticed the lack of windows everywhere immediately. He stopped at every locked gate, waiting for the guard to open it, worrying about how he would be able to sleep in these noisy conditions when he barely slept a full six hours cuddled up to Charlotte in the warm comfort of his own bedroom.

The harsh reality of prison life smacked him full in the face as he walked into the first corridor lined with cells to the sounds of inmates wolf-whistling in his direction. Arguing with each other, hurling abuse in no particular direction, they tried to intimidate the new blood, each hardened criminal attempting to climb the social ladder in this dangerous, caged environment.

"You're gonna love your new buddy, Reade, a really nasty piece of work," the guard taunted as he dragged Patrick down the white steel corridor to the last cell on the right. "C seventy-four, home sweet home," the guard said.

Patrick hesitated for a second before walking through the now open cell door. As the door slammed closed behind him, he noticed his new cellmate, Terry Race, lying motionless on the bottom bunk, facing the cold, stone wall. The cell was a standard eight feet long, and six feet wide, all painted top to bottom in dull white on cold stone walls. There was a small light bulb in the centre of the ceiling and a two-feet square window at five feet high along the back wall, naturally covered in steel bars. The view from the tiny portal was hardly glamorous: a large shopping centre strewn with cardboard boxes, pallets, and a couple of inactive delivery trucks below a grey sky.

Patrick fell to his knees next to the stainless-steel sink, tears flowing, his spirit finally broken for good. A rusty metal-framed bunk bed and a single shelf next to his bed for his pitiful handful of treasured possessions, including a picture of Charlotte and Jacob, was all his life had become. Through the trauma of his first night, Patrick thought of nothing but his late wife and little Jacob, whose future was now uncertain.

The privileged life he had led seemed a million miles away as he remembered the days of jumping into his car, flicking on his favourite Pearl Jam album, and driving to the coast with Charlotte without a care in the world. Smiles and laughter were a thing of the past. He had taken for granted those cozy nights in, watching television and sharing a bottle of wine, cooking dinner for Charlotte, or popping into the local pub after work to catch up with friends. Now it seemed like none of it had ever happened.

That first night he didn't utter a single word; nor did his new roommate. Every noise, cry, shout, and scream echoed through the hallways. He cried harder that night than he ever had before. Prison life was horrifying at the best of times, even for the most hardened criminals. Group showers, occasional bust-ups, rivals taunting each other, bland food, and minimal exercise contributed to many men becoming frail and anxious, even if they never showed it. Patrick, a softly spoken, well-dressed architect from the suburbs, still looked out of place in his prison-issue uniform, surrounded by the plethora of shaved heads and tattoos that filled the canteen on his first morning. His worst nightmare was now reality as he cowered at the slightest glance or unexpected crash of plates in the noisy kitchen, never looking up once.

He was scared – scared of not knowing what would happen; having no control over his life anymore filled him with fear. Scared of crossing the wrong kind and being beaten up or worse. His only positive thoughts were firmly focused on Jacob, a successful retrial, and getting out of the hellhole that surrounded him. Patrick spoke very little during his first few weeks, no more than thirty words a day, as he went completely unnoticed. His first month of incarceration passed without any incident. He did, however, complain about the variety and standard of food on offer, only to be laughed away by two prison officers, which he found very humiliating. And as the first few months ticked by, he gained a little weight from sitting around for long periods of the day. The stress of the trial started to dissipate, and he looked better for it, too, as his cheeks filled out, masking the now permanent grey lines marking his still youthful face.

He spent most of his time hiding away in his cell, reading whatever books were available from the prison library. Fiction, non-fiction, and a copy of the Bible was always available – he even read a DIY book on joinery out of sheer boredom. He shunned social gatherings like football matches in the yard, card games, and dice, but he did enjoy the brief hour each day when he could jog wide laps of the yard for exercise, talking to nobody.

The only other real conversation Patrick had was during planned visits from Marcus Leybourne, his solicitor, which he always looked forward to. Marcus gave him periodic updates on the timing of a retrial and on little Jacob, who now needed a more permanent home due to the sentencing.

Patrick and Charlotte had no close family, other than Lucas in New Zealand, who was unwilling to take Jacob. So, as agreed, Patrick chose Greg and Isabelle DeWitt to be named legal guardians of Jacob on a permanent basis. Patrick trusted them, having first met them when they moved in next to them over seven years ago. Greg worked at a bank, and Isabelle was busy launching her own interior design company, which was becoming increasingly popular in some of the affluent areas of London.

This offered Jacob a stable background, which Patrick took solace from, hoping Jacob would enjoy living with them rather than with complete strangers. The DeWitts had a four-year-old son, Matthew, who played well with Jacob now that he was old enough to start running around.

Marcus brought in the legal adoption paperwork for Patrick to sign. "Are you sure about this?" he asked.

"What choice do I have?" he asked as Marcus nodded back at him.

Although it all seemed very permanent and reminded him how long his sentence was, he really had little choice. Greg and Isabelle were kind enough to take Jacob into their family, and it was either that or social services. Patrick made sure that Marcus had an addendum in the paperwork, which the DeWitt's agreed to, that stated if he was released following a successful retrial, his son would be returned to him, and the adoption would be legally terminated if this happened while Jacob was under the age of eighteen.

The DeWitts had only ever been nice to Patrick and his family, and nobody wanted to see Jacob go into social care. Patrick pointed out that Isabelle and Greg might become overly attached to Jacob and find it hard to give him up in eighteen months if his retrial was successful, so he ensured the release clauses were watertight.

"What are you going to do with your time in here, Pat?" Greg asked at the final meeting to sign off the papers.

"Clear my name for starters, and if I have any spare time, I might take a law course. They have a shabby library, but they do offer the occasional educational course, which might take my mind off things. I will need to keep my brain active, or I will go nuts." After going through the fine print and confirming several points with Patrick, they both signed and dated four copies in the presence of Marcus in the hope this would give Jacob some consistency in his young life.

The first three months went by quickly; Patrick made one friend whom he had handpicked as looking less harmful in the shape of fraudster Bruce Taylor. A sixty-two-year-old man originally from Cape Town, Bruce was serving six years for selling dodgy passports to Africans and Eastern Europeans, trying to gain access to the UK. He was a creative guy who had made the silly mistake of getting caught handing over an envelope stuffed full of passports to a Nigerian man outside Heathrow's Terminal Two, right in front of an unmarked police car. He had been doing it for so many years that he became blasé, almost forgetting that what he was doing was illegal and used by terrorists, drug mules, people traffickers, and other unsavoury characters.

On one of Marcus' final visits in the first few months, he delivered three copies of the adoption papers, which Patrick felt compelled to sign.

It might take the next eighteen years, but one day, Patrick would realise that signing those adoption papers was one of the biggest mistakes of his life.

FOUR

Three years earlier
1994

The First Bank of London opened for business in 1789 and is known as one of the most prestigious and oldest banks in Europe. Arthur Thomas Yates from the south of England started the bank after making a substantial amount of money on a land deal and began lending money to his neighbours, small local businesses, and friends. Over the years, this enterprise slowly took shape as The First Bank of London, and it is attributed with helping supply funding for modern housing in the mid-1800s, most of which still stands today.

Arthur Yates later took up residence in Kensington, near the famous Jacobean mansion Kensington Palace, before passing away in 1818 at the age of sixty-one. After his death, the bank continued to grow, becoming one of the world's most respected financial institutions. Financial experts attribute its success partly to its continued owner control by the Yates family.

However, as generations passed, things changed. By the mid-1980s, the latest Yates generation had little to no involvement in the day-to-day running of the business, which was now managed by a designated board of directors. The current and previous generations of the Yates family were more interested in spending money rather than making it, often distracted by the latest playthings their substantial allowances from the bank could provide. They had less interest in pinstripe suits, the *Financial Times*, annual general meetings, business lunches, and board meetings and more interest in private jets, yachts, fast cars, and holiday villas. The biggest waste of money was designing a golf course in Port d'Andratx, Majorca and throwing countless "look how wealthy we are" ultra-exclusive parties.

As a result of some bad publicity for the family over the last twenty-five years, the bank had suffered from losing some key high-profile commercial accounts to more mainstream high street banks, as the bank's good name had become somewhat tarnished. In part, this was due to scandals involving wrecked cars, drugs, infidelity, and unpaid hotel bills across the globe. General rich family obnoxiousness followed them around on a regular basis. There were some high-profile losses due to corporate mergers and a few blue-chip companies deciding to go in a different direction and distance themselves from the scandal. Some of their longest-standing customers were no longer doing business with The First Bank of London.

As a handful of billion-pound companies no longer wished to be seen banking with such an unprofessional bank, blaming dwindling, out-of-date services that hadn't moved with the times, profits started to fall, much to the frustration of the board of directors. Every time they lost a highly profitable account, it lessened their opportunities for international travel, which usually involved lots of playing golf at some of the finest courses on the planet and boozy long lunches, all done in the name of "entertaining".

As many major commercial banking contracts were lost, the personal bank account business was thriving, mainly due to good interest rates and the pompousness of banking at such an old and prestigious bank. Even if it had a somewhat seedy undertone, it was seen as a sign of wealth and almost fashionable to bank with rather than the usual top four UK banks.

There remained a certain level of kudos associated with an invitation to bank at this organisation. Wealth was the key criterion, so when you flash a First Bank card, doors open; reservations are made; and airline tickets are frequently upgraded. Most importantly, for some of their customers, it was a polite way of telling everyone you had an annual income of more than one hundred thousand pounds a year, a lot of money now and worth even more when the bank was at its height of popularity.

The board of directors were very much old-school bankers in their three-piece pinstriped suits, handkerchiefs to match their ties, white moustaches, fine cigars, gentlemen's clubs, chauffeur-driven German cars, homes in expensive parts of London, and, for some, several rounds of golf a week at the best courses in the UK. At the top of this very wealthy pile sat the chairman, Michael Lansbury, aged sixty-two. Pristinely dressed always, carrying the *Financial Times* without fail, and driven around in a black Mercedes S-Class, a necessity.

Around the bank, Mr Lansbury kept a low profile, spending most of his afternoons watching the stock exchange monitors from his more-than-adequate corner office while drinking Earl Grey from the finest tea set. He contributed little these days to the day-to-day running of the bank as his forty-year, fourteen-hour-day career had started to catch up with him. However, he was held in very high regard by most of the team below him as the man who had achieved so much throughout his life, trying to keep the highest profile accounts on board.

Some business journalists, and even some of his colleagues, often pondered why he was still in power and not off enjoying the Mediterranean sun with his attractive pension and far less attractive wife.

Occasionally, he would invite one of the senior members of the management team out for lunch or a round of golf, but most were too busy, opting instead to socialise with each other or their younger key customers in a bid to generate more business deposits for the bank to play with.

The bank had substantial assets in the billions, zero debts, and coffers oozing with cash reserves built up over decades of successful banking that most financial organisations would likely never achieve. They made substantial profits from mortgages, personal loans, interbank lending, and foreign exchange transactions for major corporations across the globe. A single transaction commission of just 0.5% could keep some Third World countries in food and water for months.

The bank was considered by many financial experts to be one of only five institutions worldwide with such elevated levels of liquidity that they could afford for 65% of their customers to withdraw all of their cash at the same time and still be able to trade quite comfortably. A statement that was never repeated the following year after the major jolt to reality when another famous bank collapsed into liquidation, taking with it their two-hundred-year history.

In September 1991, £257 million lay in dormant bank accounts at The First Bank, and by the end of 1992, this slush fund would have swollen further due to the bank's attractive interest rates offered to its wealthy clientele.

Dormant bank accounts included both personal and commercial bank accounts that hadn't been touched for years. The owner may have stashed money for the future or for emergency purposes, gained the money illegally, or simply forgotten about the funds from fifty years ago. Less scrupulous banks denied their presence even existed and some employed heir hunters to track down the rightful owner. Still, every bank across the globe, no matter how big or small, holds a dormant bank account list, and The First Bank had more than most due to their elite clientele often coming from old money.

Being one of the largest banks in Europe, The First Bank had several million opened accounts but considered many of them to be "dormant" after more than five years of inactivity.

Some of these dormant accounts were opened over sixty years ago and created the slush funds that most people never knew existed but were the playthings of the bank directors that topped up the swollen bank accounts and helped them afford the luxury lifestyles they lived. The slush fund accounts were the main source of illegal gain for many ageing directors, as these would ooze with millions of half-penny transactions that were no good to anyone since they were demonetised by The Royal Mint back in 1984. Most directors didn't see this as white-collar crime but simply just perks of the job.

Half-penny transactions in today's economy were worth nothing, but nearly every financial transaction processed by the bank generated the odd quarter and half-penny here and there due to the complex calculations of exchange rates, stock trades, interest calculations, and dealer commissions taking 0.25% here and there.

Daily, there were several hundred thousand fractions of a penny that soon gathered pace and fell into various top-secret slush funds the directors referred to as PAN accounts behind closed doors. PAN was the secret name derived from the old days when people across the globe would pan for gold on their hands and knees in rivers and streams in the hope of getting rich.

While the directors would never be seen dead on their hands and knees panning for gold, they were all over these riches. The number of transactions automatically completed by the impressive bank software systems would frequently generate more than twenty thousand pounds per day in loose change. Aside from the standard lines of profit, such as interest from mortgages or loans and the day-to-day bank fees charged to their corporate customers.

Often, the commissions gained from these transactions were exceeded by the enormous funds amassed from odd pennies that couldn't be credited back to individual bank accounts. In many cases, the fund was fattened further by the rate of stock or currency exchange rate changing by 0.02% as the international transactions were executed with perfect timing to favour the bank further while the customer was blissfully unaware of the siphoning off going on under their noses. Rounding down was very much the policy.

As part of the annual payment of bonuses to the board of directors, some of this money was spread around the five most high-ranking directors and the chief executive, Charles Faulk, who, at the age of fifty-six, surely didn't need any more money and creamed the biggest illicit deposit. They all considered this illegal payment a pension top-up or bonus and not grand fraud punishable by twenty years in prison, which these activities would no doubt attract.

Chairman Michael Lansbury, Chief Executive Charles Faulk, Commercial Director Jonathan Matthews, Chief Auditor Giles Newbury, and Baroness Jennifer Lewis, Financial Director, were not only skimming accounts but were all highly paid and eligible for discretionary cash bonuses and long-term incentive awards. Clearly, this was not enough, and without any day-to-day intervention from the Yates family, these five people ruled the bank and its nearly fifty billion pounds in assets. The five directors had been with the bank for a collective 136 years and, between them, they knew every trick in the book when it came to taking a little extra "bonus" by grossly illegal methods.

Greg DeWitt's plan to siphon off funds from the First Bank of London was born out of both frustration and ambition. For years, he had watched the bank's board of directors amass wealth through illegal means while he received a mere fraction of the spoils. The dormant bank accounts and slush funds, meticulously built up with small, unnoticeable transactions, were the perfect targets for his scheme as a quarter penny here and there was always rounded down by the bank but, when added together over so many accounts, started to build a nice fund.

The bank's financial software platform, Verick, was both powerful and intricate, designed to handle tens of thousands of transactions in multiple currencies with impeccable precision. It was a system that required minimal human intervention, making it nearly impossible for unauthorised activities to be detected. Greg's deep knowledge of the Verick platform, coupled with his access to the bank's financial systems, put him in a unique position to exploit the bank's vast reserves.

Over the years, Greg had been responsible for maintaining the Verick system, ensuring its smooth operation and updating it as needed. His intimate familiarity with the software and its capabilities allowed him to understand every nuance of the bank's financial transactions. This knowledge was critical in designing his plan to siphon off funds.

The bank had amassed a substantial amount of money in dormant accounts, which included personal and commercial accounts that hadn't been touched for over five years. The directors were already skimming these accounts, taking advantage of the small, untraceable amounts that accrued through half-penny transactions. These funds were quietly moved to Swiss bank accounts, unreported and undetected, thanks to the involvement of the chief auditor and the intricate back-door transactions created within the Verick system.

Greg's role in setting up these back-door transactions was pivotal. Instructed by Chief Executive Charles Faulk, he had built the system that allowed these illicit transfers. In return, he received a paltry bonus of five thousand pounds annually, which was paid every December as a performance bonus, a sum that paled in comparison to the fortunes being accumulated elsewhere. Despite his critical role, Greg was kept out of the inner circle and was expected to keep quiet about the illegal activities he had helped facilitate.

Driven by a desire for more – a bigger house, more luxury cars, and the freedom that came with wealth – Greg's frustration grew as he watched the directors, who already lived lavish lifestyles, fund themselves further with the money skimmed from dormant bank accounts. The temptation to take a share for himself became overwhelming and, on a few occasions, he thought about leaving the bank altogether, just to get away from the constant lure of wanting more and more, but he never did.

Leaving would kill off any future opportunity.

His initial plans to extort his bosses and demand a larger share of the illicit profits always fell through as he lacked the nerve to confront them. However, the seed of his own scheme had been planted, and over time, it grew into an obsession. Greg began to closely monitor the dormant accounts, removing those that had been recently touched and tracking the movements of funds with bespoke reporting tools he had created in the Verick system.

Finally, the constant fermenting of his desire for wealth and the example set by his superiors led Greg to act. He rationalised that if the directors could get away with their illegal activities, so could he. His plan was simple but risky: to divert small amounts from the slush funds into an account he controlled, slowly building up his own hidden reserve without drawing attention.

If he was successful, he could see a future where he could enjoy the same luxuries as the directors without the constant frustration of being undervalued and underpaid. The risks were high, but the potential rewards were too enticing to ignore and, in his mind, were worth the risk.

And so, Greg decided to embark on his journey into financial fraud, but to do this, he was going to need some assistance.

FIVE

In the near full cockpit of the silver American Airlines Boeing 747, the captain watched on as the first officer guided the aircraft down the westerly runway of London's iconic Heathrow airport.

"V1, rotate," he instructed as the take-off speed was reached at precisely 1:32pm local time on a damp September Sunday afternoon, just seven minutes behind the scheduled departure time. With the rain beating down hard onto the asphalt, the plane began its steady climb into the wet, cloud-filled skies that had become a permanent fixture above the south of England for the last three weeks.

"Positive rate of climb," the captain called out.

"Gear up," instructed the first officer.

As the plane climbed through the thick clouds that hung over the UK and made the first of many twists and turns, jostling for position in the busy skies above South West England, the flight path over South Wales and Ireland was set and well planned. The cabin crew were released for their duties, led by cabin supervisor Amber Carter, who packed up her temporary seat in the middle of the plane, adjusted her skirt, and headed for the kitchen area at the back of the fully loaded plane.

Many of the 259 passengers that day were busy shuffling in the seat pockets in front of them, searching out the in-flight magazines, stuffing books in seat pockets for later in the flight. One elderly lady took off her shoes and sat studying the safety card intently, as if it was her first (or last) flight and that what she was reading would make a difference if the plane plummeted into the freezing Atlantic Ocean. The economy cabin was bustling with the usual post-take-off commotion as everybody settled into their tiny red and blue seats, home for the next seven hours and fifty-nine minutes on their way to Logan Airport, east of the city of Boston, Massachusetts.

"Another day, another dollar," Amber said to her colleagues, who were already busy pulling drinks trolleys from the docking stations and donning the corporate colours in the form of their deep-pocketed service aprons. The rain streamed down the windows at near right angles as the plane crawled higher and higher through the clouds that seemed to permanently hang over London these days.

"I'll be glad when this one is over; I had a great two nights in London, but now I've got ten days' leave to take in Miami," replied Brandon, the impeccably turned-out flight attendant from Atlanta, Georgia.

As the crew hurried around at the back of the plane, Greg DeWitt waited patiently for the usual packet of peanuts and whatever alcohol he could get his hands on.

Sitting in row forty-six, seat A, next to the window with nobody else in the immediate seat next to him, he was relaxed and looking forward to the next five days in the USA.

"Sir, what would you like?" came the eventual call over his right shoulder as Amber handed him the foil-wrapped peanuts and white paper napkin with the famous American Airlines logo embossed on the right corner.

"I'll have a couple of beers, please," Greg replied.

"Sure," she replied, handing him two cold cans of Heineken without a choice of brand.

Greg lined both cans up neatly on the plastic fold-out tray in front of him next to the clear plastic cup that followed. The peanuts lasted all of thirty seconds, and he was now starting to think about the late lunch, which was sure to be a palatable infusion of the finest ingredients saved for the less fortunate at the back of the plane. The first beer fared a little better than the peanuts but was still drained in less than five minutes, and as the second one was poured into the cup about to meet a similar fate, he closed his eyes, stretched his legs the best he could under the seat in front of him, and started to wonder how the next five days of his life were going to play out.

He had never been to the United States before and was keen to see as much as possible, and even though this was a business trip, he still wanted to have some fun too and take in a little sightseeing.

Greg was due in Boston for training on the bank's latest update of the mainframe computer system, known as the 9L3000, that was scheduled to go live within a matter of weeks. The bank had sent him out to the outskirts of Boston, Massachusetts, to the headquarters of Verick Computer Systems Inc., established in 1979, to learn all there was to know about their latest technological masterpiece soon to be implemented as the inaugural UK installation in London.

To Greg, this was more than an opportunity to run his eye over their latest release, which indeed was an important part of the trip. But numerous other ideas, all of which were highly illegal, were for the first time going to be spoken rather than dreamt about if the opportunity presented itself.

Through his job at the bank, he had made a few friends at Verick Computers over the years, and although he had met them plenty of times in the UK, this was his first visit to the Verick HQ. As he headed west, there was only one thing on his mind, and it wasn't their new computer system.

Greg's closest ally at Verick was Sheldon Vaughan, who grew up like any normal kid in New Jersey, loving everything any normal red-blooded male should: sports, movies, women, and cars. At six feet four inches tall, with thick black hair and sideburns to match, he had plenty of luck with the ladies, despite having an eight-year-old Ford and no money, but somehow the girls fell on their backs at the sight of his big hands, chiselled jaw, and blue eyes. Fun-loving and out for himself, he reeked of cheap everything, including the women, and was known to many as the ultimate party boy, lucky to have passed his thirtieth birthday without being jailed for more than one night. His idol was Burt Reynolds, and he did everything he could to look like his screen icon, but growing a full moustache never really suited him, so that was long gone.

The lack of money in his life wasn't an issue as Sheldon lived day by day and had no dependants; he lived for the next big sports bet, most of which were ill-advised, illegal, and born out of seduction for the higher odds of the more unlikely outcome of a basketball or baseball game. When he did hit the big time, he would spend the cash as if it was his regular income or he had just won the lottery by buying the latest Ralph Lauren shirt, which was always a necessity.

On one infamous evening, he shouted out, "Save your money, people. I am about to buy the bar", after one of those unlikely events did go his way. Surprisingly, during these hedonistic days of casual sex, big-time drinking, and gambling bordering on addiction, Sheldon managed to hold down the role of Technical Lead VP at Verick Computer Systems Inc. Since leaving college at twenty-three years old, he had worked his way up from rookie to Vice President in seven short years.

Now, just before his thirty-first birthday, he was respected by most of his older peers, some of whom liked to tag along on some of his out-of-hours crusades rather than return home to the humdrum of normal suburban life.

After moving from New Jersey five hours north to Boston with his parents when he was ten years old, he attended the local district public school, and throughout the years, he studied harder and longer in computer science than any other subject and knew all there was to know about coding in C++ and mastering the art of Visual Basic, so he fully believed he had earned his position ahead of his main rivals. He was not a geek by any stretch and certainly had the talent, which helped him surpass many of his elders at Verick Computers within a few short years. His original role was writing code in a cubicle for eight hours a day under his gruelling boss Dan Landry.

Determined not to do this forever, he kept his nose clean enough to work his way up the ranks into product development. Now Technical VP for the new 9L3000 platform, he was considered a higher rank than Landry himself, much to the latter's dismay.

The First Bank of London was Sheldon's first major overseas account, and he had become friends with Greg DeWitt over the past eighteen months during the evaluation and implementation process. The implementation of the previous release created three opportunities for Sheldon to visit London, and he struck up a good rapport with Greg, who felt obligated to host him while he was in town. They had a few nights out getting drunk and visiting various sporting venues in and around London to watch football, and Sheldon had his first introduction to Indian cuisine, taking a real liking to chicken biryani. On one visit in late 1989, Sheldon shot his mouth off to the wrong guys about which sport was superior, soccer or American football, at the Black Lion pub just off Piccadilly Circus. He nearly got his head ripped off before Greg intercepted and made a quick getaway through a side door, which Sheldon found very amusing, but his saviour was less than impressed.

Sheldon had had a few scuffles over the years, always alcohol-infused, always down to running his mouth off, and on this occasion, he knew if he'd got into trouble, his time working with The First Bank would have been over, as it was his only prestigious account at Verick.

On a different visit to the UK, Greg invited Sheldon to stay with him and his wife Isabelle rather than staying in a hotel and going out to dinner, only for Sheldon to get drunk and tell sometimes-entertaining stories of growing up in the US and sneaking into bars or casinos in New York. He appreciated the company as some of his domestic business trips were lonely, boring, and in unglamorous places outside of major cities scattered throughout the United States. He was fed up with the countless airports, car rental desks, eating alone at crappy diners next to dog tracks, strip joints, and truck stops; he felt he was wasting his life drinking alone. Sheldon and Greg had always got on really well, and on this particular meeting, little did either of them know, they were about to change the course of their lives forever.

After a quick stop for nachos at Chi-Chi's, where he had been working on the pretty waitress called Sue-Ann, for the last couple of weeks, Sheldon jumped into his battered Ford Bronco and headed north out of town towards Logan International Airport to meet flight AA158 from London Heathrow. Having already checked, he knew the flight was on time. Walking across the packed car park, smoking a Lucky Strike, Sheldon was looking forward to seeing Greg and hanging out for the week, drinking beer, playing pool, intertwined with a little work and more chasing tail. He looked forward to showing him the sights of his homeland, just like Greg had done on previous trips, and introducing him to the social scene and his superiors at work, who all knew the man from The First Bank of London was in town.

As he approached the arrivals hall, he threw his stub to the floor, narrowly missing a parked trolley packed with luggage, and walked through the automatic doors, glancing up at the information screen for the belt number of Greg's flight. The vast array of carousels were busy churning out suitcase after suitcase, which reaffirmed his lifelong decision to only carry cabin luggage and not waste his life standing around the luggage belts. Eventually, he spotted Greg in the distance, sat with his back to the wall, suitcase at his feet, and a coffee in hand.

"Hey, man, you beat me! How you doing?" Sheldon chirped as he walked towards Greg, who stood up to greet him.

"I'm okay, mate, just a bit tired but nothing a hot shower and a few beers won't sort out," Greg replied as they clapped hands briefly in a half high five, half handshake.

"Yeah, let's get you checked in downtown and head straight out to this dive bar I like. It's kinda one of my favourite hangouts and perfect to catch the Giants vs 49ers game later."

"Sounds good. What's my hotel like?" Greg replied excitedly.

"I've never heard of it before; it must be a new one. They are popping up all over town these days; it's hard to keep track. I can't remember what it's called, but it's in Boston

Common, so you're in a good spot right downtown; it should be nice enough."

"London is the same too; there must be a lot of money in hotels as they're springing up all the time," Greg replied as they headed out into the late-afternoon sun.

"You got that right. They just started building a long tunnel to connect the airport to the city too, but it's going to take something like five years to complete."

As they continued to pass the time of day with polite conversation, they loaded up the luggage and headed off into town through the busy Boston traffic, which never seemed to let up.

"So, are you looking forward to your week?" Sheldon asked, firing up a cigarette and cracking the window.

"Yeah, my first trip over here, so I'm excited. Everything looks like it does on TV," Greg replied, staring out at the impending city skyline and oversized cars he wasn't used to.

"With so many American movies and TV shows, I bet half the people in the world say the same thing, but this is just home to me."

"It all seems very different but also very familiar, like I've been here before. Quite surreal."

"You watch too much TV," Sheldon quipped before sniggering to himself as he toked on his smoke.

Eventually, they pulled up to the hotel on Avenue de Lafayette. The hotel was built inside an old paper mill, a red-brick five-storey-high building opposite two basketball courts surrounded by high chainmail fences.

"This is you," Sheldon said. "Go in and get yourself

sorted, and I'm going to park up and meet you in the lobby in about forty-five minutes."

"Okay, thanks for picking me up. See you later," Greg replied as he emptied his bags from the car.

"Not a problem," Sheldon replied, lighting up another cigarette before driving away.

SIX

Greg walked into the hotel and proceeded to wait in line for a few minutes while two Japanese men in sharp suits with nice luggage checked in before him. He guessed they were from Japan from the baggage tags on their small cases and recognising the word *konnichiwa* one of the gentlemen used.

Greg was eventually greeted by Lance, the cheery hotel receptionist, who told him all about the facilities in the hotel he wouldn't be using and offered to personally carry his luggage to the room. Greg declined and dragged his own case towards the lift.

He got out on the fifth floor and walked almost to the end of the corridor, past an ice machine he had never seen in a hotel before, and unlocked room 504. He was surprised at the size of the room, with two queen-sized beds, massive bathroom, and lounge area you would pay a small fortune for in London, he thought to himself.

He quickly ironed a shirt, headed for the shower with

the TV blaring in the background, and after a quick pit stop, he was back in the lift and soon greeted by Sheldon, who sat reading a copy of today's *Boston Globe*.

"That was quick," Sheldon said.

"I thought if I sat down for a minute, I'd probably fall asleep, so I need to keep moving," Greg answered.

"Good idea. The adrenaline of being in a different country will get you through the rest of the day, but tomorrow will be a killer, especially if you don't sleep well tonight." Sheldon chuckled, slapping his friend on the back.

They walked away from the hotel into the cool early evening breeze, which woke Greg up a little after his hot shower, as they went in search of beers at Sheldon's favourite spot, the Rock-It Bar. There, they soon found themselves two pitchers of Coors into the conversation, half-watching the various games on the big-screen TVs dotted all round the place.

As half-time approached, they were served two all-American stacked burgers and fries with coleslaw and giant pickle sides and yet more beer, which was starting to make Greg feel fuzzy, especially after the eight-hour flight and five-hour time difference, which he had never experienced before. They tucked into the food and slowed on the beer before Sheldon ranted at the TV closest to them, showing the Chicago Bears versus the Tampa Bay Buccaneers in a regular season game; one he clearly had some money riding on.

The alcohol buzzed through Greg, and he was conscious of his dialogue becoming slurred, so he stopped talking for a few minutes and continued eating in a bid to sober up as Sheldon recalled numerous eventful evenings at this and many other surrounding bars in the downtown area.

Greg wasn't really paying attention, as all he could think about was how sleepy he was getting, and the thought of defrauding The First Bank was never far from his mind. He knew he wouldn't have a chance of successfully taking a single pound from the bank without the auditors picking him up unless he had an inside track, which he hoped would come in the shape of Sheldon. Greg watched as Sheldon seemed to demolish his food in about three rapid hand movements, leaving one small piece of burger and bun on his plate. Listening to Sheldon's latest conquest from the night before, he grappled with the idea of coming straight out with his plan but worried about whether Sheldon would be receptive or too drunk to take it seriously. He opted for the tactful route, hoping to stumble across the correct opportunity, which suddenly arrived in the next conversation with the few words that happened to fall out of Sheldon's mouth.

"I hope the Bears kick their ass in the next half as my gambling debts are starting to add up this season; man, I've had some bad luck," Sheldon said, shaking his head.

Greg thought, *this is it*, as the final piece of his oversized burger hovered just below his chin.

"How much are you down?" Greg asked, cramming the last wedge of beef into his mouth.

"Around twelve grand."

"Twelve thousand dollars, bloody hell, Sheldon, are you serious?"

"Yeah, I wish I weren't, but I've wiped out all my previous winnings from the last couple of years and am now scrapping around for every bet. Wanna lend me fifty bucks?" he half-joked.

Greg smirked and thought to himself, *fifty bucks will seem like pocket change if I can just get my plan off the ground with the help of my desperate American friend.*

"Shit, that's a lot of money, Sheldon. What are you going to do?" he replied, trying to look concerned as he tried to exaggerate the losses even further.

"Do what I always do: plough through it and wait for the good times to roll again."

"Sounds expensive to me."

"You're not a gambling man, are you?"

"Nah, I can't afford to be on my wage with a wife and child to look after."

"I hear you there, my man," Sheldon replied, glancing up at the TV at the same time as sinking another mouthful of beer.

They both paused, as if to reflect on how different each other's lives were, which gave Greg a minute to compose his thoughts as they sat in the large leather-clad booth, which gave them some level of privacy from the packed bar of noisy sports fans.

"Maybe a second income would help," Greg said, leaning in but instantly starting to wish he hadn't said a word.

"I ain't into working bar jobs or delivering pizzas for five bucks an hour; a couple of big wins, it'll be cool again – I'm good," Sheldon said, brushing off the suggestion as he pulled on another big slug of beer and watched two pretty girls walk by on their way to the toilets at the back of the building. "Don't worry about me, man," he continued while straining his neck in the opposite direction.

"And what happens if it isn't cool?" Greg said, stoking the fire further. "You could lose everything if the streak continues like it has done this year."

"Lose what? A shitty car and a rented apartment, I'm hardly Burt Reynolds or Charlie Sheen, am I? And to be honest, Greg, I don't think that far ahead; shit, I don't even know what I'll be doing tomorrow."

Greg knew they would both be at Verick tomorrow trawling over the new 9L3000 and nursing some killer hangovers by the look of the way the latest pitcher of brew was disappearing.

Greg paused, knowing this could be his one and only shot, and if it all went wrong, he stood a chance of calling the whole thing an elaborate booze-fuelled joke over coffee in the morning.

"It sounds like you could do with a few quid from the dormant bank account we're sitting on back in London," he said, leaning in closer across the table and clutching the handle on his beer glass tighter.

"Oh yeah, what is that all about?" Sheldon asked with his final mouthful of the Midwest's finest. Greg scratched his neck and took a deep breath before pushing his plate to one side and leaning in with both elbows planted upright on the table in front of him.

"Well," he paused, thinking over his decision one final time and swallowing his guilt quicker than the prime beef; his stomach started to churn as he began vocalising his secret thoughts, which had been building inside for months, "I noticed a few years back a pool of frozen bank accounts littered with dormant funds that haven't been touched in years, sometimes decades, lots of them," he said as his heart readied to burst through his checked blue-and-white shirt.

"And?" Sheldon said, as if waiting for the punchline.

"It holds over sixty million pounds of untouched cash, cash that interest builds on but is never touched."

"What, one hundred million bucks with no name?" Sheldon asked.

"Well, technically it belongs to the bank customers, lots of them, and if they don't claim it or touch it, or it cannot be traced over a period of time, the bank will hold onto it for eternity as each account continually amasses the current rate of interest."

"How the hell can you lose a hundred mil, surely everything is traceable?" asked Sheldon.

"Like I said, it belongs to thousands of customers who have a bit here and there. Maybe they've forgotten about their accounts; maybe they died, moved away, kept it for a rainy day, saving for their kid's future, grandkids, lost pensions, all that kind of stuff."

"Damn, I certainly wouldn't forget about fifty bucks in the dresser, let alone a huge chunk of change like that," Sheldon said, starting to show some animation in his cumbersome posture as he shifted position in the booth to get closer.

"Well, your fancy new 9L3000 will soon be carrying

out all of the reporting on these old accounts; can you skim a few quid off the top and hide it for us?" Greg said as he sat back, realising his fanciful secret was no longer; it was unnoticeable, but he could feel his face redden by the second.

"Anything is possible when you write the code, and I mean anything," Sheldon said, lighting up a post-dinner cigarette.

"Have you done something like this before?" Greg asked, hoping for an answer in the affirmative.

"What are you, fucking stupid?" Sheldon replied, talking and blowing out a huge billow of acrid smoke at the same time.

"Yes, of course, stupid," Greg said. "I need to fight the fire; I'll be back in a minute," he continued as he stood up and headed to the toilet quicker than he normally would.

Sheldon sat back with his left arm draped across the back of the booth he was sat in as he casually lifted his head up and pulled on the cigarette, looking seemingly without a care in the world. Occasionally, he would glance up at the television for an update on his latest disastrous investment, but knowing the potential outcome, he was more interested in talent spotting, but the evening was proving slim pickings.

Greg did have a care in the world, lots of them, and as he stood at the urinal with his head resting on the wall in front of him, he considered what he had said and now wondered how much of his potentially life-changing information Sheldon had picked up on. He spent as long as he dared away from Sheldon before heading back to the booth and hoping for a favourable response.

"Feel better now?" Sheldon asked with a sarcastic laugh.

"Yes, I do, but do you?" Greg replied.

"About the money?"

"Yes, about the money, Sheldon; I know you heard me."

"I think it could be done," Sheldon replied casually.

"Done?"

"Yes, I think we could shave off a few pence here and there over a period of time, untraceable by the internal auditors at Verick."

"How would it work?"

"Simple," Sheldon said in his best attempt at a posh English accent.

"Simple, how?" asked Greg.

"It's a case of planting an additional code in the new system, which you or I could do, that essentially creates a black hole by splitting the credit transaction before it is applied to the bank account each month."

"I mean, it'll take time and precision, and it could be written into the software right under the nose of every person at Verick, and no one would notice."

"Is it safe?" Greg asked.

"As safe as the Bank of England; it's all zeros and ones, isn't it?"

"Shit, this is big, I mean, what if—"

"What if what?" Sheldon cut in.

"What if we get caught?"

"There's always a risk of getting caught, but my point is, with the right coding, it'll all be untraceable as we will simply cover our tracks; it would take years to unravel. I mean, banks get hacked all the time, don't they? It'll be fine, trust me," Sheldon replied as he drew on the last remaining smoke. "You just provide the intel on which accounts to hit up and I'll do the rest."

SEVEN

Greg was filled with excitement and apprehension for what was potentially about to happen but tired from the flight and ready to get home after all the learning and burning the candle at both ends. The idea was to keep his head down, do his job and go home to Isabelle every night, preferably without being fired and imprisoned for embezzlement, which was looking more likely following tonight's conversation.

He had a spring in his step for the first time in years, knowing the black hole could give him a very real opportunity to become seriously wealthy without having to make any changes to his day-to-day life. Now that Sheldon was involved, it almost seemed like destiny and, in a way, less illegal now someone else also agreed it was a clever idea; the thought of going to jail or losing his job had long since departed.

Having the financial means to make life more comfortable and surrounding himself with the finer things was all that he craved. Over the years, he had seen numerous jobs advertised across London, most of which offered more money than he was making, but with the extra pay came the extra responsibility and inevitable longer hours, so he continued to plod through the motions and not push himself out of his comfort zone.

This not only made him more and more miserable about his career options but also bitter towards the hierarchy at the bank, which was only made worse by their keenness to continually break the law for their own bloated financial gain. The thought of being caught internally were also long gone now that Sheldon was involved, and as they were just numbers on a screen, it all seemed like a game more than real life, but that didn't stop him from dreaming and praying that Sheldon's black hole was to become fact, not fantasy like so many of his other schemes.

Sheldon was a dreamer and always talked about how he should have been a pro basketball player or a race car driver, but he wasn't athletic enough, too tall, and too short; he had flat feet – the list went on. So, he was hoping that while this was a crazy idea, it was the one to finally unlock the treasure chest and not another failed attempt at becoming rich, like the countless failed accumulator bets and get-rich-quick schemes he had put all his hopes and dreams on over the years. If it is too good to be true, it usually is, a familiar saying that had become his motto, but this was different; this was work and something he knew he could carry off.

Sheldon was the key to Greg's dreams, and from the outset, he was the main driver, or project manager, as he would later refer to himself. Like many of Greg's peers at the bank, he wanted an illegal slice of the pie, allowing him to live the full life of international travel, expensive German cars, and all the latest fashion accessories he could get his hands on. Greg was motivated by money, pure greed, and the simplest way to gain these riches, in his mind, was to steal and steal in vast quantities and low denominations. Feeling invincible, Greg knew the chances of being caught were slim due to the design of the system, which they discussed only that one time in Sheldon's office during the trip, and this time over coffee and sickly sweet doughnuts, not beers, which made a change.

Greg was more at ease with the plan, and on the flight back to London, he had written on an American Airlines napkin what he called his "top five": a list of elaborate purchases he hoped he would soon be making with his new-found wealth, claiming a family inheritance should anyone look to query his new spending power. First on the list was a convertible Mercedes, which he would tell his wife Isabelle came with his new promotion to IT Director at the bank, yet another lie. The idea of a new house, probably down in Surrey in stockbroker country, was always the ultimate dream, but for the time being, a few smaller treats would do, like an expensive Swiss-made watch and one for Isabelle if she so desired. Then there were a couple of fancy holidays to the Maldives, Thailand, or maybe the Seychelles, plus a new set of the finest golf clubs to go with his new membership at one of the most exclusive clubs in the area. He fantasised about what all of this would bring and what opportunities might arise from moving in different social circles and networking with the elite to further personal gain over time.

He knew in doing this, he had to keep his new-found wealth a secret from his colleagues at the bank but keep up the pretence of being the successful IT director to Isabelle, piece of cake. He always wanted to visit Monaco but would tell his colleagues he was off to Majorca; he would never wear a fancy watch in the office, opting for the cheap wristwatch Isabelle gave him several Christmases ago, and as he always took the train to work, hiding various nice cars would be simple. These were his rules of engagement and ones he was going to stick to, all of which were very different from his original plans of clearing off some of the mortgage and taking a few extra short holidays.

He was excited more than apprehensive as the flight touched down back at the always overcrammed, dreary, wet, and grey Heathrow.

Battling through the usual chaos of more than a hundred flights arriving between 6am and 9am and the battle for any scrap of personal space next to the carousel, he kept his head down through the nothing to declare and was soon back in the real world. His back ached from the long flight, and he felt like someone had stuffed cotton wool in his ears, but at least he was home. Joining the queue for a taxi, Greg soon arrived back at his modest three-bedroom house on the outskirts of London at 12:03pm on Saturday afternoon, which was always a quiet time at home, as Isabelle and Matthew would normally be out at some playgroup or child's party. *So much for the grand homecoming*, he thought to himself, dropping his luggage just two feet inside the front door, realising he was alone.

Walking through the dim hall, he picked up a small stack of unopened post, which he began to pour through, perched against the kitchen counter waiting for the kettle to boil. The usual rubbish of bills and junk mail was all that was there to greet him, not even a note from his wife to welcome him back, which would have been nice. After a quick coffee and toast and an even quicker shower, he fell into bed, struggling for the first time with proper jet lag and in need of some deep sleep. He popped a couple of Isabelle's sleeping tablets he found next to the bed for good measure. As his head hit the pillow, he began to snore, despite the surge of adrenaline mixed with caffeine running through his body.

Back in Boston, Sheldon had gone into work on Saturday and sat in his office all day drafting the final additions to his masterpiece. Each microscopic transaction they planned on skimming would be collated and carefully transferred into a single file transaction to a bank in China Grove, Bexar County in Texas, where neither man had ever been, and only after the interest had been applied to the dormant accounts in London. Sheldon had set up the bank account in Texas using a copy of a dead man's birth certificate and a fake passport in the name of Jack Maine in a bid to dilute the paper trail and limit the chances of capture. He learnt how to do this from an overly in-depth how-to-catch-a-criminal TV programme. This, too, was a fraudulent act but the lesser of the various crimes they were now about to commit, assuming they were ever caught.

From Texas, the transaction would be wired immediately to ten different bank accounts: five in the Cayman Islands in five different currencies – US dollars, Japanese yen, British sterling, Spanish pesetas, and the German deutschmark – and five in the UK-controlled microstate of the British Virgin Islands, where even the official financial regulators had no idea where the influx of money was coming from or going to next. The Cayman Island accounts were in the name of Jack Maine, which were controlled by Greg, and the British Virgin Islands accounts were set up again using a dead man's birth certificate with the name Darius King, who was also known as Sheldon.

Sheldon and Greg agreed that, once a month, a sizeable proportion of the money would be withdrawn from each of the accounts and deposited at ACM International Bank in Switzerland under the name of a bogus holding company known as MUR Holdings, which Greg and Sheldon both had access to. MUR meant nothing to either of them, but Sheldon did point out to Greg that it could stand for Make Us Rich, which both found amusing.

They agreed that, on the first of every month, 75% would be taken from each account, leaving the remaining 25% in the bank accounts in the Cayman Islands and British Virgin Islands as contingency should it ever be required. They figured that although the money was safe in these accounts, the chances of the Swiss cooperating with the FBI should any money laundering charges come flying their way were less than the banks in the Cayman Islands and BVI; either way, the money was safer than leaving it in Texas.

When the layering of dirty money was available, the bank in Switzerland was under strict instructions to raise six banker's drafts in the names of Jack Maine and Darius King and post them to a PO box in Belize. Here, the drafts would pile up for a few months, ready for Sheldon to go and collect them.

"Why Belize?" Greg had asked.

"Why not?" Sheldon replied. "I've always fancied going there; it seems out of the way; they speak English there; and it just seems off the radar. Got a better idea?"

Greg did not, so Belize it was.

And at this stage of the process, the money was purely paper, but both agreed to stick to the process, and if they were to be discovered in the first couple of months, there would be no money, so no evidence to convict them, assuming some wise FBI agent was able to track the PO box and open it himself.

Assuming everything went to plan, Sheldon would fly to Belize alone, wait for a few days while he cashed in each draft, before combining their individual shares and wiring the money to their own offshore accounts, which they had independently set up and had access to from the UK and US.

Greg chose Singapore as he knew a guy out there who once worked at the bank, and Sheldon chose to send his money to either the Cayman Islands or BVI, depending on where it came from in the first place.

Greg reminded Sheldon not to take large sums of cash back into the US as the airport authorities would have highly trained sniffer dogs able to sniff out a wad of cash from five feet away. The specialist cash teams that patrolled every major airport in the developed world would love to have stopped Sheldon bringing anything over ten thousand dollars in cash into the US, which would almost certainly spell game over. Even if he came in with five grand in his pocket, the authorities would be all over him. If he were caught with undeclared cash and no watertight explanation in the form of a solid paper trail, he would end up on a watch list, making it ten times harder to spend a single dollar, let alone ten, twenty, or even fifty thousand dollars.

This tactic also limited Sheldon's gambling somewhat, which pleased Greg as he didn't want Sheldon to get greedy after big losses or, worse still, start throwing his cash around like a high roller, which was bound to draw further unwanted attention from casino bosses who were all well connected outside the gaming and hotel business. Sheldon was excited about the prospect of the money rolling in as he mapped out the final stages like an architect working on his latest magnum opus, and by the time he was finished, he was proud but frustrated as he had nobody to gloat to.

Unlike Greg, he didn't have an extensive list of purchases he was keen to buy. He already knew that whatever money came his way would be spent gambling, on cars and women; professional or otherwise. He knew this was some way off as the money had to go through its layering process before it could be pulled back in from offshore and spent at any number of casinos across the eastern seaboard. He knew the Inland Revenue Service and various other authorities would be all over any large deposits coming in from offshore, so he planned to make several one-thousand-dollar deposits on a daily basis into a couple of bank accounts in Manhattan, which would give him an instant kicker of cash.

The black hole was a complex piece of code written into the hard drive of the 9L3000 attached to an encrypted bank account using a unique algorithm technique he had developed in college. Bespoke enough that it gave him some insurance over Greg just in case he needed any bargaining chips later, as nobody but Sheldon knew the finer detail. The code was written as if it was completed by a maths major, except certain calculations came from an old school friend of Sheldon's who was prolific with numbers, never asked questions, and was always happy to help. He told "the geek", as he fondly called him, it was work-related and he would later receive a payment of three thousand dollars for his time, so the work was completed and designed to show a percentage in its entirety but calculate a fractionally lesser amount before crediting the interest to all accounts "VOID OF MOVEMENT FOR FIVE-PLUS YEARS".

This ensured that while the bank thought they were applying the current rate of interest to the dormant bank accounts, the exact amount of interest gained by the customer was slightly less and made up of two transactions. One into the dormant account for 75% of what it should be and the second transaction, the remaining 25%, into the black hole that would ultimately find its way to China Grove in Texas in the first instance. All on-screen transactions, audit reports, and balances would show the full amount had been credited to each account, but the reality was very different.

The 9L3000 system was principally developed by Sheldon as the chief architect, so he knew his way around with ease and tested every angle possible to see if a user, or even one of his technical colleagues, would be able to spot the second transaction leaving the bank. It was watertight, and as the take was only 25% of what was going to be applied, Sheldon and Greg figured it was too small for the owners of the dormant bank accounts to notice. The only other danger of forensic accountants was completely disregarded, as the chances of them being drafted in should there be any suspicion was highly unlikely from the board at The First Bank, given their own extracurricular activities. Win-win.

The final piece of the jigsaw was a not-so-clever blocky on-screen display built by Greg, which was quickly thrown together and good enough for this purpose but didn't demonstrate his technical abilities to the fullest. When launched, it would run in the background and show the money gained on the first day of each calendar month as the interest was being calculated in real time on the first working day of the month. This was the exciting window to future riches that would calculate, per second, in real time, the monies being pilfered from the tens of thousands of dormant bank accounts. Within weeks, the new 9L3000 would be implemented and running live, along with the black hole, which would start work at the beginning of each interest month. Soon the fun would begin, and the figures on-screen would be real and highly illegal.

EIGHT

Two Months Later

Greg had slept less than three hours the night before the first take, and by 4:30am, he was downstairs, boiling the kettle for his first coffee. He was a whirlwind of emotions – excited, anxious, nauseous – but managed to get to work unscathed, other than a nick during shaving, nervousness being the overriding feeling. Nervous that his plan would not work, and nervous he would be caught before he could even spend a penny. If he was going down, he wanted to have a little fun first.

"You're in early today, Greg, what did you do, wet the bed?" joked Alex, the balding, overweight security guard at The First Bank, as he let Greg in at 6:30am on Monday morning.

Greg usually strolled in long after 8am, so he claimed he had a conference call with a client in South East Asia, necessitating the early start.

"Running the foreign exchange now, are you?" Alex quipped.

"Something like that," Greg replied, gliding through the marbled, freshly mopped reception hall.

He rode the lift alone, his breath faster than normal against the whirring of the lift. Once in his office, he locked the door, drew the blinds, and settled in with his third coffee of the morning. He unlocked a drawer in his small grey cabinet, retrieved his heavy old laptop, and connected it to a private network he had set up. Sweat dripped from his forehead onto the keyboard as he sipped his coffee and started up the laptop. Using his lengthy alphanumeric password, he signed in and watched as the utility nicknamed "the window" booted up, ready for the first take.

Still doubting Sheldon's ability to pull this off, he watched as the clock ticked towards 7am on 1st December, almost two months after his visit to the US. The 9L3000 was primed to start paying interest calculations into more than two million bank accounts. Greg's stomach flipped as he picked up the phone and called Sheldon.

"Sheldon, if you got this right, by the time you get up in the morning, you could be considerably richer than you are now," Greg whispered.

"Trust me, Greg, it'll work. Now leave me alone; it's almost 2am here. I'll speak to you later," Sheldon replied, and the line went dead as the clock struck 6:58am.

How can he be so calm and able to sleep? Greg wondered, and as the clock struck 7am, he dashed for the bin beside his desk, vomiting up at least one cup of coffee.

"Ahh shit," he muttered, checking his shirt for stains. Suddenly, the on-screen utility switched status to "connected", and the stats on the screen started to move. Applied Interest Accounts: 43. Value: £0.00.

Greg waited, unsure when the interest would be processed or if Sheldon's "trust me" was just an elaborate boast and all of this meticulous planning in the last two months was a total fantasy. As the 'Applied Interest' field ticked up, the 'Value' field remained at zero.

"Asshole," Greg muttered, doubt creeping in. "Bloody nothing," he grumbled.

Five slow minutes passed before the value suddenly ticked up for the first time: £1.91.

"Small but a start," Greg whispered to himself, sweat rolling down his red cheeks. The flow of money increased: £2.37, £3.03, £3.61, £5.34, £6.56, £8.68, £11.03. *Holy shit, he did it*, Greg thought, clenching his fist. He stood up, immediately sat back down, unable to control his excitement. The value soon hit £25.27 when a sudden knock on the door revealed Chief Executive Charles Faulk. Greg snapped the laptop closed and sprang up, spilling coffee all over his desk.

"Glad you're in early, Greg. Clean that up and follow me, will you," Faulk ordered.

Greg's heart sank as fear replaced excitement. He threw some plain A4 paper on the spilt coffee and followed Charles at speed.

Calm down, he told himself. *It's just a coincidence; calm the fuck down.* His body turned cold.

Charles turned to Greg in the corridor. "Bloody hell,

old chap, are you feeling alright? You look dreadful."

"Great, thank you. I went for a run before work, and the shower obviously didn't cool me down enough," Greg lied, referencing the sweat patches on his pale blue shirt.

"Come with me," Charles instructed.

"Sure," Greg muttered, three steps behind him. *What has Sheldon done?* he thought, as they entered the much larger Chief Executive's office.

"Close the door and sit down, Greg. I've got a bone to pick with you," Charles said sternly.

"Is everything okay?" Greg retorted, searching for another bin.

"I'm a bit disappointed about your IT spend over the last couple of months," Charles said. "I thought these software upgrades were supposed to be included in our service maintenance agreements."

Greg relaxed, tension evaporating. Under normal circumstances, this would be a concern, but today was different.

"No, we must pay extra for upgrades as these are optional but required by our compliance team. They'll make the bank more efficient and watertight, so it's in our interests according to the auditors," Greg replied nonchalantly.

"Right, I see."

"Anything else?" Greg asked, eager to leave.

"Yes, what do you know about this?" Charles pointed at the screen.

Greg rose slowly, praying it wasn't anything to do with his new venture. To his relief, he saw nothing other than an amateur attempt at a scam email and returned to his chair as his heart rate finally started to slow.

"Mr Faulk, you're the chief exec of this bank, I shouldn't need to trouble you with virus fixes and system bugs. That's my responsibility. Leave it with me. I have it all under control – I think you have simply received a fishing email from a scammer – I'll tighten our firewall to prevent future emails like this getting through. There's no threat to the bank, our customers, or the money," Greg lied.

"Okay, just if you have it under control. Anything else to report? How is the new system bedding in?"

Forty-five agonising minutes later, Greg was back in his office, relieved he hadn't been caught. He tentatively reopened the laptop. The black hole had been running for forty-five minutes.

Applied Interest Accounts: 172,930. Value: £2,381.29.

Greg couldn't believe his eyes. Sheldon was a genius. He calculated that by the end of the interest adjustment run, his share would be worth close to seven grand, with 25% staying in reserve as agreed, and the rest going to Sheldon. Not bad for a day's work.

The morning flowed quickly with no further interruptions. At 10:29am, the status read "complete". Over three hours, they had purloined from more than half a million accounts. Greg dialled Sheldon's apartment.

"Sheldon, wake up. It worked. You are a bloody genius."

"Told you. How much?" Sheldon asked.

"Eighteen thousand, four hundred and forty-two pounds. About twenty-eight thousand dollars," Greg replied.

"Yeah, baby; we're going out tonight," Sheldon burst out.

"Well done, Sheldon. Check with the bank when they open?"

"Yeah, no problem, it could take a couple of days to process their end, but I'll check. Later." The line went dead.

Greg continued to stare at the screen, heart pounding. He shut the system down, closed the laptop and locked it in his desk drawer, grabbed his jacket, and headed out into the fresh air.

Taking a few twists and turns through the usual London mix of tourists and workers, he soon found solace in a bar at The Grand Royale Hotel.

"I'll have a pint and a whisky. You decide," he told the barman at the near empty bar.

"Beer, lager, cider?" the barman asked.

"I said you decide. I don't care," Greg retorted. "Sorry, crazy morning. Make it a Guinness, thanks."

Greg sat facing the main entrance, his mind racing, his stomach churning, and his body tingling with excitement. *Is it too late to go back? What the hell have you done?* He drank both drinks quickly to try and drown out the panic. Today was the day his life changed for good, and he didn't like the current feeling.

Two hours later, he returned to his office unnoticed, sobered up on bottled water, fresh air and a ham and egg sandwich before throwing in the towel at 4:45pm and heading home, hoping for news from Sheldon.

Later, Sheldon called the bank in Texas. "Good morning. I'd like to check the balance on my account."

"Certainly, sir. Can I take your account number and name?"

"Account number 0344145191, in the name of Jack Maine."

"For security, can you tell me the password on your account?"

"London."

"The balance on your account is zero, sir. Are you expecting a deposit?"

Sheldon's heart raced. "Check again."

"I'm sorry, sir. It's still zero."

"I'll try again later," Sheldon said, hanging up without any niceties.

Convinced everything was correct, Sheldon and Greg could only wait what turned out to be four agonising days before he finally hit gold.

"Yo," answered Sheldon, seeing the international number.

"Any news?" Greg asked.

"I'll call you back in five, Greg. I'm on the other line with them now," Sheldon said, flicking back to the bank.

"Mr Maine?"

"Yep."

"Thank you for holding, sir. The balance is zero…"

"Damn it," Sheldon spat, smacking his fist on the desk.

"But there is a large credit due tomorrow," the person on the other end of the phone continued.

"How much?" Sheldon asked.

"Twenty-eight thousand, six hundred and five dollars and thirty-two cents."

Sheldon gasped and punched the air. "Thanks, thanks for checking," he said, hanging up and spinning in his chair. He immediately called Greg back.

Finally, Sheldon and Greg were in business – the business of fraud. The spending and partying was about to commence on both sides of the Atlantic.

NINE

The lies continued as Greg told Isabelle an elaborate tale of a "once-in-a-lifetime" promotion to Technical Director at the bank. This came with a huge six-figure salary, an annual bonus, and a company car. He painted a picture of a future seat on the board, along with fancy hotel stays and international travel. Greg hoped his story would stop Isabelle from asking too many questions about his new-found wealth and the pockets full of fifty-pound notes that would soon follow him everywhere. Isabelle was truly elated and did not suspect anything untoward.

For the next few months, they lived a life of sheer luxury as illicit money started to pour in. Isabelle believed it was all paid for by Greg's new high-rolling job at the bank. There were elaborate nights out with friends, one of which involved a limousine ride where Greg and Isabelle ended up having sex on the way home, fuelled by their new-found love of champagne. At The Savoy, there were expensive dinners, a couple of expensive Swiss watches, diamond necklace, and Hugo Boss suits dominated the new wardrobe, with virtually every original item given to charity. One afternoon, Greg spent over six thousand pounds on clothes, secure in the knowledge that in a few days, another fistful of dirty money would be deposited in his five chosen accounts.

The spending continued with a weekend in New York on the Concorde, more champagne, and clothes for Isabelle. She only once dared ask Greg about the tremendous spending, suggesting putting some aside for a rainy day, but this was immediately scoffed at by Greg, who reassured her this was just the beginning.

"This is how things will be from now on. Lots of my colleagues live like this, better than this, so don't worry. We can afford it," he explained.

Some of their lifelong friends became suspicious of the new high-spending DeWitts, but Greg and Isabelle insisted that his new high-powered job paid the bills. They claimed the fifty thousand pounds' worth of cars on their driveway were simply company cars at their disposal. Occasionally, Greg had to dodge awkward moments when Isabelle suggested hosting a dinner party for his boss and his wife. However, most of the time, the bullshit flowed as much as the expensive wines, and nobody seemed to care as friends and acquaintances started to freeload a little.

Greg convinced himself he would go easy with the spending to avoid arousing too much suspicion, but the greedy, arrogant demon inside him soon put that idea to bed, and the spending continued.

One dreary Sunday morning followed a night out in

the West End of London with several friends, including Patrick and Charlotte from next door. They had been out for dinner and to a casino where everyone watched as Greg managed to lose fifteen hundred pounds at blackjack. He laughed it off, but for most people, that money would have paid the mortgage for several months. Some of his closest friends started to become horrified at what Greg was turning into, leading to some distancing themselves from the DeWitts altogether.

Patrick and Charlotte had noticed the change early on. Greg became more and more supercilious with his new wealth, acting like a lottery winner rather than someone who had landed a high-paying job. Meanwhile, Isabelle seemed to become more disillusioned and withdrawn. Unlike her husband, she noticed their closest friends turning away from them, reacting negatively to Greg's brash behaviour and lack of budgeting, or saving for the future.

One Saturday morning, the phone rang at 7:21am. Greg, dressed in his white dressing gown with "JD" sewn into the right cuff, walked down the long flight of wooden stairs into his white and grey kitchen, and answered the call.

"Hey, buddy, what's up?" Greg said, navigating the large oak table in the centre of the room.

"Hi, man, what's happening?" Sheldon slurred from the reception of the MGM Grand in Las Vegas. "I'm out partying in Vegas with two hot chicks named Samantha and Georgia. We're having a blast."

"Sounds like fun. I lost a stack recently playing blackjack. What time is it anyway?" Greg asked, flicking the red switch on the side of the kettle.

"Who cares, baby? I'm on Vegas time. They purposely don't let any natural light in these places or display any clocks, so nobody knows what time it is or cares either until they've lost everything."

"What time are you leaving?"

"Pick me up at Terminal Four, day after tomorrow. My flight gets in at 10am; first class all the way," Sheldon said, clearly worse for wear.

"I'll look forward to it," Greg said, hanging up, paranoid that the authorities might be listening in.

Standing in the long window of the kitchen, Greg stared into the garden as the steam from his coffee ran up the cold window. Sheldon was arriving from the US in a couple of days, and life was better than ever. He thought to himself that maybe he needed to tone down the spending to prevent further suspicion, which in some quarters was already too late.

To not raise suspicion at the bank, he kept things very quiet at work. Little did he know, his ideas of self-control were already a little too late.

Things had been running smoothly since the new 9L3000 system was launched five months ago at the bank. With the system reducing the processing time of month-end reporting and payroll by around 50%, everything was running like clockwork. The board of directors were impressed with the new system that Verick had introduced and reporting, foreign exchange, and minute-by-minute bank reconciliation was far superior to their previous system.

Greg and Sheldon were impressed too. In the first

five months, the black hole had swallowed up nearly one hundred thousand pounds, tax-free, in penny and half-penny transactions, making them richer than they could have ever imagined. They had both lost count but guessed that most of it had already been spent in various parts of Europe and North America, with Greg certainly having more trappings to show for it than Sheldon, who had gambled most of it or spent it on cheap liquor and women.

Sheldon started referring to himself as a millionaire, which Greg found very amusing. They were both happy, but Greg constantly had to push the thoughts of a criminal record and time in jail to the back of his mind or it would eat him up inside.

His conscience tried in vain to remind him that what he was doing was not only highly illegal but borderline ridiculous and already out of control. Again, he promised he would take it easy; he knew this would not last forever. Like a new lottery winner going crazy for a few months, he was starting to settle down now that the novelty of fast cars and fancy watches had begun to wear off.

With Sheldon soon to arrive, Isabelle decided to vacate the house for a couple of days on a luxury spa hotel break. She had heard all she needed to know about the loud-talking and impetuous American and didn't want to be around two testosterone-fuelled guys out for a good time. So, with Charlotte and the two boys all booked up, she packed her latest designer threads, loaded the children into the car, and headed off into the country to be waited on at the five-star hotel.

Matthew and Jacob would be taken care of at the

crèche, giving the mums some downtime. But they would no doubt enjoy splashing around in the heated indoor swimming pool at some point over the weekend.

With the families away, this left the door open for Patrick to join in the fun with the people next door. Although he wasn't too sure how much hard drinking he could tolerate, he decided to make the most of it.

TEN

A few days later, Sheldon arrived, and night one was about to get started with chilled Belgian beers at Greg's house. Patrick came over from next door to watch the football match on a very costly new television in the living room. Patrick was at ease from the steady sips of booze but regretted not picking up a Chinese takeaway and a bottle of white wine to spend some time alone. Kicking back on the sofa with the remains of a chicken chop suey seemed a far better option, but he was there and determined to make the most of it, even if he found it hard to tolerate the increasingly arrogant Greg and his ever-loud American friend.

"Come on, Patrick, suck back on that beer, bro!" Sheldon shouted as if he were fifty feet away.

"I like to pace myself," Patrick replied, the strong American accent grating on him more by the minute.

"Damn right, baby," Sheldon shouted again, throwing his beer bottle hand in the air with about as much grace as a shotgun.

"Guys, the plan is to watch the end of the match, jump in a cab, and head into the West End for a few beers," Greg said enthusiastically. "The world is our oyster."

"Yeah," Sheldon raged as he cracked open another bottle of Belgium's finest with the reverse of his oversized bucking bronco belt buckle.

"From there we'll grab some food at one of those posh restaurants, hit a club, and party!" Greg continued, launching his beer hand high into the air.

"Yeah!" Even louder came the response from the party boy. "Don't forget the strippers too," Sheldon quipped on his way to the toilet for the first of many times that night.

Slouched on the sofa, Patrick started to get nervous at the thought of being in a posh restaurant in the middle of London with these two loud boys.

"What do you fancy eating?" Greg asked.

"I'll go with the flow," Patrick replied, not taking his glare off the match being played in Serie A in Italy.

By the fourth beer, Patrick's uneasiness had passed, and he was becoming increasingly louder himself. In fact, he was quite enjoying himself. Being called Pat instead of Patrick by Sheldon no longer vexed him. As the match finished, they headed into town.

Several more beers were downed, and the night was going well until they realised they were down to two.

"Where is Sheldon?" said Greg. "He's been gone ages."

"I have no idea. The last I saw, he was over there talking to some girls," Patrick slurred, slouching back in an oversized red leather chair in one of London's finer strip clubs.

"I've been on many nights out with him before, and he's never disappeared. I don't even think he knows where I live," Greg said, sipping a tall glass of champagne.

"Who cares?" said Patrick. "He's a big boy. I'm sure he'll be back soon."

The evening passed quickly and had pretty much gone to plan: beers, football, beers, cab, beers, T-bone steaks, wine, beers, dancing, beers, G-strings, boobs, champagne, high fives, tequila, and Chinese food, all done and dusted by 4am. The only downside was that Sheldon was still missing, but Greg and Patrick were too drunk to care.

The following morning, Patrick finally arose from his drunken stupor. Despite the pain, he had enjoyed himself. The night was made even sweeter by Greg and Sheldon insisting on paying for everything and throwing their money around like The Rolling Stones. Patrick recalled Sheldon stuffing over one hundred pounds in ten-pound notes into the G-string of a lovely blonde girl who had been writhing around in his lap for a good half an hour. *One hundred for thirty minutes of "work"*, he thought to himself. His mind boggled, and his head ached as he hauled himself out of bed and proceeded to the kitchen in search of painkillers, bacon, and black coffee.

Next door, the scene was very similar: strewn beer bottles, empty Chinese food cartons, discarded clothes and shoes, the toilet seat up, and the mother of all hangovers in full effect. Greg was in a deep sleep, lying face down on his bed, mouth wide open, when the sound of fists banging on his front door jolted him awake. He glanced at the green digits on the digital clock next to the bed: 11:26am. By the time he got to the front door, it was almost hanging off its hinges from the continual banging.

"Sheldon, where the hell did you end up? Let me guess, you went home with a stripper?" Greg said, opening the door to the highly dishevelled party boy.

"I wish it was that simple, Greg. I got into some serious trouble," Sheldon said as he clutched Greg's arm with intent and led him into the kitchen.

"Where the hell did you go last night? We couldn't find you anywhere, what trouble?"

"I ended up leaving the strip club with some chick who took me to a poker game with some high rollers, and I lost twenty grand!" he said with full animation.

"What? Slow down. What are you talking about, twenty grand? What poker game?" Greg replied.

"I know, I thought I was going to get laid, but then she started talking about playing poker for money and my priorities changed. I couldn't find you or Pat to say I was going, and to be honest, it was all a blur. How much did we drink?" Sheldon said, looking sheepish and tired as he sat slouched at the kitchen table.

"You bloody idiot, Sheldon," Greg belted as he turned to fill the kettle.

Neither said a word as the kettle slowly boiled until Greg finally spoke first, handing a much-needed coffee to Sheldon.

"What were you thinking? How much cash did you have on you?"

"I thought I could win. The booze gave me confidence. I play poker all the time back home with my buddies, and I got carried away. You know I love to gamble," he explained, burning his lip as he slugged the coffee.

"The guys seemed legit, and I know it all seems crazy in the cold light of day, but I've done this before back home and made thousands. But this time, I was ten grand down by 2am. The buy-in was three grand, but they extended me a line of credit when I gave them my watch. Now, I owe the money to some dodgy dude called Liam who has threatened to scar me unless I pay him back in cash by tonight."

"Oh great, you sure know how to pick your card games, don't you?" Greg expelled. "They don't know where you come from or anything about you, do they?"

"They took my driver's license from my wallet when I could only get another five hundred out of the ATM machines, so they know my name. And they know where you live."

"Jesus Christ, Sheldon," Greg screamed, throwing both hands over the top of his head.

Sheldon walked out the back door, lit a cigarette, and sat on the white plastic patio furniture, glaring at Greg. Greg looked pale, either from the hangover or the realisation that all his dreams were built on party boy USA and his huge gambling addiction. Without Sheldon, there was no black hole. Without the black hole, there was no cash, no new house, and just his normal salary from the job he got sick of years ago.

"You do realise the banks are closed today?" Greg shouted from inside.

"I've never run out on a bet in my life, and I'm not

going to now. I'll go and pay it if you can lend me the money," Sheldon shouted back.

"I'll go and pay it, you idiot. That's almost forty thousand dollars. I've got a safe upstairs. I'm going back to bed," Greg seethed as he walked out of the kitchen.

Sheldon, relieved at the offer, smoked two more cigarettes before lying on the sofa and falling asleep.

A few hours later, the daunting task of stuffing twenty thousand pounds in cash into a backpack and taking it across town to someone who had threatened to maim his friend started to weigh down on Greg. He was seething at the thought of dropping off that amount of money and determined to make Sheldon pay every penny back.

The drop was scary; the guy didn't say very much other than "tell your American friend he's welcome here any time" before laughing and telling him to "fuck off". Greg didn't need to be told a second time and was out the door faster than when he arrived.

ELEVEN

Two months after the infamous visit of Mr Vaughan, things were settling back to normal – or as normal as could be when you're stealing tens of thousands of pounds a month. On an uneventful rainy Tuesday morning, the illegal game they had been playing looked all but up.

The unexpected arrival of the bank's chief executive, Charles Faulk, walking into Greg's office completely unannounced, was enough to stop anyone in their tracks.

"Hi, Greg, got a minute?" he said, pulling up a chair without waiting for a reply.

Greg instantly felt the sweat seep from the back of his neck, dampening the collar of his new twill shirt as Charles sat, crossing his legs right over left and flicking his tie to the side.

Greg was far from comfortable and could not even muster a hello. He began to think he must look guilty as hell.

"Greg," Charles said, drawing in a deep breath past

his cigar-stained yellow teeth he had clearly given up worrying about years ago.

"Hi, Charles," he managed.

"Let's cut to the chase. I know you have been involved in high-stakes poker games, as a few weeks ago, an acquaintance of mine watched you pay off a substantial debt to someone known to be involved with one of the worst criminal gangs in London."

Greg felt the words like a full-force gut punch but decided to stay quiet and motionless, desperately thinking back to the only two people in the room when he paid off the debt for Sheldon.

"I really don't care what sort of gambling addiction you may have, but what does concern me is how someone in your position can afford to lose such large sums of money," Charles continued. "What are you up to, Greg?"

By this stage, Greg was in complete panic but tried not to show it, even though he could have passed out at any moment. He sucked in a few breaths before launching his defence.

"An American friend of mine got himself into some trouble when visiting here and asked me to pay off the money on his behalf after he had left the country."

"I see." Charles seemed to ponder the lies with real gusto, for all of two seconds. "The same American friend that works for Verick?"

Greg nodded without opening his mouth.

"So, tell me about your new Porsche and the Saville Row suits you've been wearing to work over the last few months – think I wouldn't notice a two-grand suit when

I saw one? You must be stupid; my wardrobe is full of them."

Greg half-chuckled nervously and took a huge gulp of water from the glass atop a stack of reports on his desk. He had become complacent, taking his car to work on the odd occasion but still careful enough to park it away from the office. He was certainly better dressed than at any stage of his career, but it was too late to look back now.

Shit, he thought to himself in disgust at how casual he had become. In such a short space of time, he had become accustomed to the money and too relaxed, especially for a man who could be facing twenty-five years in jail at the drop of a hat.

"Listen, Greg, before you try to dig a big enough hole for you and your Porsche to fall into, I'll continue if I may," Charles said, leaning in with intent.

Greg did not move as the sweat started to pour relentlessly down his back. He felt cold as ice but was burning up at the same time with guilt, trepidation, and a little remorse.

"I understand there can be certain benefits to working for a big old bank like this," Charles said, waving his right hand out in front like he was Lord of the Manor. "After all, I have been here a lot longer than you." His voice started to become noticeably sterner. "Let us assume for just one moment the money was yours and that you have another income; one that far outweighs your salary here. One assumes you don't get let into any old card game without a decent-sized wager to start with." He scoffed.

Greg could hear his heart pounding as he watched the

equally corrupt Charles Faulk continue and suddenly offer him the unlikeliest of lifelines.

"Now, Greg, I'm leaving the bank at the end of the month to take early retirement, partly so I don't have to deal with that arsehole chairman anymore, but with me leaving you alone, it should help things and make life easier for you."

"I'm not sure what you mean, Charles," Greg said quietly, trying not to look guilty.

"We could be a team. You continue doing whatever it is you do, and I'll keep quiet, provided I receive, say, two grand a month," Charles requested.

Greg recoiled in his seat, enraged and astonished by the audacity of this pompous prick in his pinstriped suit, sitting in his office, blackmailing him. *It should be the other way round; I should be calling his bluff*, he thought to himself.

"I appreciate your concern, but I did inherit some money a while back, which helps me afford a few niceties in life. And like I said, the card money wasn't mine," he retorted.

Charles stood up abruptly, interlocking his fingers and stretching them outwards in the process, seemingly unruffled by the response.

"I like you, Greg, and if this is the case, perhaps we can forget this little conversation. But if there is anything you'd like to discuss, you know where I am."

Greg didn't respond, and Charles walked away.

As soon as he was gone, Greg decided to take off for some much-needed fresh air. *Wait until Sheldon hears of this*, he thought to himself as he stepped onto the busy street to consider his options.

He soon learnt about the "hush money", and went crazy but was told to "live with it" by Greg, who said it was a necessity, and after no arrests were forthcoming, they soon forgot about the extra honey pot that needed its monthly furnishing. Sheldon was too busy with his trips to Belize, living his best life, and being three thousand miles away, he was far enough detached from the goings-on in London so, as a result, felt far more relaxed than Greg.

Month after month passed, each of them with two thousand pounds in cash being handed to Charles Faulk's trusted driver, on the first Friday of each month outside the Dog & Duck public house at 1pm sharp. This made Greg start to feel more invincible than ever, like he was above the law – people knew, and he was still doing it. The only tricky part was pulling together that amount of money in cash, as most of the wealth he and Sheldon were accumulating was on paper, stashed away in bank accounts all over the world.

The latest instalment was to be the fifth payment, and prior to this, the handover was no different than any other. The whole amount was to be delivered in used notes, mainly twenties and fifties, in a brown envelope with no bank wrappers or elastic bands, just cold hard stolen cash or, as Faulk was led to believe, cash won at the high-stakes poker games. Greg pulled up on the corner of Pit Lane and Rupert Street and waited for the luxury black Mercedes to arrive, always on time and always without Charles Faulk. As the car pulled up, Greg glanced up and down the street before walking to the driver's side of the car, ready to pull the envelope from deep within his black jacket. The window rolled down on cue, and the delivery was complete, or so he thought.

"Mr Faulk will be expecting three thousand a month from now on."

"What?" Greg spat. "Is he taking the piss?"

"You heard. Nothing to do with me, DeWitt. Take it up with the boss."

The window rolled up; the envelope was gone; and the car sped off.

Greg walked back to the office, muttering, "Three bloody grand a month, that son of a bitch" as the chilly autumn air whisked around his ears, doing little to cool his temper.

Greg knew three was still a good deal in the grand scheme of things and was easily affordable from the little black hole, which was now making them more than £150,000 every six months, so 2% in "tax" didn't seem all that bad. Greg started to fret that Faulk knew exactly what they were doing and how much they rinsed from all those bank accounts monthly, so he was upping the ante. He chose not to think about it any further and headed back to the office, still smarting at his new outgoing but determined not to become paranoid.

This was not supposed to be some big internal fraud, just a lucrative plaything to give Greg enough cash to make a difference in what he thought was a sorry life. Sure, Sheldon had to get involved because, without him, there would be no black hole, but now a third party taking a sizeable "donation" made things far less comfortable. *Where is it all going to end?* Greg asked himself.

That afternoon, he could hardly call it work; he punched a few figures into the calculator repeatedly and spoke to Sheldon briefly, who was equally pissed off as now they were down fifteen hundred a month each instead of a thousand. Both agreed their options were limited, and while three thousand miles apart, they both planned the same thing that evening: getting drunk.

TWELVE

Another twelve months flew by at three thousand a pop, but little did Greg and Sheldon care as they had now amassed over three hundred thousand in illegal gains in a little over a year, most of which was now being stacked up high in cash at various bank security deposit boxes in Boston and London. Greg kept a few uncashed banker's drafts and twenty-five thousand in cash in his side of the wardrobe, hidden in an old shoebox underneath a pile of his shoes, confident Isabelle would never go near them. He treated her to chauffeur-driven nights out, first-class trips to Rome and Milan with enough new clothes and accessories to start her own clothing line.

Sheldon, living the life of a bachelor, was a little more orthodox in his stockpiling and stacked over a quarter of a million dollars in new one-hundred-dollar bills in a four-foot-square Milson and Reeves bank vault. All was going well for the Vaughan-DeWitt partnership until the first Friday of May, when Charles Faulk stepped up his extortion by demanding eight thousand pounds a month, which Greg instantly dismissed.

Up until now, the regular three-thousand-a-month payment was a well-automated process of stuffing the cash in a large brown envelope, handing it over, and doing it all again thirty days later.

This month, Greg was more nervous than ever for some reason; as he waited for the window of the Mercedes to roll down, he once again looked up and down the street. To his surprise, it was Faulk himself sat at the wheel. Greg's heart raced as he saw the unmistakable tan leather driving gloves Faulk was always seen wearing when driving.

"Get in," he said as Greg got within two feet of the gleaming German build.

Greg's pace slowed as he walked round the front of the car and entered through the passenger door. He glanced round quickly, and with nobody else in the car, he said, "I'm only paying you three; that's a good deal and you know it."

"Buckle up," came the reply without any eye contact as Faulk pushed down hard on the accelerator.

They drove in complete silence for twelve minutes as the car zigged in and out of traffic aggressively. To Greg, it felt like a lifetime as he thought of a hundred questions he could ask, only to receive the same response. He kept quiet for another eight minutes before the car turned into Kew Gardens and straight into what seemed to be a disused warehouse. The panic really kicked in as the roller shutter door came slamming down as both men exited the car.

"Mr Faulk, you know three thousand pounds a month

in cash is a great deal for doing absolutely nothing," Greg shot across the bows, his heart racing like the first meeting over a year ago where they agreed on two grand a month in his office.

"Listen here, DeWitt," he said without showing any interest in his opening statement. "I have brought you here today to find out what your long-term aspirations are, as I know you aren't playing cards. I've had you watched for the last three months, yet the money is coming from somewhere."

Greg stared at Faulk and did not utter a single syllable. *Think fast, DeWitt, think fast.*

With nothing coming to mind, Faulk continued, "Why would a middle manager at a bank be so willing to hand over three thousand pounds a month – the net equivalent of more than his entire salary – if he wasn't hiding something untoward?" Faulk demanded to know.

It was now or never for Greg. "I have another, more substantial, income that does need hiding," he divulged, much to his displeasure.

"Go on; I presume this has something to do with the bank?" Faulk said, pulling up an old plastic patio chair in the near-deserted lock-up.

"Yes, it does have something to do with the bank, and my plan was to keep going as I have done without getting greedy," he said.

"Well, Greg, I think now is the time to up your game somewhat and cash in quickly before you do get caught."

This was certainly not the plan, as Greg had always intended a long-drawn-out project that would keep the volume of gains low enough to stay under the radar. Pulling large chunks of cash was a stupid idea, one to get you caught out by some senior financial analyst or auditor, even if the black hole continued to hide the majority of gains.

"I disagree, Mr Faulk. I think the smaller transactions are harder to trace, and we wouldn't want to increase them too much more and run the risk of getting caught, would we?"

Faulk suddenly snorted and chuckled to himself in self-amusement. "Greg, you are the only one at risk of getting caught. I have nothing to do with this little operation you have going here."

Greg sensed the glint in his eye as he plunged both hands deep into the outside pockets of his rather fetching and very expensive brown Italian jacket. Faulk was right; he would never be traced back to the source and could easily blow things up with one phone call that would bring the whole thing crashing down around him. In a bid to get himself out of this uncomfortable situation rapidly, Greg reluctantly hit the negotiations trail, hoping to stop the idiotic thought of pulling millions out and the subsequent guarantee of incarceration.

"How about I increase your monthly to six grand?" he asked.

"Six grand is neither here nor there," Faulk said, brushing off the generous offer. "I want eight, but originally, I was thinking more in the region of ten grand."

"Ten grand a month? Are you bloody stupid?" Greg

spat, seriously starting to lose it now. He laughed aloud as sarcastically as he could muster under such circumstances. "You surely cannot be serious?"

No risk and more profits were on Faulk's agenda today.

"Oh yes, Mr DeWitt, I am deadly serious; you are forgetting this was my bank you are defrauding, so consider yourself lucky that I don't call the police to investigate your new-found wealth," he replied with a steely, cold grin.

Greg stared up at the broken glass panels high up in the ceiling and counted five pigeons sitting without a care in the world, preening themselves next to rows of wooden panels covered in cracked white paint.

"I could do the same thing and ask the police to sniff around your affairs at the bank over the last ten years," Greg shot back.

"You really are getting desperate, aren't you? There is little, if anything, to trace, certainly now that I've left."

"Okay," Greg said slowly. "I'll give you your eight grand—"

"Make it twelve," Faulk interrupted.

"You really are a prick, Faulk," Greg said, raising his voice and starting to get a little desperate. "How many months do you want twelve for?" he muttered, slowly realising he had no position to bargain.

"Why, planning to take off sometime soon?" he quipped.

"No, I just can't see this as a long-term plan, and with all the risk on my shoulders, I could just say no."

Greg stood his ground as best he could under wobbling knees, safe in the knowledge he was more lucrative alive than he was dead. By now, his stomach was swirling like a washing machine on spin.

"No is not an option, Greg. Maybe you need some persuading. I am a charming man, Greg, with many high-society connections, several holiday homes, and the police commissioner I can call on as a friend. But I also have friends in the gutter, linked to the underworld of organised crime, who are desperate to impress me."

Greg wasn't sure what he meant by that and involuntarily spat on the floor, which he figured was a way of his nervous system telling him to stop planning on launching himself across the front of the car and strangling Faulk. Surely, there was someone watching nearby; after all, the doors didn't close by themselves, so he assumed the driver was lurking in the shadows.

"You're deluded if you think we can get away with this level of pilfering on a long-term basis, Faulk."

"Who said anything about long term? Besides, I have no idea how you are gaining these funds, so you must be good and have all of your tracks covered."

Greg stood motionless, with a cold look of dread and anger etched across his face like a condemned man waiting to be executed. His spine shuddered, which quickly flipped his head from side to side.

"I'll give you ten a month," Greg offered, having carried out some quick mental arithmetic in the few seconds of silence that ensued.

"This isn't a flea market in Morocco, DeWitt. There's no negotiation. I want the full twelve for a year, then I'll walk."

The options were simple enough: pay him his seventy-two thousand in total for what would undoubtedly loiter for longer than the six months, or do not pay him anything more than what they had originally agreed and run the risk of being beaten, sacked, investigated, jailed, or worse. The final option was to up the percentage taken, which was riskier but helped cover some of the losses incurred by the ludicrously high twelve thousand a month Faulk was intent on swiping. Greg weighed up the options as Faulk pulled a small business card from his inside jacket pocket, providing Swiss bank account details for the transfer, which made it more difficult to hand over than cash.

"My Swiss bank account, Greg. I haven't got all day. Make sure the money is forthcoming, or there will be dire consequences, and I'm not fucking around."

With that, he pulled on his brown leather driving gloves, nodded to the far dark corner of the garage, and jumped into his car, reversing slowly as the rollers started to grind a rusty track skywards, pulling the shutters away from the oncoming luxury car. Greg was left to find his own way back, with plenty to think about along the way.

He knew for certain that Sheldon would be ready to disobey all instructions from Faulk when he caught wind of this latest demand.

THIRTEEN

1997

The decision took many late-night phone calls between Sheldon and Greg, but eventually, they agreed to cut off Faulk's payments, hopefully serving as a stern reminder that they were in charge. Greg meticulously erased all traces of the black hole monitor from his laptop and switched to a more secure pilfering method, using a hotel room once a month rather than his office. His position as head of IT networks gave him the freedom to carry out these operations discreetly, away from the office. With Faulk no longer the chief executive at the bank, they decided to eliminate him completely. The set-up was foolproof, with no traceable links back to Greg, Sheldon, or Verick. If cornered, Greg could always blame a bug in the system that he neither created nor could detect.

A month after asserting dominance over Charles Faulk, things were about to change; Greg and Sheldon were about to find out just how deep they had got themselves in the worst possible way.

Patrick was in police custody following the brutal murder of his wife, Charlotte, at their home next door.

Greg was devastated and in utter shock when the news came through from Isabelle, who was now six miles away at her mother's house while the police carried out their investigations next door. He learnt the grim news during a frantic, tearful phone call just as he was about to leave the office after a routine day at work.

Returning home to Millfield Road at approximately 6:35pm, he was greeted by yards of police tape, police controlling traffic at both ends of the street, the sounds of a helicopter circling above, police cars, unmarked vehicles, and news crews. The surreal scene struck him as he pulled up to the yellow tape.

Instructed to park at the end of the road, Greg walked up to the police tape and pointed to his house next door to the crime scene as two officers stopped him from going further. He was temporarily allowed to collect overnight supplies for Isabelle, Matthew, and himself. As he approached his front porch, his heart pounded faster. A large white tent covered the entire driveway, porch, and front door of Patrick's house, blocking any view inside. A huge floodlight illuminated both houses as forensic teams in white suits and blue plastic boots worked in a makeshift lab on the small, paved garden next to Patrick's ageing Volvo.

"Where's the boy?" Greg asked a young female officer.

"He's in safe hands and wasn't harmed in any way," she replied. Greg nodded in relief. "Did you know them?"

"Yes, very well. That is my house," he replied, pointing to his quieter home next door. "I cannot believe he would do this; no way."

"What were they like?"

"Just a normal, nice family who kept to themselves. I've known them for years. What happened?"

"I guess you will find out in the papers at some point. Poor woman. I feel sorry for the child," she said.

Greg didn't respond further. He walked towards his front door, thinking about little Jacob while trying not to look at the crime scene. He avoided any graphic sights as he quickly entered his house, grabbed clothes, and stuffed them into plastic bags. He tried to block out thoughts of Charlotte's body possibly still lying next door. Within minutes, he was done and slammed the door shut behind him, not looking back as he hurried to his car, avoiding eye contact with anyone.

In the days, weeks, and months that followed, Greg visited Patrick, who had recently been charged with murder, something he struggled to believe from day one. During one prison visit, Patrick pleaded his innocence so emotionally that both men were in tears as they discussed their devastation over Charlotte's death and the police's decision to charge Patrick with so little evidence. Isabelle had not stopped crying since her best friend's death and resented Greg for visiting Patrick, the man charged with the murder. Despite Greg's attempts to convince her of Patrick's innocence, Isabelle insisted on waiting for the jury's verdict. "What the jury comes back with will make up my mind for good," she repeated. "If he is found guilty, we will adopt little Jacob for Charlotte, not for Patrick."

The jury soon delivered a guilty verdict. A few months later, legal papers were drawn up at Patrick's request for Jacob to be adopted by Greg and Isabelle, who now insisted Greg sever all ties with Patrick. "Don't befriend him or comfort him. That bastard killed his wife, my friend, right here next door to where we are raising Matthew," she fumed one evening after several glasses of pinot grigio. "We're doing this for Charlotte, not for Patrick. I can't live here anymore. I want to put the house up for sale," she ranted.

Greg didn't know what to think and went through every day like it was the day before.

Weeks after the adoption was finalised, with Jacob showing no signs of trauma following counsellor assessments, he was officially released to Greg and Isabelle. Despite witnessing his best friend's sentencing and dealing with the stress of stealing large sums from his employer, Greg's life returned to a semblance of normalcy. However, he remained unaware of the continued threat from Charles Faulk, who had been quiet in recent months but was merely waiting in the wings for the right moment to strike back.

During a late-night phone call with Sheldon, Greg joked, "Things are quiet again now after the trial and we haven't heard from Faulk; we sure showed him who he was messing with."

Neither Greg nor Sheldon realised the extent of Faulk's patience and cunning as the trial took its course as, within days of that conversation, Greg was walking through

Central London when he was suddenly bundled into the back of a black van and frogmarched into the Park Plaza Hotel, where he experienced easily the worst day of his life.

As the door to room 432 opened, he was greeted by a stocky man in his forties, dressed in a black suit with an open white shirt revealing greying chest hair; Greg's unease grew stronger. The man, who seemed capable of cracking walnuts with his large hands, instructed Greg to take a seat, informing him that Mr Faulk would join him shortly.

As Greg sat nervously in the luxurious surroundings overlooking the London skyline, sweat seeped from his hairline down the side of his face. He wiped it with his cuffs as Faulk suddenly emerged from a side bathroom, casually drying his hands with a small white towel, which he soon discarded on the bed before seating himself six feet away from Greg.

"Thank you for coming, Greg," he said, as if he'd been given a choice. "I wanted to tell you in person how disappointed I am that our arrangement ended, but seeing as there was a well-publicised trial happening next door with your friend and neighbour, I thought it best to let the dust settle," Faulk began.

"I thought you'd be enjoying your retirement by now," Greg replied, staring straight ahead.

"Oh, I have been enjoying myself, but I believe there's still an opportunity for us to work together," Faulk said calmly.

"Work together," Greg scoffed, "blackmail is not a

form of working together, and besides, the money has now stopped, Faulk, so you're not getting any more as I simply don't have it," Greg lied.

"That's a shame for you, Greg, a real shame, because you need to know something that may change your mind, which is why I brought you here today," Faulk continued as he sat across the large, round table in the window.

"I don't give a shit what you've got to say; I'm not interested," Greg said, now looking out the window.

"Fredrick," Faulk swiftly called out, which made Greg sit a bit more upright. The heavy re-entered, holding a clear plastic bag containing a green knitted cardigan, which Greg instantly recognised as his own. His heart rate spiked.

"What the hell is going on, Faulk?" Greg demanded.

"Do you recognise this cardigan?" Faulk asked, as Fredrick dangled the bag close to Greg's face, revealing a large, dark-red stain covering more than half of the front section.

"Yes, it looks like one I own," Greg replied, trying to mask his anxiety.

"Owned, I think you might find. This is indeed your cardigan, with your DNA and hair fibres on it, plus a large patch of dried blood that once belonged to Charlotte Reade," Faulk revealed.

The bombshell hit Greg hard. His body went cold, and he struggled to process the reality of the situation.

"Your clothing with Charlotte's blood; how damning for you. How could this be?" Faulk continued in mock confusion.

"You fucking killed poor Charlotte?" Greg blurted, tears welling up as the realisation dawned on him.

"Not me, Greg. I contemplated ordering the demise of your wife, but I needed you focused on our arrangement, so I chose someone close but not too close," Faulk replied coldly as he stood up and walked towards the large window.

"What the fuck are you talking about, an innocent woman murdered over money!" Greg shouted as he leapt from his chair and lunged violently at Charles, slamming him hard against the glass, which was immediately met by one rapid, blunt punch to the side of his ribs by Fredrick, sending him to his knees.

Greg gasped for air for what seemed like over a minute as the room fell silent.

"Got your attention now, haven't I?" Faulk sneered.

"Who the hell are you?" Greg asked, crumpling back into his chair.

"Twenty-five grand a month, Greg. I want twenty-five grand," Faulk said calmly as Fredrick handed Greg a piece of folded paper with details of his Swiss bank account.

"I said there is no more money, Faulk," Greg said as he pulled himself to his feet.

"That's for you to figure out, Greg; after all, how much value do you put on your own family? And don't forget, I know where you live, and we have a nice little insurance policy of your clothes and her blood. Now get the fuck out," Faulk instructed as his demeanour became increasingly cold.

Greg didn't need another invitation and quickly left

the room, slamming the door behind him and sprinting down the corridor, not looking back.

Faulk sat back and lit up a cigar. "I think that went very well," he said to Fredrick with a wry, smug smile.

From that day onwards, Greg never fully recovered; psychologically scarred for life, he now carried the burden of knowing his actions indirectly led to the demise of a close friend and an even closer friend being framed for her murder.

He told Sheldon that Faulk's men had threatened his family, which infuriated Sheldon but didn't stop him from contributing half of the ransom. Greg's work suffered as he became reclusive, paranoid, and plagued by panic attacks. The stakes were higher than ever, and there was no turning back. What was supposed to give Sheldon and Greg the ultimate freedom became a deadly trap and a noose around their necks.

Greg knew he needed to take drastic action to protect his family, and Sheldon suggested moving to the United States, offering to help him secure a consultancy job at Verick.

"If we completely disappear to another continent, we can continue to lead our lives without the threat of Faulk," Greg said to Sheldon during an emotional conversation.

"You got that right, Greg, and don't forget, we can still run the black hole from here and keep a hundred per cent of the rewards for ourselves," Sheldon replied.

From the moment the idea was proposed, she needed hardly any convincing. Her enthusiasm was immediate, her agreement unwavering. With her support firmly in place, Greg wasted no time. He marched into the bank with a quiet determination, handed in his notice, and gave his reasons simply: personal matters, the weight of stress. It was as though a new chapter had already begun, the old one neatly closed with the stroke of a pen. He never revealed the true reason for their abrupt move, hoping neither Patrick nor Isabelle would ever discover the truth.

Greg contemplated telling Patrick of the move and, for a brief second, he also thought about coming clean and trying to help him clear his name but ultimately chose to protect himself and his family. If Faulk could seemingly get away with murder, Greg's family were in danger, so he decided to keep quiet.

They boarded the plane to New York, safe in the knowledge an offer was about to come in from Verick and with enough money in the bank to tide them over and help them apply for work permits in the US.

Greg's conscience was far from clear, but although his imprisoned friend was seemingly innocent, which he had thought all along, he deemed his life more important, so he put this phase of his life behind him as he readied himself for the next.

FOURTEEN

2015

Eighteen years: seventeen birthdays, seven lawyers, three unsuccessful appeals, fourteen minor scuffles with fellow inmates, a handful of trips to the warden's office, and hundreds of restless nights had all taken their toll. Patrick was finally a truly broken man, a pale shadow of the successful family man he once was before his friend and neighbour inadvertently ruined his life and took his beloved wife from him.

Incarceration can drive any man insane; a jail term, no matter how long, can see grown men reduced to tears, staring at the sky for hours each day, wishing their sorry lives had been different. Some prisoners' lives were so wretched that guards regretted taking the job; even though they were free to go home to their families every night, they were haunted by what they saw on a daily basis.

Every inmate had an elaborate story to tell about

his notorious past, but few would share, keeping it to themselves in fear of attracting too much unwanted attention. Only a few hard men sought the spotlight, knowing they could handle the heat if someone challenged their authority. Most kept quiet, and all pleaded their innocence to the crime that put them there in the first place.

Patrick was lonely and kept himself to himself as much as he could, troubled by the amount of drugs in prison and not willing to go anywhere near them. Within days of being locked up, he started to notice regular scabs or specks of blood on the inside of both arms of his cellmate, Dereck Weekes. He never mentioned anything to the guards despite his concerns for fear of retaliation and later found out Dereck died nine months into his sentence from a colossal heroin overdose. In the early days, Patrick questioned the guards about the availability of drugs and how control should be tightened, but that all stopped after several threats from inmates and occasional prison staff, all no doubt involved in making money, taking drugs, or banking favours.

Some inmates read; some lifted weights; some wrote; some sold cigarettes and drugs; some played cards; some studied; some talked non-stop; some listened; some worked; some hid; but most simply did nothing. Some became violent with others and, over time, he saw many were violent to themselves, leading to high suicide rates throughout the jail, with a couple not making it through the first night.

Over the years, Patrick had tried his hand at most

things: the compulsory work in the kitchens, playing football, basketball, and dominoes, painting, smoking a pipe, and always reading and writing.

A shadow of the well-dressed professional man he once was, Patrick had now become streetwise, resourceful, and hardened, but most of all, bitterly angry that his dear Charlotte and comfortable life had been taken away from him, along with his good family name being tarnished.

All his old colleagues, friends, and neighbours would now refer to him as a violent convicted killer – a tag he detested but could not shake. He had no escape from the pain of being an innocent man locked up like an animal, and on many occasions during the long and cold eighteen years, he had considered suicide himself but never attempted it. He could have jumped head first over a balcony to his death or found something strong enough to tie round his neck, but every time, his thoughts turned to his long-lost son, Jacob. Sometimes things became so tough he almost convinced himself it was the only way out, as the pain was unbearable, each day seeping away exactly the same as the day before and the day to follow.

Breakfast in the canteen was the same dour experience day after day – the usual cold eggs, cereals, hard toast, and lukewarm, weak coffee or tea that had clearly been through the strainer more than once – and lunch was not much better. The one hour of exercise per day was like being a lion at a zoo to the inmates, pointlessly walking, pacing, or running back and forth within the confines of their captor's lair.

After two unsuccessful appeals, he had accepted the

unthinkable: that the peak years of his life were going to be spent locked away with some of the world's worst human beings. The prime of his life was taken away, never to be replaced.

During the early days, he was scared, often intimidated, by the slightest glance from an inmate, regardless of whether they had stolen a car or murdered their whole family. Jail makes people look meaner than they actually are, and Patrick kept clear of everyone as much as he could for the first few years.

Some of his later friends would come and go as he hand-picked them based on the severity of their convictions. Murderers, paedophiles, and rapists were the scum of the earth, people he wouldn't look at, let alone spend time with voluntarily. He would only make conversation with inmates on lesser jail terms for driving offences, fraud, or minor drug running – people he would never have chosen to associate with had his life taken a different path, but he was forced to choose alliances from a bad stock. Glances and stares no longer filled Patrick with anxiety; it was all just a big game, like one giant pantomime, and it's surprising what a man becomes used to if subjected to certain things for any amount of time.

Cell 33B on the third tier had been home for the past seven years, and even though he shared this cell with convicted fraudster Bill Alexander, he felt fairly at ease and out of the way. On a regular basis, Patrick, having just returned from his usual two-hour shift cleaning the canteen after lunch, would spend the afternoon lying on his bed talking with his roommate, reading, or napping.

Bill had been in the same cell as Patrick for two and a half years, and while they had their moments, they mostly looked out for each other, and Patrick would call him a friend if cross words broke out with other inmates. During many conversations, Patrick had convinced Bill he was innocent, and he believed him, but there was always a piece of the puzzle missing: if he didn't kill Charlotte, who did? Sometimes they would laugh behind grated teeth at the awful predicament of him being caged without reason. It was the occasional laughter that helped keep them both semi-sane, or they would go crazy feeling sorry for themselves, which would ultimately cause them to reconsider checking out of life early, but Patrick's thoughts always returned to Jacob.

He resented Greg and Isabelle for leaving the country without telling him. It took over twelve months for him to find out, after contacting an old neighbour on Millfield Road who kindly informed him that they had all left to live abroad, but he didn't know where. Patrick hated the thought of Jacob being brought up by two different people in a foreign country. He couldn't understand why – so soon after Charlotte's death, his guilty verdict, and Jacob's adoption – they suddenly packed up and bolted to a different part of the world. He often wondered where they were, narrowing it down to English-speaking countries like Australia, Canada, or the US.

The question of Jacob's whereabouts and well-being constantly occupied Patrick's mind, and he clung to the hope of one day seeing his son again. If he could just spend ten minutes with his son now, it would be like winning the lottery, but those days were seemingly gone forever, and his regret over not spending more time with Jacob was deep and painful.

He had tried to contact Greg and Isabelle on several occasions, writing to the bank and sending letters to his old house next door in the hope of them being redirected, but nothing ever came back. Every now and then, he would write a letter and cling to a small thread of hope for a few weeks after posting it, but nothing ever returned. He had asked friends on the outside to track them down, but all failed with one story or another about them falling off the face of the earth.

Now, years later, with the internet at his fingertips, Patrick started researching software companies in Boston after remembering a night out with Greg and Sheldon, who mentioned he was from the area. With the power of the internet now available to him under the supervision of a guard, he spent hours each week sending emails to every software company in Boston, all with the same title: "Please Forward to Sheldon Vaughan", hoping one of his emails would reach him.

Sheldon eventually received one of these emails over coffee one morning and replied to Patrick, telling him his son was in New York and fast approaching his twenty-first birthday.

> *Dear Pat,*
>
> *I heard what happened all those years ago; life must be very tough for you, and I'm truly sorry about what happened to your wife. Greg says you*

are innocent, and I believe him. As far as Jacob goes, he is well and healthy, living in a nice suburb of New York City with Greg, Isabelle, and Matthew, where they have been for many years now. They treat him as one of theirs from what I can see, and I understand he is doing well at school too. I am sorry I cannot be more help; I cannot divulge any further information as it is not my place to do so, but I will tell Greg you wrote to me so he may contact you if he chooses.

All the best, Sheldon

Patrick was delighted to have learnt of Jacob's whereabouts and how he was but took little comfort from Sheldon and Greg thinking he was innocent. He wrote several more emails packed with questions, one containing a letter for Jacob, which he hoped Sheldon would pass on, but there were no more replies. He followed this up with several harshly worded emails to Greg and Isabelle, calling on her motherly instincts to let him have some contact with his only child. The pleading went unnoticed, as the emails were not delivered as Sheldon blocked all further contact from Patrick; he had said enough and didn't want to get involved.

Without ever receiving any further correspondence, Patrick took some comfort knowing Jacob was doing well in school in New York, even though it did little to boost his hope of ever tracking him down when he eventually got parole. "One day we will be reunited," he kept telling himself out loud during many tearful nights.

FIFTEEN

One afternoon, at precisely 3:36pm, a small ray of light appeared at the end of the long, dark, lonely tunnel. It came in the shape of Liam Phelps, the prison warden for the past nine years and three months, not that anyone was counting, but he was just four years from retirement and kept a little countdown calendar on his desk. This was an unusual visit to 33B, indeed to any cell, but one that was fully justified by the warden himself.

"Patrick," Liam said, standing in front of the steel door.

"Hi, Warden," Patrick replied, swinging his feet off the bed and sitting upright with concern. "Have I done something wrong? We had a drug sweep here yesterday," he continued, a puzzled wrinkle sweeping across his brow.

"Come with me, please," Liam said, showing no warmth as he pointed towards the now-open cell door.

"This is a surprise. What's going on?" Patrick asked with urgency.

"I'll explain. Just follow me, please, Patrick," he replied.

"Is everything okay? Is it my son Jacob? He lives in America now," Patrick asked, worry now clearly visible in his eyes.

"Relax. It has nothing to do with your son," Liam said, walking down the blue-painted steel stairs towards the warden's office.

The only other time Patrick had been to the warden's office was to be told his appeals for a retrial had been turned down. This room reminded him of cold disappointment as he was instructed to sit.

The warden's office was basic, with a thinning rug covering most of the stained black wooden floor; an old laptop flickered in the corner next to a kettle and two stained coffee mugs full of teaspoons. An overstocked bookcase demonstrated the varying tastes in literature the warden enjoyed, none of which were arranged neatly, with some lying horizontally in places.

Without warning, Liam started to divulge. "Ever heard of Fredrick Milne?" he asked.

Pausing for a couple of seconds to watch the rain slip down the large windowpane to his left that overlooked the south exercise yard, Patrick replied, "No, why? Who is he?"

"Have you heard of Charles Faulk?"

"The name is vaguely familiar. Wasn't he the head of that bank in London where that son of a bitch, Greg DeWitt, once worked before he stole my son and ran off to the States?" Patrick spat with unusual venom and a hint of sarcasm.

"Patrick, Fredrick Milne was a distant cousin of

Charles Faulk and someone he worked with for many years, a fixer if you like. He died yesterday morning."

"Who? Milne or Faulk?" Patrick said nonchalantly.

"Faulk disappeared years ago. Milne died at a hospital somewhere up in Hertfordshire, but before passing, he confessed in some detail to killing your wife."

Patrick's heart exploded, racing faster than ever before, as if he were on the twenty-fifth mile of a marathon. His gaze was firmly fixed on the messenger, who had never seen the look on Patrick's face, or any face for that matter. His eyes burnt bright and round as Liam watched the man, found guilty and locked up for eighteen years, physically pale and break down into a flood of tears. He felt the emotion in the room; tangible was an understatement.

"Take a minute, Patrick; I know this must be a huge shock," Liam said, sitting down in silence, glancing at a prison memo while Patrick wept into cupped hands and used his sleeves to wipe his eyes and nose for nearly three minutes.

"I know this is a shock, but statements and photos taken from the scene have been compared already and show an uncanny resemblance to what Fredrick Milne described," Liam continued.

"Did he say why he did it?" Patrick finally managed to muster.

"No, just that you were innocent and that he may as well confess now that he was about to expire."

"Could this have been an act of revenge against Charles Faulk? Was he somehow involved in the death of

Charlotte? What happens now?" So many questions but only one answer.

"It depends on a complex appeals process that is going to take months, so don't set your sights too far ahead just yet."

"Appeals process? I've always maintained my innocence, and now somebody else has confessed. I should be allowed to walk; you know I should."

"I'm afraid it's not as easy as that, Patrick. Like I said, you need to slow things down and take one stage at a time," Liam said, standing up from his desk and resting against the radiator underneath the window to warm his backside.

"There is no signed confession. It was only heard by a few people – five at best – and the man is now dead. It could have been a sick joke on you, knowing he was about to die."

"But if he talked in great detail about what happened on that day in my house, then surely that means something?"

"It does, and I'll be pushing for new DNA testing, which is a lot more accurate than it was back when you were first arrested, but remember this is a long time ago now, and there will be little to nothing worth testing."

"How long does that take?"

"Again, it depends. First, we have to get the courts to prevent Milne from being buried and agree to DNA testing. Then we have to see what tagged and bagged samples, if any, taken from your wife and the surrounding areas at the time remain on file."

"This is absolute bullshit, and you know it."

"Hang on," the warden said, holding up his hand as if to stop traffic. "Then a medical examiner must complete their work, and depending on their schedule, this could take some time. These labs get horrendously backed up, you know."

"I've waited eighteen years for this day, and it feels nothing like I expected it to," Patrick said, wiping his face of old tears and pulling himself together.

"I must warn you, your parole hearing could come round quicker than the results of any tests, and any appeals process will be notoriously slow and drawn out."

"I should be allowed to leave today, not in a year. I want to rebuild my life and find my son," Patrick said, putting both hands on the warden's desk.

"I'll keep you up to date, and I'm sure the investigation team will be in touch with me in due course."

"In due course? What does that mean? I'm innocent – he's confessed – let me go."

"Sorry, Patrick, you know I can't make that decision. There is little comfort in this, but I'm pleased this has happened. You are a model prisoner, and we cannot change the past, but we may be able to change the future. Now head back to your cell, and I'll be in touch when I hear anything," the warden said as he walked towards his office door.

Patrick suddenly found himself back in his cell in a numb daze. He sat in silence on the corner of his bed with his hands clasped together in his lap, thinking of nothing but Charlotte and Jacob. He didn't utter a single word or one sigh as he sat remembering the smoothness of her skin, how he used to run his fingers through her long, brown hair, and as he closed his eyes, he could hear the gentle tones of her voice.

Thinking of Charlotte always filled Patrick with emotion – sometimes rage, but mostly love and a great, sickening feeling of loss. He could no longer make her smile, hold her hand, cup her face, or make love to her, and the pain was made so much worse by his conviction for her death. Surely, he had suffered enough in losing her. So many years had passed, and after several unsuccessful appeals, he had lost the will to continue the fight to clear his name.

He closed his eyes tighter, hoping the images of Charlotte would become clearer and brighter as the tears started to roll towards his chin once more. He lay back on his bunk, the crease of the grey blanket encasing the destroyed soul of a man who had lived someone else's life.

He always knew his existence should have been different, and now maybe other people would start to believe there was a chance he should have been allowed to continue his middle-class life as a free man, even if it was without his beloved wife, Charlotte. The harsh reality was so far removed that he would have never dreamt of sharing a cell with a complete stranger for almost eighteen years after being wrongfully convicted of killing his wife, whom he adored.

SIXTEEN

When the DeWitts first moved to the US, things were exciting; Greg was in a better place mentally and felt he didn't need to look over his shoulder at every turn as he had done back in London. As a result, the marriage and the family unit flourished in the early years as Greg was able to successfully block out the anguish and guilt he felt at being told Patrick was innocent, which he never acted on.

He pushed the green cardigan with Charlotte's blood stain on to the back of his mind and moved on with his life.

Greg and Isabelle originally fell in love with a sprawling two-storey home in New Jersey with a basement complex when they first arrived that served as a perfect den for their boys. The house, just ten years old, boasted spectacular river views and was located in an exclusive community of fourteen similarly priced homes. Each home had extended gardens, long, looping driveways, expansive entrance halls with full-height vaulted ceilings and impressive chandeliers illuminating wide, open spaces.

They were happy in their first home, and with a permanent base, the family explored many new places, most within a few hours' flight. In the first year alone, Greg took eleven weeks of "holiday" from his position at Verick, taking Isabelle and the boys to Disneyland, Naples, Cancún, Hawaii, Aruba, Cabo, and on occasional boys-only weekends with Sheldon to Las Vegas, Chicago, and New Orleans. Greg also indulged in fishing trips off the coast of San Diego, shooting in Arizona, and gambling thousands of ill-gained dollars in Atlantic City with Sheldon, who showed no signs of slowing down his ultimate party boy image.

The family had everything they desired, with plenty of money rolling in from Greg's less-than-high-ranking consultancy work at Verick, which covered their extravagant expenses. Greg's job appeared very lucrative, though in reality, he was a little used consultant that picked up thirty hours a month at a flat rate of four hundred dollars an hour and most of the work, if you could call it that, came from his good friend, Sheldon.

Greg didn't need the income from Verick but went through the motions of completing tasks for his employer in order to keep his green card; without this, he was faced with a return to the UK, which was definitely not on the cards.

And, after nine years and with the boys growing up fast, they decided to move for what would be the final time in their relationship. They purchased an elegant six-thousand-square-foot home in the leafy suburb in Westchester County, New York. Greg and Isabelle chose the area for its good schools and proximity to New York City should they want to go shopping or catch a flight, which was convenient for Greg for work, while being far enough from the city's hustle and bustle.

The house was set in an acre of well-manicured gardens with a four-car garage to the right. Above the front door, which was flanked on either side with large, white pillars, was an elegant balcony with a large arched window that added so much light to the entrance lobby. The balcony gave a regal feeling to the property, which was instantly appealing to Greg.

A large central fireplace with brick cladding to the ceiling, which dominated the main reception room, a real open fire furnished by a huge log store at the rear of the property, and open-plan living were the many features Isabelle loved the second she viewed the property.

On occasion, Isabelle wanted to return to the UK, knowing nothing about the possible dangers of the criminal underworld in London that could be lurking round any corner, but Greg was always quick to dismiss the idea, saying the boys were happy and settled.

Isabelle spent her days having her nails done and lunching with "the girls" as she affectionately called them, who were all local in the neighbourhood and of similar age to her. Most of them were like Isabelle: didn't work thanks to their wealthy, high-powered, and often inattentive, serial cheating husbands, who would often stay out late, sometimes all night, with their younger secretaries.

As the overspending continued through the years, and as their eldest and only biological son, Matthew, prepared to go to college, the initial excitement of the move to the United States had well and truly worn thin. Greg and Isabelle had no more children and found themselves stuck in a relationship that had turned into a facade, maintained mainly for the sake of their boys, their social standing, and lack of desire on either side to part ways.

Greg had become bored with life; he would take the odd "business trip", as he called it, which were always in the US, but the reality was, he was heading to the Cayman Islands, Belize, and other tax havens to move money around, as he relied heavily on the cash reserves he was still amassing from The First Bank of London, which was still operating but at a much smaller rate of pocketing.

The money began to run low due to Greg's excessive spending and pending college fees and Sheldon's overindulgent lifestyle that showed no limits. In response, they started working on identifying a new black hole opportunity in Manhattan, something they swore they would never do; just as long as the Verick system continued to be the platform of choice at The First Bank of London, the money would continue, but they became complacent, and greed started to set in.

Greg read the financial pages of major newspapers in New York, scouring reports to identify which companies were doing well, which were hiring, and who was climbing the corporate ladder the fastest. This gave Greg a sense of purpose, which was sorely missing in his life, as he started to pull together a list of key targets.

Meanwhile, in Boston, Sheldon scoured through a list of financial organisations using their products and cross-referenced it with the target list to find a suitable, and more importantly vulnerable, mark.

Eventually, they set their sights on the well-established Gold Leaf Bank, where Sheldon had long-standing connections due to the bank using Verick's banking system, BN1000. Greg instructed Sheldon to arrange a series of "account management" meetings at Gold Leaf Bank to find their next target, as they looked to create a new digital black hole, which was easy enough to do, but they needed someone on the inside to identify the dormant bank accounts.

After several meetings over as many weeks, and with background checks being carried out on several people, the deliberation was over. Some marks were discarded because they had law enforcers in the family; some had families that were too big; some had a history of moving from one job to another. Eventually, they landed on Securities Manager Hill Copeland, who was perfect for the task in hand. He was a loner with a modest, rented one-bedroom apartment in Queens, who frequented seedy brothels in four of the five boroughs, excluding Manhattan due to its expensive women and proximity to his workplace.

Greg had arranged for photographs to be taken of him leaving various establishments in case they needed to resort to extortion and obtained his bank statements through the Verick platform, which revealed his constant use of a free-of-charge overdraft due to lack of funds towards the end of the month.

Greg built a fragile relationship with Hill at first, visiting him under the pretence of conducting a Verick audit, which only worked because of his naivety and unwillingness to challenge authority. But Greg was patient, and after a few months of meeting Hill, watching him, having him followed and grooming him, he finally made a breakthrough and invited Hill on a night out with the promise of a free and fun evening on Sheldon's company credit card. Hill, eager for companionship and excitement, accepted enthusiastically.

The play was in motion as Sheldon caught the train from Boston to Penn Station and checked into an expensive hotel in Midtown near to the Empire State Building.

They agreed to meet at 8pm at a local bar chosen by Greg, an eponymous spot that opened in the early sixties and was named after a local boxer. Poor Hill didn't expect a thing as he had worked with Sheldon on a previous project and was looking forward to a Friday night out that didn't involve paying for company and late-night pizza.

The three of them stumbled out of a speakeasy, their laughter echoing through the narrow streets of the Lower East Side as they headed to the next bar. Sheldon, always the loudest, slung an arm round Hill's shoulders, a cigarette dangling precariously from his lips as he shouted something unintelligible into the night.

Hill, grinning like a man who had forgotten all his loneliness and financial troubles, waved a half-empty bottle of bourbon like a victory flag. Behind them, Greg trailed slightly, quietly observing, cautious to make sure Hill was definitely their man, but tonight his eyes glittered with mischief, cheeks flushed from whisky and the thrill of the chase. They zigzagged through the neon-lit streets, dodging cabs and catcalls with their own brand of reckless energy.

As the evening finally started to wane, Greg said, "We should do this again, Hill. Have you enjoyed yourself?"

"Absolutely, I have, and I can't thank you enough for your very generous hospitality," Hill said, climbing into a taxi as the sun started to rise.

"Any time, Hill, we'll be in touch – we had a blast," Sheldon stated as he closed the door on Hill and waved him off.

"What do you think, Shel?" Greg said as the taxi pulled away into the empty road ahead.

"Oh yeah, he's our guy," Sheldon said, grinning from ear to ear.

SEVENTEEN

For months, Hill had been living what he considered "the dream": expensive trips to strip clubs, casinos, high-end restaurants, bars, and ice hockey games, all paid for by Greg and Sheldon. Each time Sheldon arrived in town, they would go on a spree, throwing cash around like it grew on trees, paying for pretty girls, and plying Hill with the finest wines money could buy. It wasn't hard to loosen him up.

Hill – short, balding, and slightly overweight – was a forty-year-old from Arkansas. Lonely, friendless, and aching for excitement, he found himself caught up in their whirlwind of excess. After a few of these lavish nights out, Hill genuinely believed they were friends, real friends.

But Greg and Sheldon saw him for what he really was: the perfect mark. They had a plan, and Hill was nothing more than a piece on the board.

The night it all came to a head started at a steakhouse just off Sixth Avenue in Manhattan, the kind of place where the waiters wore white gloves, and the wine list came in a leather-bound book. Hill had just devoured a fifty-ounce steak, wiping his mouth with a napkin as he leant back in his chair, flushed from meat and wine. He looked over at his two companions.

"How do you guys get such large expense accounts?" he asked, genuinely curious.

Greg and Sheldon exchanged a quick glance, an unspoken conversation flashing between them.

"What's your limit?" Sheldon asked casually, taking a sip of his bourbon.

"Honestly?" Hill shrugged. "I don't have one. They don't trust me enough, I guess. I'm not that important."

Sheldon chuckled, throwing a look at Greg. "We have all sorts of fun up and down the East Coast, don't we, Greg?"

Greg nodded, swirling the amber liquid in his glass. "Absolutely. Why don't you join us, Hill? You could be doing the same."

Hill raised an eyebrow, the ice in his Manhattan cocktail clinking as he chewed on a cube. "Join you doing what?"

Sheldon smirked. "Yeah, we've got jobs at banks and Verick, but you'd have to be pretty naive to think all the fun we're having is paid for by company credit cards."

"I just assumed it was all part of the deal since I'm your customer," Hill replied, a little uncertain.

"You're not my customer; I'm merely a consultant for Verick," Greg pointed out.

Hill hesitated. "But aren't I Sheldon's?"

"Nope," Sheldon replied, eyes gleaming. "We just like hanging out and getting wasted. Right, Greg?" He flagged down the waitress for another round.

Hill, now several drinks deep, leant forward. "So where does the money come from?"

Greg gave a slow smile, leaning in as well. "Well, Sheldon and I found a little loophole a few years back. Ran a scheme out of a bank I used to work at in the UK. To this day, no one has a clue."

Hill blinked, processing. "And how can I get in on this?" he asked, his voice slightly hushed, though he wasn't quite sure why.

Greg and Sheldon exchanged another look. "I don't know if this is really your thing," Greg said slowly. "It's... not exactly legal."

"I see," Hill said, cautious but intrigued. "Still, I'm interested."

Greg leant in closer, lowering his voice. "All we need is for you to help us identify some static bank accounts that haven't been touched in years and help Sheldon install some covert code on the Verick system at Gold Leaf. You open the firewall, let Sheldon provide the latest 'update', and we take care of the rest. It's completely undetectable."

The waitress appeared, setting down the round of fresh Manhattans. The pause gave Greg a moment to gauge Hill's reaction.

Sheldon grinned, raising his glass. "Tell him the best part."

Greg leant in even further, his voice barely more than

a whisper. "We'll start you off with a four-grand-a-month commission. Tax-free, of course."

Hill blinked again, trying to appear nonchalant as he leant back in his chair. "What do I have to do for that kind of money?"

"Nothing," Greg replied. "Just help us set things up and sit back and relax. We'll be up and running in no time."

Hill swirled the drink in his glass, the uneasy sense that this was too good to be true gnawing at him. "What's the catch?"

Sheldon gave a grin, lifting his glass higher. "That's the beauty of it – there isn't one."

"Cheers," Greg added, his voice smooth as velvet, as their glasses clinked in a quiet toast.

As they drank, the realisation of what Greg and Sheldon were proposing settled in the pit of Hill's stomach, but the lure of easy money – of real camaraderie, of excitement – was too strong to resist. He smiled, feeling the warmth of the alcohol, and nodded.

He was in. Their inside man.

Things ran smoothly, and in the first month, they cleared a cool forty-three thousand dollars, with Hill receiving his payment in cash from Greg at the end of the first month under strict instructions not to flaunt his new-found income. Over an eighteen-month period, they amassed over four hundred thousand dollars between them, and Hill was soon boosted to a 10% share, plus occasional bonuses.

Sheldon continued his partying lifestyle, while Greg,

feeling increasingly isolated from Isabelle, stockpiled money after slowing his spending. Despite his new income stream doing exactly what they expected, Greg was unhappy, resenting Isabelle and yearning for freedom, yet he stayed with her for fear of being investigated should either of them file for divorce. Not to mention his desire to continue to ride the gravy train as much as possible. Over the years of taking that dated back to London, Greg had collected Swiss watches, driven every imaginable car, and flown first class around the world, but he continued to grow in discontent.

Hill Copeland enjoyed his wealth too, moving to a much larger apartment in a more desirable area. Unable to build relationships, he remained a classic loner, happy to buy friends and pay for female company. One afternoon, his unease grew when Greg and Sheldon invited him to Chicago for the weekend, a first that filled him with trepidation, sensing that something was about to change.

Sheldon and Greg had become complacent and increasingly greedy after years of successful larceny, and Hill was well on his way to joining them.

"You're booked into Hotel One Point on East Wacker by the river. Meet us at the House of Blues on the other side of the river. Go through the doors, up the stairs, and we'll be at the bar on your right," Greg had instructed in their last phone call before they were due to all meet in the Windy City.

The idea of the meeting made Hill slightly uneasy as they had never met outside of New York before, but with the Gold Leaf project well up and running, a less local meeting was needed, and with Verick based in Boston, that was no good either.

After landing at O'Hare International, Hill moved quickly through the airport, his mind buzzing with uneasy thoughts. The black car he'd arranged was already waiting outside, its windows gleaming with the rain that had just begun to fall. He slid into the middle seat in the back, clutching his worn leather carry-on bag like his life depended on it. His fingers drummed nervously against the bag's handle as he stared out at the rain streaking across the car windows.

With everything going so well, why the hell do they want to meet me here? he thought, feeling the pit in his stomach tighten. I hope they aren't planning to get rid of me.

The car sped through the wet streets of Illinois, and Hill watched the bright, blurred lights of oncoming traffic cut through the rain. He couldn't shake the feeling that something wasn't right. Sure, he'd been on a hell of a ride, living large, spending freely, even paying off some of those debts that had been haunting him for years. He'd got comfortable. Too comfortable, maybe.

He was soon at his hotel, where he freshened up with efficiency, keen to get the night over and done with. A quick change of clothes, a splash of cold water on his face, followed by aftershave, and he was out again, walking briskly across the bridge on North State Street that arched over the Chicago River, his collar turned up against the biting wind the city was renowned for.

The rain had settled into a steady drizzle as he

approached the House of Blues, its neon blue sign buzzing like an omen in the damp air. Hill spotted Sheldon immediately as his short legs carried him up the stairs and into the bar.

Sheldon waved; Greg was nowhere in sight.

Hill forced a smile, but his mind raced for no reason.

"Hill, you fat bastard, how are you?" Sheldon jested with his usual aplomb before pulling in the last of the good stuff.

"Oh, hello, Sheldon. Yes, I'm fine, thanks. Is Greg here?" Hill replied nervously.

"He sure is, over in the corner," Sheldon said, standing up at the bar and putting his right arm round Hill's shoulders, tucking him under his wing.

The drinks soon arrived, and as they walked through the busy bar, Hill clocked Greg sat at a small table near the back of the noisy bar, busy tapping away an email or text into his phone.

"Hi, Hill, come and sit down," Greg said, pointing to a chair next to him, placing his phone on the table in front of him with the screen still lit.

"Hi, Greg. Thanks, how are things?"

The bar was full of Friday-night boozers, parties out to try the nachos and burgers, mixed with a few tourists enjoying the music. Tonight, a solo blues guitarist sat on a stool in blue jeans, a scruffy polo T-shirt, and an even scruffier goatee beard and cowboy hat. He didn't look great under the bright spotlight, but he could definitely hold a note.

"I haven't been here before; nice place," Hill mustered,

trying not to show his nervousness as he twitched in his seat like a child needing to use the toilet.

"Hey, thanks for coming to see us, Hill. Yes, this is a cool place. I've been here a few times," Greg said, brushing aside the remnants of the beer label he had been peeling off his bottle as he waited for Hill to arrive.

"Oh, no problem," Hill replied as they sipped on the frothing beers in large glasses complete with oversized handles.

"Twenty-six bucks for three damn beers," Sheldon moaned as he took his first slug. "There's a 7-Eleven round the corner; I could have picked up a cooler of six-packs for less than half that," he continued before pouring another huge mouthful of brew down his gullet.

"Moan, moan, moan, that's all he bloody does," Greg quipped, slapping Sheldon across the back of his large head.

Hill, Greg, and Sheldon hadn't spent much time together lately, even though they had been in "business" for well over a year, so the night was always going to start off a little slow.

"Look, Hill, you look shit scared, so just chill out and enjoy the music and have a few beers," Sheldon said in a jovial Friday-night, let's-drink-beer kind of way. "We can talk business later."

This suited all parties, and over the next three hours, they tucked into steak and shrimp dinners and at least six beers each, enjoying the ambiance and the steady flow of blues from the stage. The evening reminded Greg and Sheldon of their first meeting back in 1991 when they sat in Boston watching football, only to end up talking about the idea of the black hole for the very first time.

Sufficiently lubricated, the agenda changed as they started to discuss pushing the percentages for more and more cash. *This thing is about to go through the roof,* Hill thought to himself as the plan was spelt out by Greg.

Hill knew he couldn't say no to his paymasters; after all, they could just walk away and leave him to clear up the mess; he was the one on the inside who had facilitated the black hole.

Finally, he now knew why he was in Chicago: to agree to up the tempo and identify pensions, foreign exchange calculations, and mortgage transactions that created the odd irregular amount that could be rounded down to take more than just from the frozen bank accounts. There was no turning back for Hill; he was in way too deep.

EIGHTEEN

Patrick's fury was fermenting at the lack of any change in his circumstances following Fredrick Milne's confession almost three months ago. The prison service and the courts would not take a dying man's confession seriously, even if it could clear the name of an innocent man who had spent the last eighteen years behind bars – there had to be more proof.

The warden had repeatedly warned him not to get ahead of himself, often regretting that he had shared the information at all, as it would have made his life quieter. These things inevitably took time and required extensive research. Patrick had been warned that cases like this were rare, with few legal precedents, so it was unlikely he would be released before his parole hearing.

After meeting with the warden, Patrick spent several days sobbing in his cell, eating very little, and refusing all leisure time. He struggled to process the tiny snippet of information about what had actually happened to his beloved wife, Charlotte. He felt sick as he tortured himself with images of what had been done to Charlotte on the day of her death.

He screwed his face up in sheer frustration, thinking repeatedly about how Milne could have entered the house without a trace, killed Charlotte, and left without any sign of his presence. The mangled mess of her remains on the floor, the blood everywhere, would haunt Patrick for the rest of his life. The burning pain inside him now stemmed from not knowing why Fredrick Milne, a complete stranger to his family, would commit this dreadful act without any obvious motive.

Was it just a random act of violence?

Did he know her?

Were they having an affair?

Was he high on drugs?

How did he get in?

How did nobody in the street see or hear anything?

The questions kept coming, over and over, without any answers, driving him insane.

The circles round his eyes became redder and redder as his impatience grew. Almost a month after hearing about the confession, tired, unshaven, and unable to cry anymore, Patrick suddenly stopped feeling sorry for himself. His thoughts began to clear from the haze of sorrow and helplessness.

He cleaned himself up, ate regular meals, called a meeting with his legal brief, and arranged with the warden for additional time away from his cell to study Milne in the prison's library. His legal brief held out some hope of an early release based on the confession but warned Patrick not to hold out too much hope. The likelihood was he would have to wait until his official release date, six months from now, before he could walk the streets as a free man. Patrick wanted to clear his name, but his number one priority now was getting out of prison in sound body and mind.

At 9:05am on a Tuesday morning, 6,670 days after he was jailed for a crime he did not commit, Patrick sat down in the library. With the internet at his fingertips, he started to read every news report he could find on Fredrick James Milne and his life of crime and recent death.

Why would a notorious gangster from London's East End suddenly decide to kill Charlotte? he thought to himself.

Pondering this question over and over drove Patrick to distraction, but he remained focused on his quest to seek the truth. He knew it was unlikely he would find all the answers, but if he had any aspirations of getting out early and clearing his name, he had to start somewhere.

The hours of research, both in his cell through printed materials and in the library, were a welcome distraction. But after three days of getting nowhere, he had only managed to find out that Milne had been in jail for numerous acts of violence over the years, ranging from wounding with intent, to attempted murder, racketeering, and arson.

Over the past twenty-five years, Milne had served more than nine years in jail. Crucially, Patrick discovered from an old newspaper cutting that Milne was released from one stint in jail just five months before Charlotte's murder, confirming he was almost certainly not in jail at the time of her killing. The stories started to add up, and through his perseverance, Patrick managed to piece together further information about Charles Faulk. Now retired, he had flown back to the UK from Tenerife to attend Milne's funeral just two days prior.

Patrick was soon hit with the bombshell that DNA tests would prove inconclusive, which wasn't entirely unexpected, considering the amount of time that had passed, so it did little to dissuade him from continuing his research.

Determined to dig deeper, Patrick requested additional records, tracing connections between Milne and anyone who could have had a motive to harm Charlotte. As he delved into the seedy underbelly of Milne's past, Patrick stumbled upon a series of events and relationships that painted a darker picture. He found whispers of a possible connection between Charlotte and an old business associate of Milne's: a man named James Talbot. Talbot had been involved in a number of shady deals that Milne had orchestrated, and there were rumours of a falling-out between the two.

Driven by this new lead, Patrick requested an interview with Talbot, hoping to extract any useful information. The waiting period was excruciating, but Patrick held on to the hope that this line of inquiry might finally yield some answers. Meanwhile, he continued to build his case, amassing every bit of evidence he could find to support his innocence and expose the truth behind Charlotte's murder.

Every morsel of information about Faulk, Milne, and

DeWitt – who he had now thrown into the mix following his unexplained disappearance from the UK with his own flesh and blood – was invaluable. Somehow, these three were involved in Charlotte's demise, he surmised, almost convincing himself.

One late afternoon, as the sun beamed through the high windows in the library, Patrick started to sketch out a timeline that would set him on the road to redemption:

Milne released from prison.
Charlotte murdered.
His arrest.
The trial.
Greg and Isabelle adopt Jacob.
Faulk retires from The First Bank.
Greg and Isabelle flee the UK without any warning.
Milne jailed for attempted murder.

All of these events, starting with Charlotte's murder, happened within the space of around eighteen months. They could easily be dismissed as coincidences, but one question remained unanswered: why flee to the States with Jacob if you have nothing to hide? No letter, birthday card, or phone call in eighteen years made Patrick realise that Jacob probably didn't even know of his existence back in the UK. This, combined with the timeline of events, made him more and more suspicious about the good fortune Greg had been enjoying in the lead-up to Charlotte's murder back in 1994. While he was still in jail, Patrick would need help on the outside.

There was one other person in the world who might share the same level of motivation to uncover the truth about Charlotte's death, but that person simply didn't know it yet – that was about to change.

Patrick called in a few favours with a guard he had befriended over the years. The guard, in turn, contacted a police friend who did a bit of digging and found out that Jacob DeWitt, as he was now known, went to school in Boston, Massachusetts. If this mess were ever likely to get untangled, Jacob would be his only saving grace and perhaps the source of information about why Greg and Isabelle left the UK so quickly without even selling their house. Why did they agree to adopt his son, telling Patrick everything would be fine and they would help him clear his name, only to suddenly bolt from the UK with his son and never allow any contact?

Something didn't add up in Patrick's mind. He needed to pull a few more favours and finally get in touch with his son. A long shot, but the only shot.

At the age of twenty, Jacob DeWitt had everything he could have dreamt of. He had a gleaming black BMW 4x4, good teeth, good hair, money in his pocket, one or two girlfriends, and good grades at a prestigious university. Life was good, and he had few cares in the world, although he would probably admit to needing a few more friends. In the main, he was happy and had a plan for how he wanted his life to unfold.

His young life was very similar to those of his peers. He grew up playing in the streets of tree-lined suburbs or in the deep back gardens of sprawling homes in the finest neighbourhoods. He knew he was different from most because the two people he called Mum and Dad were not his real parents due to some tragic accident he tried to block out from time to time. All in all, Jacob and his friends were very similar, and few knew the family had a terrible past. Through his parents' accents, they knew they had come over from England, but that was about it.

The one very dark fact from his past was shrouded in secrecy. Greg and Isabelle had told him both his parents were killed in a car crash, and as their good friends and neighbours, they legally adopted him soon after. Jacob could never bring himself to enquire further and drag up what was sure to be a depressing and upsetting past, so he knew little else about them. He was so young when it happened that this life was all he knew, and he wanted to keep it that way rather than drag up the worst moments in his life.

Jacob was a tall, fair-headed young man with an almost lanky appearance, standing at six feet two inches and not yet reaching his full adult weight. He dressed like most his age, with expensive labels afforded by just over three-quarters of his peer group and didn't really stand out from the crowd in any way. He wasn't part of the testosterone-charged sports crowd and didn't quite fit the bill as a classroom geek, so throughout his education, he scored good results and languished somewhere in between.

In recent months, he had been sporting a small, shaggy goatee that needed grooming, but it made him look older, and the occasional girl he met didn't seem to object to his new facial scruff. An academic by nature, he wasn't, but with dedication, he had climbed the educational ladder of success the best he could with the tools he was born with. He wanted to make something of his life rather than live off his parents' money like his brother. Growing up, Jacob and Matthew were very different. Jacob was tall, slim, and athletic, perfect for the golf course, whereas Matthew was under six feet with a stocky build more suited to rugby.

Both liked sports, films, and cars, but that was where the similarities ended. Especially during their mid- to late-teenage years, they cared very little for each other and were always fighting, sometimes verbally but mostly physically. Matthew cared little for education, spent most of his time wrapped up in sports, and starred in the baseball team throughout school and college but lacked the discipline and, probably, if he was honest with himself, the talent, to make it to the majors.

Jacob watched and seldom played any sports, preferring computers, books, and films. Since university, beer and girls had become a regular vice but not to the detriment of his studies.

Unknowingly, today would be the day his life would unravel in a completely different direction from what he had hoped and worked towards. Literally round the corner was a shock, closely followed by a period of utter disbelief, panic, and unsettledness that would ultimately turn into curiosity.

Jacob's day started the same as any other on campus at the University of Massachusetts Amherst. The weather was cool and breezy, and the coffee was hot and bitter as the same old faces crowded the public spaces. He was two years into his studies for a computer science degree, hoping it would eventually land him a good job in the city.

He admired his adoptive father, Greg, who he believed had reached the pinnacle of his career. Jacob wanted to enjoy similar trimmings of success – the big house, country club membership, vintage sports cars, fine wines, Cuban cigars, and international travel – all afforded having written his own ticket rather than handed down from parents like plenty of others he knew. He and his brother, Matthew, were raised to appreciate the finer things in life, thanks to their parents' success, which inspired Jacob.

As he walked through the shaded grounds with his navy backpack slung over his left shoulder and a cup of takeaway coffee in his right hand, his college pal, Parker, rambled on about his latest conquest, wishing he could stay in school forever just for the "chicks", an idea Jacob found lame. They turned towards the science block for their 10am class just as Jacob noticed a man clearly too old to be a student and not a teacher he recognised. The man, wearing dark-rimmed glasses and sporting a shaggy mop of greying hair, walked towards him at pace.

"Jacob DeWitt?" the man said in a British accent.

"Yes," Jacob replied.

"Do you have a minute? I have something important to discuss with you."

"How do you know my name? Who are you?" Jacob asked, noticing a small tattoo behind the man's left thumb.

"Jacob James DeWitt, born Jacob James Reade in Ealing, West London, 8th July 1995, to Patrick and Charlotte Reade. Moved to the US after being adopted by your now-parents, Greg, and Isabelle DeWitt, in 1997, aged two. Currently studying computer science here at UMass. Shall I continue?"

"Parker, I'll catch up with you," Jacob said, nodding towards their destination. Parker, disinterested, headed off to class.

"Who are you?" Jacob asked again.

"My name is Michael Hough, and I've just travelled three thousand miles from London to meet you. If you want to know why, I suggest you come with me."

With his heart racing, Jacob agreed to follow Michael to a nearby coffee shop, and as they sat down without ordering anything, Jacob jokingly asked, "Are you a scout from another university? Because if you are, you've got the wrong guy. I've got two left feet."

Michael, looking serious, checked over his shoulders before turning back to Jacob, who was gripping his coffee tightly.

"Look, I'm not here to harm you, so relax. It took me six weeks to track you down, so just chill out. I'm here on behalf of your father, Patrick Reade," Michael said, unzipping his jacket.

"My real father is dead," Jacob replied coldly.

"Is that what Greg and Isabelle told you?"

"Who the hell are you, and how do you know so much about me and my family?" Jacob demanded, lowering his backpack to the floor next to his seat.

"Patience, kid. I don't mean to freak you out. I'm a friend of your father's – your real father – and he is very much alive but couldn't come himself."

"You're mistaken. He is dead, and that's probably why he couldn't come himself."

"He's alive and in jail," Michael replied, placing his hand on the table. "I worked as a guard in the jail where your father has been for the last eighteen years, and I believe he is innocent, which is why I'm here."

Jacob, now fully engaged, stared at Michael, who ordered a large cappuccino from the waitress and a Coke for his young friend before continuing.

"I know this is a lot to take in and probably not what you want to hear, but if you calm down, I'll explain," Michael said.

"You were born in the UK twenty years ago, correct?"

"Yes."

"Your real parents were Patrick and Charlotte Reade, correct?"

"Yes, we've established this."

"When you were just over one year old, your mother was murdered, and your father, Patrick, was jailed for her murder."

Jacob's eyes widened, and his body chilled at the words. After a moment of silence, he muttered, "I don't believe you", his heart aching at the thought of his real parents.

"Your father has been in jail for eighteen years, always pleading his innocence. Now, after all this time, some random guy in London confessed to killing your mother on his deathbed."

"This is too much. What the hell are you telling me?" Jacob questioned, looking round the coffee shop.

"The truth," Michael said, leaning forward.

"Where is Patrick now?" Jacob asked.

"Waiting for parole in Pentonville jail in London."

"If someone else confessed, why is he still in jail?"

"There's no signed confession. The man died a few hours later, so there's no concrete proof. There are only witnesses to the conversation, which seemed to match the events of the day your mother died. Other things he mentioned are being investigated."

"Where exactly is this jail?"

"Pentonville, just outside London. Patrick is due for parole in about four months and wants you to visit him. He asked me to give you this," Michael said, handing over a large brown envelope.

"What is it?" Jacob asked, accepting the package with his name handwritten on the front.

"Various news clippings, a letter, some family memorabilia. Your real father is desperate to see you. Have you never been told any of this before?"

Jacob shook his head in silence.

"Take this home, read it, and when you're ready, you can reach me at The Westin on Copley Place. I'll be here until Thursday."

"Okay," Jacob said, stuffing the envelope into his backpack, clearly in shock.

"What are you going to do now?" Michael asked, pulling cash from his wallet to leave on the table.

"I'm taking the day off," Jacob said, standing quickly and dashing out of the shop.

As Jacob walked away, Michael stepped outside, lit a cigarette, and shouted, "Don't hang around, Jake. Look everything up on the internet if you want. Remember, Westin on Copley Place, I'm telling you, Patrick is innocent."

Jacob wandered a few blocks to a diner on the corner of South and Finch. Inside, he ordered another Coke and took a seat in a booth at the back. He stared at the envelope for a moment, his heart racing as he opened it and pulled out a newspaper clipping with a handwritten note attached. A copy of his birth certificate fell onto the table, confirming what he knew about his birthplace, but with different parents' names. Carefully putting the certificate back, he read the note.

Jake,

This will be hard to read, but I promise you it will explain a lot. Listen to what Michael has to say and then decide what to do for your mother's sake. I hope you will listen to your heart and come visit me soon so we can talk face to face. I swear I didn't and would never have harmed your wonderful mother.

Your loving father, Patrick

The newspaper clipping was from *The Times*, dated 24th September 1997, and read:

Reade Guilty of Wife Slaying

Patrick James Reade, aged thirty-nine, was sentenced to life in prison for the murder of his wife, Charlotte Reade, aged thirty-three. Reade, who will serve a minimum of eighteen years, always claimed his innocence but, due to the lack of any alibi, was the main suspect in this horrific murder case. As Patrick Reade heads to prison, his two-year-old son, who cannot be named for legal reasons, will be cared for by family friends before a permanent family is found.

Jacob read the article three times, each word sinking into the pit of his stomach. His real mother was killed by his real father. It seemed authentic, even though it was a photocopy. He couldn't remember his biological parents but knew he was adopted. Only now was he realising the true extent of what had happened to his family. Tears welled up in his eyes as he glanced outside the diner.

The second newspaper clipping was a modern, full-colour piece titled: "Notorious Fredrick Milne Confesses on Deathbed to Killing Charlotte Reade in 1997 Murder".

The short news bulletin read like a rap sheet of Fredrick Milne, detailing his convictions and claims. The reporter, James Wallace of the *Daily Times*, noted the possibility of sensationalism from a dying man trying to hit the headlines one final time.

Jacob rushed to the bathroom and vomited several times as the enormity of the situation hit him. After tidying himself up, he returned to his booth, staring at the clippings. The final item in the envelope was a compliments slip from The Westin Copley Place in Boston, with Michael's room number.

Jacob had to find out why his father was contacting him after all these years. Surely a man in prison for almost two decades would have found a way to prove his innocence if he were indeed innocent. As he left the diner, his mind raced with questions. *Why did he do it? Did he really do it? Why now when he is due for parole in four months? Why not come and see me himself in four months?* He needed answers.

Jacob fired up his tablet and started researching newspaper articles from *The Times* in the UK from 1997. He spent almost three hours reading every word about his parents and the tragic events that unfolded in February 1997. The headlines ranged from "Suburban Slaying" to "Reade Convicted of Killing Wife", all detailing the same horrific story.

By the time he left the diner, Jacob felt betrayed, angry, and deeply upset. Walking slowly through the reception area, tears rolled down his cheeks. He took a detour to the bathroom and bawled his eyes out, vomiting again from sheer devastation. Knowing his life would never be the same, he splashed cold water on his face and stared at his reflection in the mirror, his eyes red and swollen.

At that moment, he knew he was going to London.

NINETEEN

Jacob met Michael for a brief meeting the next day at the sprawling open-plan reception lounge at the hotel in Copley Place. They sipped coffee by an empty fireplace where Michael filled in a few blanks and emphasised the importance of telling no one, travelling alone, and being cautious when he got to London.

Over the years, Greg had always refused Isabelle's pleas to take the boys back to the UK to see their homeland and meet with family and friends. He insisted on them coming to the US, which they often did, as he would cover the expenses. Isabelle could never understand his refusal to return or even let her travel alone with the boys. She found it very upsetting but had long given up trying to change his stubborn mind.

Greg was hiding a dark secret that could blow up in his face at any time. He vowed never to travel back to the UK since leaving nearly eighteen years ago. Despite being over three thousand miles away, he lived in constant fear that his past would one day come back to haunt him. This would be the first time a DeWitt had set foot in the UK in nearly two decades, and Jacob was filled with overwhelming apprehension about seeing the father he thought was dead, who had been imprisoned for more than eighteen years. Not only was he anxious about seeing his father for the first time since he was a small boy, but he also felt uneasy about betraying his adopted parents and lying to them about his upcoming travels.

Jacob headed straight back to his apartment to gather his things before heading back to New York the following morning to collect his passport. His mind raced with all the details, minor and major. He left a note for Greg and Isabelle, telling them he was going to Vegas for a break from his studies, as he had no classes for the next week and was keen to blow off steam.

Leaving the DeWitt family home, dressed in a black designer shirt, beige chinos, khaki boots, and a smart tweed blazer, Jacob dodged the rain as he left for the waiting black Suburban that had arrived at precisely 5:20am. With the seat belt pressing against his stomach, stirring with emotion, making him sweat, he sat uncomfortably, looking through the window at the dank outside, hoping his stomach would not play up for the next ten hours of travel.

The taxi navigated the Van Wyck Expressway towards JFK International Airport in heavy traffic, with most cars exercising extra caution due to the heavy rain. The driver tried twice to strike up a conversation about sports and then the weather, but Jacob was too consumed by his thoughts and wasn't having any of it.

Since finding out about his parents' fate just two days ago, Jacob struggled to come to terms with what Michael had told him, but the internet didn't lie – it was all there, and he had consumed it over and over.

Despite confirming many facts through incessant research, he was still confused and upset about meeting someone he thought was dead and who was found guilty of murdering his mother. As the car neared the airport, he stared at the newspaper cuttings that Michael had given him in Boston and was soon jolted from his thoughts as the car drove up to the drop-off zone, littered with limousines, buses, taxis, and police cars.

"Here you go, kid, Terminal Eight, American Airlines. That'll be sixty-five bucks," said the driver without looking over his shoulder.

Springing two crisp notes from his wallet, Jacob told the driver to keep the change as he slid across the seat, looking to exit onto the pavement. He paused for a few seconds to look out the back and side windows, all of which were steamed up by the wet weather, before exiting the car. Once outside, he continued scouting the area for people he knew or unknown people who might be keeping an eye on him as paranoia kicked in.

Surely, this is all in my head, he thought, trying to think logically as he shoved his hands deep inside his jeans pockets. He waited under the shelter as the rain continued to pour while his black suitcase was unloaded by the driver, before racing off into the terminal building, keeping his head down and avoiding eye contact.

Walking through the newly refurbished terminal

building crammed with people and luggage, Jacob felt the knot in his stomach tighten, prompting him to glance round for the nearest toilet. Sixty million passengers would pass through JFK this year, so the chances of bumping into someone he knew were slim but not impossible. The thought of going to London alone didn't trouble him; being caught by his adopted father or learning the truth about his real family was far more worrying.

As he continued walking, he glanced up at the departure boards, quickly scanning around the terminal and clocking two blue-suited airport workers looking up and down the concourse, talking quietly into their walkie-talkies. Were they talking about him? "Shit," Jacob muttered under his breath. "Keep calm." *This must be how a drug mule feels when they arrive at an airport with a stomach full of cocaine*, he thought, walking towards the escalator to departures. His stomach rumbled with emptiness, except for one black coffee. He was hungry but too distracted to think about food.

He read down the long list of destinations: Amsterdam, Atlanta, Delhi, Denver, Las Vegas, and finally, London Heathrow. Check-in desks eighteen to twenty-five for American Airlines flight 8:35am. Jacob stood in the check-in queue, watching people around him going on holiday, returning home, and businessmen talking on their mobiles. *You can always spot a businessman at an airport*, Jacob thought, trying to distract himself. The guy standing alone with one small suitcase, a laptop bag, a worn-out passport, looking like he's slept in his suit for two years and not stepped inside a gym since high school. *I wish I were that guy right now,* he thought to himself.

Back to reality, he finally arrived at the front of the check-in queue at desk nineteen and forced a smile at Eve, the nice-looking forty-something woman behind the desk.

"Passport and tickets, please, sir," she said, sounding more like she was on autopilot than interested in being at work.

"I'd like a window seat, please," Jacob said, handing over his passport.

"I'll see what I can do," the woman replied. Jacob looked nervously over his shoulder, paranoid he was being followed and wouldn't make it to that window seat.

Having been born in West London, Jacob had dual citizenship, allowing him to have both a British and American passport. His British passport had never been used in the five years since he applied for it. He planned to use his UK passport in London and his US passport when he returned to avoid long immigration queues and, more importantly, cover his tracks as neither passport would have an immigration stamp proving he had been in and out of the country.

After the routine questions and false smiling, Jacob was through security and on his way to a coffee shop with his boarding pass tucked inside his passport, confirming flight AA142 and seat 32A, the window seat he requested.

A flood of thoughts rushed through his head, making him dizzy. None of them were about coffee or the status of his flight. Jacob opted for a large cappuccino and a jam doughnut, sitting with his back to the coffee shop window as he forced the sugar into his system. *Maybe this will stop the headache*, he thought, pouring two sugars into the large coffee. In the ensuing ten minutes, he checked his watch eight times, spent exactly thirty-nine seconds stirring his coffee clockwise, and looked up from his table just once.

During the ninety-minute wait for boarding, Jacob did all he could to remain inconspicuous: reading magazines without paying for them, sitting in a toilet stall for twenty minutes, and even going into the prayer room to keep out of sight from other passengers and potential prying eyes he was convinced were following him. He was not religious and had never been in a prayer room, but it served a purpose for a quiet thirty minutes, allowing him to calm down and relax. Eventually, the wait was over, and the announcement was made – he was on his way to the plane.

"American Airlines is proud to announce the boarding of flight AA142 for London Heathrow. Would all passengers needing assistance and first- and business-class ticket holders please make your way to the gate," the woman's voice bellowed from the tannoy.

Jacob stood waiting patiently for his time to board, counting twelve airport or airline staff hovering round the desk or near the doorway to the air bridge. He counted them, thinking it was massive overkill for boarding a plane, but for a brief moment, it took his mind off things. Eventually, he was up, and as he walked down the air bridge to the silver Boeing 777, he realised he was just an average Joe, a needle in a haystack. The chance of knowing someone on the same flight was a long shot. He had made it. He smirked, showing his boarding pass to the waiting cabin crew. Although he had sweaty palms and an uneasy stomach, he was well on his way to London, looking forward to settling in for back-to-back films for the next seven hours.

Sitting next to him was a couple returning to Wales after an enjoyable two-week tour around the US, culminating in their engagement in Central Park. He was not up for much conversation but managed the usual pleasantries of congratulations when someone tells you news of pending nuptials. This was his first time across the Atlantic since arriving as a small child, and he soon realised the benefits of free films and free food, as he started to relax for the first time since entering the terminal building. *Today is definitely a day to remember*, he thought as the plane's engines roared and the plane sped off down the runway.

For the next seven hours, Jacob read some of the documents Michael had provided in a brown envelope, trying not to be too conspicuous to his new neighbours, while watching two films and sipping several Cokes, before trying to get some shut-eye.

With the flight thirty minutes ahead of schedule, Jacob arrived at Heathrow's Terminal Three just a shade after 8pm and was soon met with the usual chaos of any major international hub. Suitcases piled high on luggage trolleys, passengers hovering in groups with vacant looks on their faces, police at every exit, some wandering with sniffer dogs, limo drivers, airport workers in smart uniforms and cleaners trying to keep the place as tidy as possible. His head whirring with all the information he had recently received and the change in time zone, Jacob quickly collected his backpack, splashed water on his face in the men's toilets and headed for the exit marked green – nothing to declare.

Standing behind the line and sifting through his brand-new passport for the picture page, he heard the clerk in front shout, "next" while pointing at him. Jacob walked forwards, feeling a bit anxious about using a UK passport for the first time, especially with his American accent. But after a quick glance and scan of his passport, he was through.

"Welcome back," the clerk said.

"Thank you," Jacob replied, unnecessarily adopting a fake British accent in an attempt to avoid drawing attention.

After collecting his luggage, which was one of the first off the carousel, he walked briskly towards the nothing-to-declare green line. Pulling his suitcase behind him, he moved straight through customs and couldn't wait to get to his hotel and blend in, becoming just another guy on the street without uniformed people seemingly monitoring his every move.

Walking out of the gate, he saw rows of limousine drivers with placards standing behind barriers like baying dogs waiting for their prey. Casually walking through, he happened to glance to his left and saw the name "Jacob Reade" on a board held by an Asian man dressed in a dark suit and white shirt. *Shit*, Jacob thought to himself; he wasn't expecting anyone to meet him and purposely walked past the guy. A nervous shudder ran down his spine as he continued to the nearest shop to buy himself some thinking time. He bought a Coke while pondering his next move.

He decided that this person had nothing to do with his folks back home, as he had been known as DeWitt for so many years. Standing at a good distance away, he watched the man waiting patiently for Jacob Reade to appear and present himself. Jacob didn't have to wait long to build up the courage.

"I'm Jacob Reade," he said, standing to the side of the Asian man.

"Hello, Mr Reade. I am your driver today. Shall I take your bag?"

"No, I've got it... thanks, but I wasn't expecting a driver, and I didn't book one," Jacob replied.

"I'm a friend of your father's. Come on, the car is not far from here," the man answered.

Walking out of the airport towards the ground floor parking garage, Jacob thought of a million questions he wanted to ask, but before he got the chance, the driver spoke up.

"So how was your flight?"

"Okay, I guess. It's about the same time flying from New York to LA as it is to London."

"Huh, I bet. Never been that way myself, although I'd like to go one day. I've got a package in the car for you," he said, pointing at the back seat of the black BMW.

"Oh really?"

"Yes; your father asked me to give it to you and to make sure you got into London okay."

Jacob started to relax, telling the driver he was grateful for his help and desperate to get to his hotel for a shower.

"Which hotel are you staying at?" the driver asked.

"Uh, I think it's Park Plaza," Jacob replied, pulling flight confirmations and hotel printouts from his jacket pocket.

"Got an address?"

"Yes, here somewhere."

"Great, we'll let the sat nav do its job."

Climbing into the back seat of the car, Jacob saw a white envelope with large black writing on the front saying "Jake Reade". He decided not to open it until he was at his hotel, clutching it with both hands for the duration of the journey through the crazy London traffic.

As the car meandered through the busy streets of London, Jacob tried to remember being there before but quickly became frustrated as he didn't recognise anything, even though he knew he wouldn't since he was just a baby the last time he was here. None of it looked familiar except for the double-decker red buses, something a kid would always remember, he thought, but only because he had seen them on numerous television programmes.

When he arrived at the hotel, the driver wished Jacob good luck and told him he would be safe there as it was in a nice part of town near Leicester Square with plenty of places to eat and drink. After having his offer of payment declined by the driver, Jacob walked into the hotel and was soon relaxing in a hot bath in his surprisingly small hotel room.

Until now, he had resisted opening the envelope, but

after a few more minutes soaking in the tub, the lure of the envelope given to him by the driver got the better of him. He was soon out of the bath, wrapped in a towel, and sat on the edge of the bed. He opened the envelope and peered inside, finding a single page and a small plastic envelope containing a SIM card for a mobile phone.

The handwritten letter read:

Dear Jacob,

Welcome to the UK and thank you for coming. I know this would have been a big decision for you to make. I am looking forward to seeing you after all these years and I know it can't have been an easy decision to make to travel here alone. I have arranged a visit for tomorrow, at 11:30am at Pentonville Prison, where I have been wrongly imprisoned for the last seventeen, almost eighteen, years. During this time, I have had three appeals tried unsuccessfully, but with a parole hearing set for four months from now, I'm counting the days to getting out of this hell and rebuilding my life. I will explain more when I see you on Friday. Enjoy your time in London. Now that you are an adult, I'm sure you will find plenty to do!

Please don't take any chances and make sure you are not followed; this may all seem strange to you now, but I cannot stress enough how important it is that nobody knows you have visited me or even travelled to London, especially any members of the DeWitt family.

You should have received a SIM card, which inserts into a pay-as-you-go mobile phone that you can pick up from any number of shops in the city. Use this instead of your normal mobile phone, which you should keep switched off and in your hotel room at all times.

Again, I cannot thank you enough for coming all this way to let me say my piece; I have waited so long for us to finally be reunited.

Love, your father, Patrick Reade

Jacob read the letter several times, finding it strange that a complete stranger called himself his father. At the same time, he was intrigued and looking forward to their meeting, albeit with a little apprehension.

He didn't believe the pleas of innocence, wrongly assuming that the justice system had done its job properly and he was indeed guilty as charged. But he was here with a half-open mind and willing to listen. He knew the SIM card was a good idea as mobile phone calls can be tracked not only from number to number but from country to country, leaving a permanent record of where he had been and who he had been talking to. His usual mobile phone was switched off and in the bedside drawer and hadn't been turned on since arriving in the country. No signal, no trace.

After drying off from the bath that helped wash away the past twelve hours, he couldn't resist jumping into bed for a long ten-hour sleep; after all, London would always be there and could wait until he started feeling more human again in the morning.

TWENTY

Claire Gains worked behind the bar at the exclusive Bakers Point, just off Leicester Square in Central London. An attractive twenty-three-year-old, standing at five feet six inches with a slim and fairly athletic, yet slight, frame, she was a confident young woman with a sparkling personality. She was never short of admirers while working every spare hour she had available for the last nine months to get herself through the last year of her law degree at the University of East London.

After leaving university, she intended on working sixteen-hour days as a trainee solicitor at one of London's largest firms like Sloane and Wright or Bellingham Brothers, where she could practise corporate law and, with any luck, fly through the ranks.

For now, reality was Bakers Point until gone midnight, followed by days, and sometimes very early mornings, studying, £7,347 and rising in debt to various different creditors, including her parents Carol and Roger Gains. At the last count, the debt had increased and not decreased as planned.

Although her job at the bar was not really the answer to her financial woes, it did manage to just about help keep her head above water. Well, that and the student loans and overdraft that most of her student friends were also reliant on, apart from the occasional rich kid or overseas student that seemed to have endless amounts of money being pumped into their accounts on a regular basis. One of her friends, Sushmita Rai from Mangalore, had recently divulged her personal information, which included a four grand a month allowance from her father back in India. Claire could not even dream of that much money per month, even when she started working as a solicitor, let alone as a student.

Her main characteristics at first glance were her shoulder-length, thick, glossy, brown hair, cut straight across her forehead with a deep fringe; her pouty lips; and a small mole next to her right nostril that she liked to call her beauty spot, which contributed to her smouldering looks. She had a tattoo of a small arrow across the back of her neck that was hidden most of the time by her hair unless she wore it up.

The locals liked her for her sense of humour, her kind manner, and her ability to remember every favourite tipple, from Jim Beam to tomato juice with extra hot sauce, and of course, her obvious good looks. The tips were good from the regulars; the tourists enjoyed the view from the other side of the bar as most left generous tips and the occasional phone number or hotel room number that she always threw straight in the bin the minute they left.

"Hello, Mr King, how are you today?" Claire said, greeting one of her regulars with a big smile. "The usual?"

"Yes please, dear," said Mr Randolph King, a retired British Airways airline pilot and a daily visitor to the bar for the last seven years since his wife Dorothy passed away from heart trouble. He had seen his favourite pub, known as The Oak, revamped into the slick Bakers Point five years prior, but he wasn't put off by the smell of coffee or the lunch menus that covered most tables in a bid to stay up to date with tourists' demands rather than the local drinkers'.

Randy was one of only a few regulars at Bakers Point, as it was mainly airline crews and tourists due to the location next to all the major hotels. The pub usually enjoyed peace and relative quiet during the day, despite the brisk trade, and then would come alive most evenings with a fresh batch of cabin crew fresh in from all over the world, coming in to wash away their tiredness. The Australians and the Americans always enjoyed getting drunk and ending up spending the night in each other's beds. Randolph, by this point, would be safely stretched out on the sofa back at his two-storey townhouse after his usual three or four fixers.

Having slept again after breakfast, Jacob finally decided to venture out and stretch his legs for some fresh air. At 3:41pm, he exited his hotel, turning left onto Panton Street in the direction of Leicester Square. The dense pavement traffic was made up of shoppers and office staff mixed in with a few beggars and police. Dressed in dark-blue jeans, a freshly ironed black shirt, and his usual blazer, he fast paced his way down the road, quickly drawing out his long legs. His back ached from the flight across the Atlantic and the firm bed he had slept in, so he hoped the exercise would be beneficial, and a little sightseeing enjoyable, as he searched for an outlet that sold prepaid mobile phones that could not be traced.

Walking at his usual fair pace, Jacob admired the very different city feel he had become so used to in New York and less so in Boston; sure, it was still hectic but certainly quieter than the noisy streets of the Big Apple. The roads were not bumper to bumper; there was little rubbish piled up outside every shop and restaurant, which blights many pavements in New York; and the soundtrack of the city he had become so accustomed to – the constant car horns and police sirens like an automobile orchestra – were noticeably absent. He liked the novelty of the black Hackney cabs instead of the famous yellow back home, and the fact they all drove on the wrong side of the road amused him.

As he continued to walk and glance in the odd coffee shop window, he realised he needed to change some US dollars into pounds. He made an unscheduled stop at an "Authorised Currency" shop and exchanged ten fifty-dollar bills in return for brightly coloured notes and three small gold coins.

Jacob had come prepared with plenty of cash as credit and ATM cards would leave a trace that can be electronically tracked around the globe within seconds of the transaction being completed; he was determined to leave no trace if possible. If he had been caught out because of bank statements, he would have been annoyed at himself, and he even booked his hotel room with the email address Adamjj12@worldnet.com and checked into the hotel under the name of Adam Judge just in case he was being tracked.

With the now correct currency neatly folded into several pockets for security, and some in his wallet, Jacob headed straight for the nearest pub with only one thing on his mind: a cold beer to sip while he watched the busy world outside go by. The sheer novelty of ordering a legal beer was too much of a temptation. Walking into the first pub he came across, he clocked an empty table in a far corner and sat near the window, waiting for a server to appear.

He looked round the pub to see if anyone was watching him. He did not expect to see anyone he knew, but he was still mindful of the warnings Michael had given. If Greg had suspected something, there would be no doubt in his mind that he would send someone to follow him all the way from America to this very pub. Most people in the pub sat in small groups talking and laughing or watching the cricket flickering on the TV in the distance; at least, he thought it was cricket. One elderly man sat on his own towards the back of the pub reading the *Racing Post*, occasionally scribbling his ideas down for the next big win.

After a few minutes gazing out of the window, watching people go about their business, he soon realised he was not going to get service at his table, so he left his blazer on the back of the chair and slouched towards the bar with his hands deep inside his pockets.

"What can I get you?" the bartender asked.

"I'd like a beer, please, but I'm not sure which one – this is all a bit new to me," Jacob enthused.

"Well, do you want a lager, a stout, or an ale?" the tall barman asked.

"I don't want a Budweiser or a Heineken; give me something different," Jacob said, calling on his adventurous, exploratory nature.

"How about Guinness or Speckled Hen?"

"Speckled what?"

"Speckled Hen. You'd be hard-pressed to find that in the States," the barman said, reading his accent correctly.

"What the hell, I will try your Speckled Hen, sir," he said with a beaming smile and a half-decent English accent.

He paid and returned to the table with a dark-brown pint of ale in front of him. With barely a sip taken, Jacob started to recall the contents of the letter he had been given. Wrongly jailed, three appeals and no success – *can a guy be that unlucky?* he thought. Again, he couldn't quite believe this was the reality of the situation, but full of intrigue, he had promised himself the chance to investigate in search of the truth.

By the third gulp of Speckled Hen, he had already made up his mind that the next drink would probably be something like a Budweiser or Heineken, and by the third pint, he was ready to get something to eat and was in the mood for steak.

With change from his drinks rattling in his front left pocket, Jacob tossed his jacket over his right shoulder and headed for the door he'd walked through ninety minutes earlier. After a more relaxed stroll for around a mile, he noted the name of a bar that read "Bakers Point at Cavendish Square". He looked round to savour the moment; he had never heard of Cavendish Square but was happy to be there. With the alcohol starting to take effect, he stopped looking over his shoulder for the time being and started to relax, forgetting the very reason he was in London in the first place.

As he walked into the bar, he instantly realised this was your more pretentious drinking establishment with decorated walls, spotlights in the ceilings, dark wood tables, picture frames to match, well-printed white menus, and contemporary leather sofas next to magazine racks full of *Time* magazine, *GQ*, *Cigar Aficionado*, *Cosmopolitan*, and *Vogue*.

For the first time, his eyes met Claire's, and for a fleeting moment, he was caught in the warmth of her welcoming smile. It spread across her face like sunlight breaking through clouds, drawing his attention for just a heartbeat too long. Shaking himself free, he chose a seat by the window overlooking a small courtyard, a leather sofa tucked towards the back of the room. The menu card resting on the small table quickly gave up its secrets, and he settled on his choice. Timing his approach to the bar with an unspoken rhythm, he found Claire waiting to serve him, their interaction charged with a quiet, unspoken ease. *Smooth*, he thought to himself.

"Hello, sir, what can I get you?" she said, wiping a cloth with her right hand across the bar in front of him.

"I would like steak, rare, and fries please, and a bottle of Budweiser," Jacob replied, clocking the white name tag Claire pinned on the left side of her chest.

"Not a problem; can I get you any side orders to complement your meal?" Claire responded.

"No, that'll be fine, thanks, Claire," he replied with an overenthusiastic smile.

"Are you going to stay at the seat in the window or move to a more formal dining table?"

"Oh, there is fine," he replied, handing over two twenty-pound notes. "Keep the change."

"You can pay at the end; would you like to open a tab? All I need is a credit card; you can pay cash at the end," she asked before taking the cash from his outstretched hand.

With every intention of staying for the duration, Jacob was never going to chance the use of a credit card, so he opted to stick with untraceable cold, hard cash.

"I'll pay cash, thanks."

He watched Claire glide elegantly to the opposite end of the bar and punch his order into the register. His eyes followed the shape of her almost brown copper hair cascading down her crisp white blouse and tight black skirt, which concealed what he could only dare to imagine was a very pert derrière. His lustful gaze only lasted a couple of seconds at most but had a lasting effect on him for the rest of the evening.

Jacob felt more at ease than he had in a long time. The

sense of relaxation washing over him was, once again, courtesy of the alcohol coursing through his veins. It dulled the sharp edges of unease that came with being alone in an unfamiliar land, wrapping him in a haze of comfort that made the foreign feel just a little less daunting. Jacob had never been inside a jail, let alone to visit his father, whom he had not seen since he was a child, couldn't even remember for that matter. This was going to be a weird trip, he surmised, as his steak arrived, sadly delivered by a far less attractive server.

After a couple more anaesthetic-like beers and a fill of rare beef, Jacob was happy watching the street outside fall to darkness and decided to head back to the hotel if he could find his way. As he stood up, trying to recall the route he had taken from his hotel, and looking like every other tourist in the bar, he decided to ask for directions, and there was only one person he had in mind.

Claire was keeping herself busy wiping down the bar again in between customers as Jacob approached, complete with clammy hands and thick tongue.

"Excuse me, Claire," he said.

She looked up and smiled. "Is everything okay, sir?"

"Please don't call me sir; I get enough of that rubbish in the States. I'm Jacob," he said, awkwardly shoving his hand out in front of him as if he were flagging down a cab, complete with flailing arm.

"Where are you from?" Claire quizzed as they shook hands.

"I grew up in New York with my family; well, my other family. It's hard to explain, but I'm originally from

London, but this is my first trip back since I was a kid," he blurted out.

"What part of London were you originally from?"

"Uh, Ealing, I think, but to be honest, I don't know a lot about my days here."

"I see."

"Are you from London?"

"No, I'm here studying, hence the bar job," she said, pointing out her standard-issue uniform. "I'm from Bath."

"I'm at university in Boston, studying computers, for my sins; what are you studying?" he asked in a bid to keep her attention.

"Law; I'm in my final year, and it has been hard, but I guess I don't know the meaning of the word, as the training is supposed to be brutal."

"I can imagine."

"So how come you're over here during term time?" Claire asked with a quizzical look on her face.

"Long story; a very long story. Maybe if I call in tomorrow sometime, you can give me the heads-up on your competition; I'd like to find a traditional boozer."

"Sure; I'm working the day shift tomorrow, so maybe I'll see you then… Jacob." She smiled once again, which seemed to talk directly to his heart.

They wished each other goodnight after Claire had given him vague instructions on how to get back to his hotel.

The walk home was a few degrees cooler, but the warmth created by his first experience of Claire seemed to fight off the cool late-night air. More likely, he had

had excessive amounts to drink to go with his jet lag. On finally making his way back to the hotel, that night he fell asleep thinking only about the lovely, well-spoken Claire and not the cold jail and murderous father he was about to encounter. He closed his eyes and wished himself to sleep, looking forward to seeing Claire again tomorrow. *What time do bars open in the day?* he thought to himself as he started to doze off.

TWENTY-ONE

Jacob woke up well before the 9am wake-up call, thoughts of Claire briefly occupying his mind before anxiety about meeting his father took over. Lying in bed for forty minutes, he pondered the many questions plaguing him: Patrick's innocence, his sudden move to the States, and why Greg and Isabelle told him both parents were dead. These unanswered questions fuelled his suspicions.

A sluggish morning followed, thanks to last night's alcohol and his growing trepidation. After finally dragging himself out of bed, Jacob took a long, hot shower, hoping it would wash away his unease. It didn't work. His breakfast in the hotel restaurant consisted of a bowl of cornflakes, a croissant, and two cups of coffee, was spent mostly staring at the wall, and occasionally observing other guests. The smell of greasy bacon stirred his stomach but not his appetite, so he quickly finished, thanked the staff, and grabbed a green apple on his way out.

After brushing his teeth and collecting his jacket, he exited the hotel and climbed into one of the waiting taxis. Checking his watch before glancing over his shoulder, he wished he had skipped breakfast as his stomach began to churn. The car edged slowly through the traffic towards Pentonville Prison. A glance at his expensive watch revealed it was 10:14am. Jacob closed his eyes, placed both hands on his knees, and drew in a long, slow breath, trying to calm his nausea.

The taxi ride felt interminable, with every stop and turn intensifying his nerves. Finally, he arrived, paid the fare, and stared up at the towering, whitewashed walls of the prison. He couldn't believe his father belonged in such a place. With a sense of dread, he approached the huge double green doors leading to the visitors' vestibule.

Raised in an affluent New York borough, Jacob found it hard to reconcile his background with this prison. But he needed answers. As he entered the prison for the first time, his apprehension intensified. His goal was to quickly uncover the truth so he could return to his life in Massachusetts.

The reception area was crowded with police officers, security guards, and visitors from all walks of life. Jacob felt out of place. He quickly moved through the queue, his hands getting sweaty.

"Hi. Jacob DeWitt. I'm here to visit Patrick Reade," he said quietly, placing his hands on the counter.

The prison clerk checked the register. "I've got you down as Jacob Reade. Is this you?" asked Rodney, an overweight guard.

"Yes, that's right. Eleven o'clock, right?"

"Yes, for a thirty-minute visit. Sign here and show me some photo ID."

Jacob signed the register and handed over his New York City driver's license. "My legal surname is DeWitt; I guess he must have forgotten."

"That's fine," she said, handing him a white plastic bag for his possessions. "We'll lock these here and give you the key."

Jacob took his key and sat in the waiting area, his anxiety momentarily eclipsing his nausea. As he waited, he wondered if he would recognise his father. A loud siren signalled it was time to proceed, and Jacob joined the queue for the pat-down. Suddenly feeling sick, he dashed to the toilet, entered a cubicle, and vomited.

Cleaning up, he rejoined the queue. Inside, he saw a large room with tables bolted to the floor, each with an inmate on one side. Jacob scanned the room until he locked eyes with a tall man, Patrick, who looked back at him with a mix of anticipation and anxiety. Jacob sat down opposite the man he thought was dead.

"Jacob, I can't thank you enough for coming," Patrick said, his words heavy with desperation.

"Hi," he replied flatly, his voice betraying nothing.

"So, how've you been? Life in the States treating you well?" Patrick asked, trying to break the ice, his eyes searching Jacob's face, taking in his now adult son.

"It's fine, I guess," Jacob muttered, his eyes cold. He didn't know how to answer the question.

Patrick's eyes widened, a faint look of surprise crossing

his features. "Wow, didn't think you'd have an American accent"

"It's been a minute. So anyway, why am I here?" He leaned forward, his arms crossed, the tension almost palpable.

"I— I just needed to see you, Jake," Patrick stammered, his voice strained, "I've spent years hoping for this moment… but I need you to understand. I didn't kill your mother."

Jacob's eyes narrowed with anger, maybe even pain. "You know, I thought you were dead. And now, I find out you're alive, but that's not the worst of it. You killed my mother, they said. Do you know what that does to me?" His voice was low but edged with fury.

Patrick seemed to shrink under Jacob's gaze, but his voice was unwavering. "I would've never hurt your mother, Jake. I swear. I… I loved her. I loved you both more than you'll ever know."

Jacob looked away, his jaw tight. "You didn't answer my question. Why the hell am I here?"

"Because I need you to listen to me," Patrick insisted, his eyes pleading. "I don't expect you to believe me, but I need you to hear this. I swear to you; I had nothing to do with her death."

Jacob's expression remained stone-cold, and he didn't flinch when he spoke. "The court says otherwise."

Patrick's hands trembled as they flattened against the table, his knuckles white. "Did you read the articles I sent you?" he asked, with desperation creeping into his voice.

"I did, who is Fredrick Milne?"

Patrick leaned in. "He was connected to the London underworld and a distant cousin of Charles Faulk who worked at the bank the same time as Greg. This was all around the same time as your mother's death. And listen, Jake, the details he gave about that day, about our house, about your mother... it's too accurate. I'm telling you he did it."

Jacob shifted in his seat, the seed of doubt beginning to sprout in his mind. "OK, I can understand how you might be unsettled by this. But why does that mean Greg is involved?"

Patrick became animated. "Because Greg and Isabelle never, never talked about moving away, not in all the years we knew them. They mentioned buying a place in the south of France, sure, but they never said a word about leaving permanently, especially so far away."

Jacob's eyes narrowed, the puzzle pieces starting to fit, but he wasn't convinced. "That doesn't exactly scream 'they're guilty,' does it?"

Patrick's voice dropped to a whisper. "Jake, I know this sounds crazy, but I need you to trust me on this. I loved your mother, and the day you were both taken from me, that was the day my world ended. I get why they convicted me. But they were wrong. After you were adopted, Greg and Isabelle vanished, no warning, no consultation. They left without a word, and I believe they know something. Maybe they were part of something bigger."

Jacob sat back, his mind whirling. He could see Patrick's desperation.

Patrick nodded urgently. "I don't know how, but

Milne's confession is the only thing that makes sense. The system's a mess, and no one is willing to listen to me. I'll be due for parole soon, but I can't afford to wait."

Jacob's eyes softened ever so slightly, but he held himself back. "I've read every article I could. I won't lie to you; I see why you might think there is a connection."

Patrick's face tightened with a mix of relief and desperation. "Thank you, son. Just... help me. You're the only person I've got left."

Something in Jacob's gut told him there was more to the story. He couldn't shake the thought. "I'll help you, but I don't know how much use I'll be."

"You're all I have," Patrick said, his voice cracking as he reached across the table. "Anything you do from here on will help more than you know, do it for your mother."

His words hung heavy in the air.

As the guards signalled their time was up, Jacob stood and shook Patrick's hand, their eyes locking for a moment, both unsure of what the future would hold. He turned and walked toward the door.

With mixed emotions he climbed into the back of the waiting taxi and contemplated everything Patrick had said. Despite his doubts about unearthing anything of interest, he felt compelled to uncover the truth, more so for himself and his mother than for Patrick.

Clearly Greg and Isabelle held a lot back from him.

Redirecting the taxi to Bakers Point, Cavendish Square, Jacob hoped to find some solace in meeting Claire again.

TWENTY-TWO

Arriving outside Bakers Point with a sharp stop, Jacob paid his taxi fare and paused for a second to look in both directions up and down the street; it had become a habit to look out for unwanted followers.

"Keep the change," he instructed as he passed over a worn twenty-pound note before exiting to the left onto the pavement.

Without any hesitation, he walked into the bar, which was empty apart from the staff and an old guy sat in the corner trying to complete a crossword with two beers in front of him. Jacob stuffed his hands into his jeans pockets and walked to the end of the bar where Carlos, the rather less attractive member of the bar staff, suddenly greeted him.

"Hello, sir, and how are you today?" Carlos said, rolling his R's while polishing his English.

"I'm good, thanks. Has the lunchtime rush been and gone?"

"Yes, yes, it has. Quiet now," the barman replied, picking up a couple of empty glasses and stacking them in the dishwasher behind the bar.

"What can I get you?"

"Just a diet Coke," Jacob replied before taking a seat near the bar, clearly disappointed Claire wasn't around.

The drink arrived on a beer mat in front of him, and as he watched the fizz bouncing around the ice packing the glass, he called out to the barman, who had already turned his back to fiddle with the optics set across a large, mirrored wall behind the bar.

"Is Claire around?" he asked, more in hope than expectation.

"She'll be in later," Carlos replied without turning back round.

Jacob picked up his drink and sat alone on a sofa in silence with his legs extended out in front of him, crossed left over right. He started to fidget in his seat as he recalled the conversation he had had earlier in the day. There was so much information poured on him in such a short space of time, he really did not know what to make of it all, but he kept hearing Patrick's words:

I did not do it.
Fredrick Milne.
Revenge.
Work with me.
I love you, son.
Do it for your mother.

Although he felt some loyalty to Isabelle and Greg, he needed to find out the truth, and for the first time in his life, he felt a small pang of affection and allegiance towards his real father. He was tired but decided to order another drink when the quiet of the afternoon lull was disturbed by the door of the bar opening as three businessmen in varying tones of pinstriped suits walked in, laughing, and telling stories loudly, clearly celebrating a big trade in the city. Jacob picked up his drink, ordered another one at the bar, and retired towards the back of the bar where the dark wooden floors met the lush cream walls papered in a luxurious silver pattern and several padded booths, with low-hanging lights hanging on long trailing wires from the ceiling, were situated.

Claire suddenly appeared from a side door and immediately waved him over. She was wearing her neatly pressed black work gear, waiting for her shift to start. Fresh-faced after a brisk walk to work, she smiled as Jacob walked towards her.

"Hi," Jacob said.

"How's things?" Claire asked, with a pleasing smile on her face.

"Good, thanks. How are you?" he replied as they both sat down opposite each other in a booth.

"Oh, I'm okay, thanks, just about to start my shift," she said, putting her phone in a small rucksack that was sat beside her. "So, the wanderer returns. I didn't think I'd ever see you again."

"What do you mean?" Jacob asked with a puzzled look on his face.

"I see hundreds of people a week; some talk, some don't; some say they will pop in again but never do." She shrugged, bunching up her lips and raising her eyebrows as if showing her disappointment.

"Well, I'm back and glad I caught you. I kinda need a friend right now, and I literally know nobody in the UK."

"Okay, this place is dead, so I'm sure they can cope without me for a while. What's going on?"

"Can I get you a drink?"

"No, I get free drinks here, but I'll gladly take the money," Claire joked with a beaming smile across her face as she gazed into his eyes.

Jacob laughed as he pulled at his left sleeve before taking off his jacket; he felt nervous inside but liked the way she looked at him.

Claire started to make polite conversation. "So why are you in the UK if you don't know anybody? Work?"

"It's a long story," Jacob responded with an exhale of breath. "I came here to see a family member I didn't even know existed until a few weeks ago."

"Oh wow." Claire exhaled. "Some kind of inheritance coming your way?"

"Not exactly," Jacob replied.

They ended up talking for close to half an hour, and Jacob probably told her more than he should have, but having bottled everything up inside, he needed someone to talk to, and Claire seemed to respond with good advice and compassion to everything he had to say. He liked her; she seemed kind-hearted, and she liked him; he seemed a little lost and quite gentle, despite the harsh American accent.

"Are you sure this is all true? This really does sound like some sort of elaborate scam," Claire enquired. "It all seems too far-fetched, but I guess you need to try to find out something more," she said as she swung her legs outwards to exit the booth they were sitting in. "Maybe there is some element of truth in this, which, if there is, you deserve to know. Why don't you crack on, and I'll meet you later? My shift finishes at 8pm."

"Are you sure you don't mind? I don't want you to waste your evening off on me," Jacob said, looking up at her in the hope she wouldn't change her original offer.

"No, not at all. Anyway, are you kidding? This is much more entertaining than the crap on TV," she quipped. "Sorry, bad joke. I know this is your life. If your dad is innocent, I might be able to help you – I might not have my law degree yet, but I do know a thing or two. I would be happy to help, and it'll give me a distraction from this place and studying all the time," she said, throwing her left arm in the direction of the bar.

Jacob smiled. "I do owe it to Patrick to at least look into this, don't I? After all, I didn't travel all this way for nothing."

"I think you do, and if not for him, certainly for your mum" Claire said. "Meet me here at 8pm?"

"Sure," Jacob replied keenly.

Jacob headed back to his hotel to freshen up and do some more research online about Patrick's court case and arrived back at Bakers Point ten minutes before Claire's shift was due to finish. They headed round the corner to a different bar and, after an uneasy first twenty minutes, the drinks were flowing, and so was the conversation as they sat across a round table from each other on small, dumpy stools.

"I grew up in Bath, a beautiful place to live about one hour west of here, and I have one sister who now lives in Perth in Australia with her boyfriend."

"Wow, have you visited?" Jacob asked.

"No, maybe one day if she's still there, but I have no money to spend on long flights; I can just about pay my rent."

"Universities aren't cheap," Jacob said, as if he knew the financial pain she was going through and wanted to keep in her good books rather than divulge his millionaire lifestyle.

"Tell me about it. My parents have zero money, so I'm working as many shifts as I can here and am up to my eyeballs in student loans."

Claire was a family oriented girl, which Jacob admired, and after she spoke about her parents' lifelong ambition to retire to Spain and spend six months of the year poolside in a sangria-induced coma, Jacob talked about his less-than-conventional upbringing in the States.

He recalled how his adopted parents told him at the age of seven that he was originally from London and that his real parents were no longer alive but how much they loved him.

The drinks continued to flow, with Jacob drinking bottled beer, picking at the label, and Claire sipping on a Bacardi and Coke as the conversation unsurprisingly turned to his recent shock at discovering his father was still alive and, worse still, in jail for killing his mother.

"Literally a week ago I knew nothing about this."

"It really is crazy; how do you feel?" Claire asked with genuine concern.

"Honestly, I don't know what to make of it," he replied, slugging the rest of his beer.

"Have you decided to help Patrick?"

"I guess. I really don't know what I can do at this stage, but after this Milne guy admitted to killing Charlotte, and with Patrick constantly pleading his innocence over the years, maybe there is something in it." He shrugged. "Another drink?"

"Sure," she said, finishing her last one. "I think it's a noble thing to do – imagine if he is innocent and has been stuck in there for eighteen years. I don't know how much I can help, but I am happy to try and use my law degree, well, you know what I mean."

"I really appreciate this conversation, more than you know, and any help would be great," Jacob said as he stood up and strolled to the bar.

The whole evening was a bonding session for Claire and Jacob, and as the evening wore on, she showed him a few sights of the city and probably the insides of a few too many pubs along the way as both of them started to relax, laugh, and forget for a brief while the very individual circumstances of their lives.

They eventually found themselves back at Jacob's place, where the night ended in truly climactic style as Claire decided to seize the moment and spend the night, which was a rarity for her to do. The couple found themselves in a drunken yet passionate embrace that was over in less than ten minutes but certainly worth the effort on both parts.

TWENTY-THREE

At 3:43pm, American Airlines flight AA345 was 289 miles off the East Coast of the United States, on route to New York's JFK International Airport. Jacob had not slept throughout the flight, nor had he watched a single minute of entertainment on the blank screen in front of him. The burden of troubles weighed heavily on his mind as he returned home. His thoughts were only lightened briefly by the occasional swooning over Claire every thirty minutes or so. Doubts, plans, and retribution swirled round his head, making him feel dazed with too much information as his imagination got the better of him, concocting various conspiracy theories.

He now knew that Greg and Isabelle had lied to him about his parents, which was his main motivation for seeking the truth about what exactly had happened to him and his parents eighteen years ago. Patrick had convinced him that Greg could not sustain the country club lifestyle they had all enjoyed over the years by simply heading up the IT division of a large bank or moonlighting as some hotshot IT consultant. He hadn't won the lottery. Jacob knew deep down that the maths simply didn't add up, and the chances of a jackpot win were even less likely than Greg being involved in some illegal activities.

During the flight, Jacob thought through the many occasions that he might have questioned his parents had he stopped to think about it at the time rather than just accepting it as his life. Greg and Isabelle could seemingly afford all types of luxuries, although money was never mentioned in either a positive or a negative way. In fact, Jacob could not recall Greg or Isabelle ever saying no to a request for money – whether it was for a school skiing trip, clothes, music, pocket money, a new bike, the latest games console, and so on. Even his and Matthew's first cars were both Mercedes, fully loaded with all the extras available.

Jacob could not be blamed for not questioning where all the money came from. Growing up surrounded by wealth and not knowing any different prevented him from questioning it. However, the more he thought about it, the more it made him wonder, fuelling his motivation to seek the truth. His desire to find out more was certainly ignited from his trip to the UK. If seeking the truth directly benefited Patrick and his quest for revenge, then so be it.

During the flight, he listed on an American Airlines napkin things that he now thought Greg couldn't afford on an average salary or even one that was five times an average salary. The list made interesting reading:

- Cars: Porsche, Ferrari, two Range Rovers and one Mercedes Benz – estimated one million dollars in cars sat on the drive.
- First-class airline tickets and hotels – one million dollars plus.
- Designer handbags and suits – one hundred thousand dollars.
- Swiss watches – one hundred thousand dollars.
- Country club membership for as long as he could remember – ??
- Private education for two kids – ?
- Six thousand square foot home – two to three million dollars.
- Apartment in Miami – one million dollars.

The list was extensive and certainly not exhaustive, but this was enough for Jacob to calculate millions of dollars spent over the last fifteen years. Even if it were all on credit, there was no way even a huge half-million-dollar salary could generate so much consistent wealth or substantial line of credit to purchase all of this.

Jacob was intrigued, he was definitely onto something here, and he kicked himself for not identifying this earlier.

His first thoughts were of a long, hot shower, followed by a short sleep, so he opted for a hotel in Manhattan instead of heading back to the DeWitt family home and the inevitable questions about his trip. The confusion surrounding the last five days of his life ensured the sleep was uninterrupted. At 6:30am the following morning, Jacob took the subway to Chinatown in the hunt for some unofficial, unbranded hardware.

He had read an article in a magazine about technology available to monitor keystrokes and search for passwords on a PC. He soon acquired a surveillance USB key and the relevant software for $150 from a sketchy-looking guy in Chinatown calling himself "Tip Top". He also offered an impressive array of fake Swiss watches, handbags, and designer clothes, all of which Jacob could afford the genuine versions of, so he politely declined and settled in twenty-dollar bills for the surveillance kit only.

Tip Top reliably informed him that installing the software onto the target machine and leaving the USB stick in place would allow him to copy all files and keystrokes in real time. This would enable him to intercept all passwords, emails, attachments and so on from the target PC. *If I could gain information on bank and email accounts, I might be able to establish where the money was coming from, how much of it there was, and who else was involved, if anyone* he thought to himself. Now he just needed an opportunity to gain access to the PC in Greg's home office.

He decided to take a taxi back to the family home in the hope that both Greg and Isabelle were out so he could target the PC and then lie in wait for the activity to begin. As the yellow taxi rolled north out of the city, Jacob hoped that neither Greg nor Isabelle would be at the house. The information he had learnt during his visit to the UK was still fresh in his mind, and keeping a lid on it might prove difficult, especially if he ran into Greg.

Why have they lied to me for all these years? he continued to ask himself.

The uneventful ride home of just thirty miles took longer than he had hoped, with the usual sheer weight of traffic causing most of the delays. This gave him plenty of opportunity to gather his thoughts and gain some composure just in case either parent – or worse still, both of them – were home. As the car drove into Westchester, his heart started to race, and as he swung round the last bend, the imposing iron gates were open; he glanced at his watch – 3:49pm – both Isabelle and Greg were out, much to his relief.

The sweat moistened his palms as the tension bit harder; he was now feeling the full strain of his heart pounding in his ears as the car stopped outside number 1479 Cedar Tree Avenue, the very exclusive suburb everyone in the area wanted to live in.

Jacob paid the seventy-one-dollar fare, leaving a nine-dollar tip, collected his luggage from the boot, and walked as calmly as possible towards the front door, turning the key slowly as the large, twelve-feet-high door clunked open in front of him.

The house was cold and seemed empty, so he quickly slipped inside and pressed the door closed before carefully lowering his backpack onto the floor near the large grandfather clock that was dwarfed by the huge entrance hall. He rolled his suitcase quietly to one side and headed through the dim morning light past the grand white staircase to his right and into the kitchen.

He walked past the half-empty coffee pot and tapped the still-hot glass on his way to the side door that opened into a corridor, linking the main house to a vast array of garages and a games room with a pool table and shuffleboard, which he virtually live on as a teenager. There were slot machines, a fully stocked bar as good as any you would find in an upmarket hotel, and large screen TVs everywhere. Jacob recalled the many endless days and nights with Matthew watching sports with their friends, sneaking the occasional alcoholic drink. Sometimes Greg would join in if he was in a good mood or needed a drink, but these visits had become less frequent in recent months.

He turned on the lights, and as they blinked to life, he stared at the bay always used to park Greg's beloved black 911 Carrera S4, complete with personalised license plate "IT KING". The bay was empty, much to his relief, and Isabelle's Lexus jeep, which would always be parked next to a red Ferrari covered in a red dust sheet adorned with the yellow prancing horse logo, was also missing. The coast was clear and, within a few seconds, his heart rate started to drop rapidly, knowing Greg couldn't confront him any time soon. Stay calm, they know nothing, he told himself as he edged back inside.

He headed quickly back into the corridor through the kitchen and past the foot of the grand staircase, back into the main entrance hall. The stone floor was polished most days by the housekeepers, so his rubber-soled boots squeaked as he walked towards the large study Greg called his office. Once inside the study, he tried to calm himself down by acting natural; he often used Greg's printer, so his presence would not have caused any suspicion, just a general interest in what he was doing. Jacob turned on the light and left the door wide open in a bid to act as normal as possible and, of course, to listen out for Isabelle rising. He fired up the PC he knew Greg used for both work and home life and located the black tower under the antique solid teak desk originally from Denmark, before realising he had left his backpack in the main hallway.

He squeaked towards the grandfather clock that suddenly bellowed out eight chimes just as he bent down to pick up the bag, stopping him cold in his tracks. His heart skipped several beats; he bolted upright, his completely straight and vertical spine tingling. He physically could not move for a split second before jumping and spinning round all in one impressive movement, backpack now in tow. His heart raced further, and sweat covered his cold back. *Relax*, he thought to himself, *just relax*, but he could not seem to even look remotely calm, let alone feel it inside.

He quickly skipped back through the door of the study, got down on his knees, and plugged the USB hard drive into the port on the back of the PC tower under the desk. The red light started to glow, which caused Jacob some concern, but when he turned the tower back into its original place, the glow was facing inwards and no longer noticeable. He opened the CD drawer, inserted the software disk, nudged it closed, and sat in the comfortable leather chair behind the vast, and predictably very tidy, desk. The disc started to spin, and the software began to load.

"INSTALL NOW?" appeared on the screen, followed by some text Jacob assumed was Mandarin, possibly asking the same question. *Cheap Chinese software, it had better bloody work*, he thought.

He rolled his eyes as the crass software performed at an unusually low speed while Jacob tapped his fingers relentlessly on the desk in front of him. He hit "Y" on the black keyboard in front of him, and a new window appeared:

Installing 0%
Twelve Minutes Remaining

"Shhhhiiiiit," he mumbled, "twelve damn minutes."

He sat patiently waiting for the blue bar to wipe from left to right across the screen as he listened out for any signs of movement along the landing above. Firing up the internet, he headed for his favourite search engine, trying to look as normal as possible while waiting impatiently. He typed in "Sony laptops", which brought up thirty-one thousand links, one of which he clicked and printed, after flicking the on switch on the laser printer located behind him under the huge window covered in dark wooden blinds.

Twenty per cent ticked by as he heard Isabelle call from near the front door.

"Greg, is that you?"

"No, Mum, it's me."

"Hi, honey, I didn't know you were back. Everything okay? How was your trip?"

"Yes, fine, thanks. The trip was great."

"Oh great, I'll just take a shower, I've been at yoga, and I'll be down soon."

Jacob returned to the PC and glanced at the pop-up window on the screen.

33%

Eight Minutes Remaining

"Come on," he scoffed before closing the door quietly and zipping back through the hall to the kitchen, leaving the Sony laptops internet page on the screen.

His heart pounded as he poured the coffee pot into the sink and stocked up the percolator with fresh coffee granules from the side cupboard. He took two white china cups from the cupboard, poured milk into one, and added sugar to the other. Black and sweet, he needed his coffee today, so he poured in extra sugar for good measure.

He turned on the big flat-screen TV that resided on the back wall of the kitchen near the laundry room and set it to the Fox23 News channel before walking back across the hall to the study to stand patiently behind the desk for a further few minutes, nervously willing the software to complete.

68%

Four Minutes Remaining

Having not had the chance to test the software, Jacob thought this could be one huge waste of time if it didn't work, and all of this stress could have been avoided. Yet he stood behind the desk, waiting patiently for it to finish and the coffee to percolate in the kitchen. Suddenly, he looked up, and standing in the doorway was Isabelle, dressed in a camel-coloured towelling dressing gown with her dark-brown wet hair twisted to one side, cascading down her left shoulder.

"Hi," Jacob blurted out in surprise, quickly walking towards her.

"Hi, Jakey, coffee?"

"Sure, it's just brewing, should be ready by now," he replied as she walked back across the large, tiled entrance hall towards the kitchen.

75%

Three Minutes Remaining

"How was Vegas? I didn't expect to see you back here before you go back to Boston?" she called out to him.

"Great fun, thanks. We stayed at the Bellagio on the same floor we all stayed on last time we went," he lied. "I thought I would fly back via here to pick up a few things before catching a train back to Boston later," he answered without taking his eye off the screen. "Any bagels?" he asked, looking to delay her further.

83%

Two Minutes Remaining

The longest twelve minutes of his life ended with the software finally wrapping up the installation process and spitting out the CD. He clicked "OKAY" when it had finished, quickly switched the PC off, and then wandered leisurely into the kitchen for the well-earned coffee, leaving the USB key plugged into the tower under the desk.

He started to relax and enjoyed two cups of coffee with Isabelle. Despite there being so many questions on the tip of his tongue, desperate to leap out of his mouth at any time, he managed to keep his composure.

He planned a quick turnaround to avoid running into Greg and any further time spent with Isabelle, who was soon to be on one of her usual three-hour drinking sessions with her friends in the middle of Westchester. He collected some fresh clothes, took a shower, and headed for the train back to Boston and college.

TWENTY-FOUR

Patrick sat on the cold, hard concrete step in the exercise quarters, staring west towards the high concrete walls topped with razor-sharp wire, typical of most prisons across the UK. Pondering his game plan for the sixth time that morning, he thought of Jacob being back in school, possibly carefree and far away. The cooler-than-normal morning was filled with the noisy, often immature, and sometimes aggressive, banter from the other inmates as usual. Patrick had already turned down a game of chess from Howard, one of the old cons still serving time for an armed robbery conviction back in the early eighties.

Patrick had spoken to Jacob the day before and told him that a girl he had met in a bar near his hotel was going to help him should he need any assistance now that he was back in the US. He felt uneasy about Claire, the stranger, though under any other circumstances, he was sure he would have liked her from what Jacob had told him.

Patrick was wise enough to understand that if he

were to forge any kind of lasting relationship with his son, he would have to accept that Jacob was an adult now; choosing his own friends was up to him. There would always be many people in Jacob's life Patrick would never know anything about. Exploring the past and potentially gaining revenge from a prison cell against a man who lived over three thousand miles away was never going to be a cakewalk. In a way, he surmised, the extra pair of hands would surely be useful.

Claire was due to visit in less than five days, and although he had plenty of plans, more information, and tactics for her, he could not stop feeling apprehensive about divulging everything to a complete stranger, which kept him up at night. Claire would be feeling equally apprehensive too, he thought to himself. What young woman wants to visit a complete stranger in jail, let alone a convicted murderer?

The Chinese software was working, and in ten days, all 262 emails to and from Greg's Elite and TMAIL online accounts found their way to Jacob's Blackberry. Most of them seemed like the usual mixture of junk and a startling number of social invitations from people he had never heard of, many of whom were women. As yet, nothing had aroused Jacob's suspicion, which was about to change.

At 7:32am one morning, out of the cool, dark morning air, his phone started to bleep and vibrate on the side table next to the bed, waking him instantly from his deep sleep. He wiped his eyes with his left hand as he rolled over to locate his phone. As he scrolled through the various emails, he quickly sat up upon noticing the first email from Sheldon titled "Miami". This email stood out as Sheldon hadn't emailed him to date, so ignoring all the other emails that had been sent to his phone, he opened this one, which read:

> *Greg,*
>> *Heading down to Miami today, I'll arrange with*
> *HC and be at the usual on Biscayne Blvd.*
>> *Keep you posted as always.*
>> *SV.*

Although vague and disappointingly short on detail, there was one word that drew his attention the most. While he had not planned to get up early that morning, the word "usual" got Jacob moving as he hoped the chase was finally on. And who was HC?

He sprang to his feet, rubbed his eyes again, and pulled on a pair of jeans that had spent the night crumpled on the bedroom floor.

He sat at the more-than-adequate desk in his student accommodation on campus, which he opted to pay more for to keep his privacy and not share a room when he first enrolled at the school; he could afford not to share with strangers. As his PC fired up, he clicked Internet Explorer and, after a few seconds, typed in "private investigators Biscayne Blvd, Florida", which brought up plenty of options to choose from. But Jacob needed one close to Miami and fully registered.

Larry Branstone was a retired cop from Indiana's Metropolitan Police Department, where he had managed to attain the high rank of Captain over thirty years in the field of fighting crime, before deciding to cash in his long-awaited pension. Too many of his colleagues had either got close to retiring or had, in fact, retired only to be cut down with a heart attack, cancer, or a brain tumour. "I'm not going to make the same mistake," he regularly told his wife, Lorraine.

Sadly, fate dealt its cards again, and soon after retiring and moving to warmer climes, Lorraine died from sustained hypertension, ending in a stroke and, two weeks later, her untimely, yet peaceful, demise. Following Lorraine's death, with his two children Luke and Joanna living their own grown-up lives, Larry missed the chase of being in the force and needed to ease his boredom. Based in Miami Gardens, a suburb in north-central Miami-Dade County, he had eased himself back out of retirement and was busy topping up his pension by running his own small private investigation bureau.

Florida had been their choice of retirement location in the Sunshine State for many years prior to Lorraine's death due to the weather, like most people. They purchased a duplex condominium overlooking a large lake and were happy in the short-lived time they had left. Mainly other retirees and the occasional tourist or professional, lucky enough to afford a holiday home in the sunshine, surrounded a peaceful network of lakes and two-storey units he now called home.

To date, his normal assignments were employee

monitoring, insurance fraud, and investigations of suspected infidelity – all easy-to-handle, short-term assignments. So, the next call he was about to receive was to prove a little more taxing.

Jacob had chosen Larry specifically for his location twenty miles north of Miami and because he liked the look of the picture, which his son Luke had posted on his basic website, of him draped in his beige Miami Police uniform prior to his retirement.

"Larry Branstone," the old guy said, flipping open a pay-as-you-go mobile phone and glancing at his watch: 7:49am.

"Hi, Larry, my name is Matt Williamson. I have just picked up your number off your website and need your services. Are you free for the next couple of days?"

"Yes, sir, I am," he replied, walking into his home office with a fresh cup of coffee clutched in his left hand.

"How are you fixed for a couple of days in Miami?"

"Not too far from here, but I guess you know that already. When are you thinking?"

"Today, ASAP."

Jacob explained he needed Sheldon tracked for the duration of his stay in Miami and that he would be willing to pay the published rates on his website: five hundred dollars per day plus expenses. He emailed several pictures of Sheldon he had copied from the Verick website, along with a general description and the details on Biscayne Boulevard, which both could only assume was a hotel, seeing as there were plenty along that stretch.

After ten minutes of trading information back and

forth, Jacob pulled his credit card from his wallet and rattled off the sixteen-digit card number in order to complete the transaction and get things moving. The line soon ran dead following Larry's sign-off as he continued topping up his notes from the conversation.

"I'll be in touch, Mr Williamson."

Not entirely convinced Sheldon was involved with the lifestyle Greg and Isabelle led, Jacob knew he was worth tracking for a few days at least. He switched the computer off, stored Larry's number in his phone, and headed back to the sack.

Always prepared for a quick exit, Larry was soon packed and ready for every eventuality. Dressed in his usual grey trousers, green shirt, and faded red baseball cap – his minor attempt to blend in and not attract attention – he backed out of the driveway in his navy-blue Chevy Malibu and headed for I-95 south and the short drive to Miami.

Arriving on Biscayne Boulevard in the heart of Miami just a few hours later, Larry immediately counted all the hotels that lined the street, and after driving back and forth for several minutes, he parked in the Best Western car park and headed into reception.

To his left, he had The Plaza, a tall, pastel-pink-painted building, the Marriott, Intercontinental, another Best Western, Hilton, Days Inn, and a handful of small motels that he certainly would not rule out. Assuming the target was staying in one of these hotels, he thought he shouldn't have too much trouble tracking him down as he monitored the day-to-day activities going on around him.

So, with a newly purchased plain navy baseball cap pulled firmly down over his ever-receding hairline, Larry sat calmly sipping free coffee from the polystyrene cup emblazoned with the green and grey hotel logo on the front. Several flight crews checked in and out; an elderly woman with three yapping chihuahuas, who looked like she was the one being taken for a walk as they dragged her across the hotel lobby on their leads, soon followed. An executive in a not-so-smart suit checked in, and among the many others, he observed a family of five with three tired-looking children.

Four hours and six hotels later without a bathroom break, he knew he had his work cut out as he walked into the lobby of the Intercontinental, where he decided against helping himself to the complimentary beverages sitting on a hot plate in the reception area. Once again, he nestled in a quiet corner contemplating his approach after failing to track down Sheldon under his real name at any of the lodges, raising further suspicion, which he'd been hoping for.

Again, more people poured in and out: holidaymakers, businesspeople, honeymooners, or couples seemingly on their honeymoon, or possibly a romantic weekend with someone else's spouse, and plenty more flight crews from all over the world. Sheldon wasn't about to walk straight into his life, and he knew he would have to return to his bloodhound ways of track and trace. But so far, after five hotels, two diners, three bars, and a handful of shops, he was starting to run out of hope.

Walking to the front desk after fifteen minutes of

watching in vain, Larry pulled a picture of Sheldon from his inside jacket pocket and introduced himself to the check-in clerk standing behind the desk.

"Larry Branstone, Bail Enforcement Officer. Have you seen this man today?" he asked, shaking his right leg to ease the cramp.

The blonde lady in the hotel's navy uniform studied the picture for a second and then glanced up at Larry with the reply, "No, sir, I have not, but I only started my shift thirty minutes ago."

"Who was on before you?" he asked a little kinder.

"Jamie, but she has gone home by now. Our supervisor may be able to help."

"Can I talk to him, please?"

"Her, and yes you can. One minute, please," she replied, rising to her feet and walking into the back office marked "STAFF ONLY", with a few letters missing.

Less than a minute later, out came Gloria Westwood, holding the photo of Sheldon.

"What has this guy done?" she asked Larry.

"I'm afraid I cannot tell you that, ma'am, but he is not a violent criminal, so there is no need to panic," he said, sensing he was on to something.

"He checked in about 11:30am; I did it myself."

"What name did he use?"

"Can I see some ID, sir?"

Larry quickly flashed an accurate copy of a bail bondsman ID that had come in handy on a few occasions since his retirement, which a friend of his had kept from his bondsman days. Gloria nodded in approval before tapping several times on the computer in front of her, then picking up a pen and jotting down the result, which Larry hoped was the start of a great adventure. She handed over the slip of paper and passed a brief smile at Larry.

"Very good of you, thanks," he said, before returning to his original seated position, this time without the coffee.

He glanced at the note, which read: *Vincent Claremont, Room #365, 1 night, returning the day after tomorrow for another one-night stay.*

Larry now knew which room Sheldon was in, and he'd used an alias, so something was going on – he had to find out before he left town, or he would have nothing to show for his endeavours and risk missing his day's pay. He immediately pulled his mobile from his trouser pocket and tapped in the hotel's number on the information board in the lobby.

"Welcome to the Intercontinental Hotel, how may I direct your call?"

"Room 365, please."

"One moment, please."

Larry waited, cool as ice, for the line to pick up at the hotel he was sat in. Three rings later and bingo.

"Yeellllow?"

"Good afternoon, sir. My name is Daniel. I'm with hotel relations and I'm sorry to bother you. We have recently launched our new customer service programme, where we contact every guest on the day of arrival to make sure everything is to your satisfaction."

"Send me two more pillows and four bottles of Bud Light in an ice bucket."

"Yes, sir. Anything else?"

"That'll do it," Sheldon said before hanging up.

Larry now just had to sit and wait for Sheldon to move and, of course, arrange for the pillows and beers to be sent to his room so as not to blow his cover. The wait would be a long one, as Sheldon didn't move for a further five hours, but when he did, Larry was ready.

As the target walked out of the hotel, Larry followed him at the textbook twenty-five paces behind, perfectly timing his footsteps as he crossed to the opposite side of the road, glancing infrequently at Sheldon only to keep him in sight.

Eventually, after a ten-minute walk, the target predictably headed into Miller Brewing Co and took up a stool at the bar in front of a vast array of beer taps. Larry opted for the sanctuary of a booth towards the back, along the side of the bar in full view of Sheldon. He ordered a sparkling water from a passing waiter while the target tucked into three different beers in quick succession.

Larry stayed with him all evening as he worked his way through a plate of chilli, several beers, and even more females. Larry pushed the remains of his chicken finger platter to one side as he closely watched Sheldon's lecherous gazes being rebuffed by every female unfortunate enough to come into his sight.

Eventually, Sheldon headed back to the hotel alone, or so he thought, as Larry was in tow twenty-five paces behind, and after a brief conversation with the clerk behind the reception, Sheldon retired to room 365.

Heading back to the reception, after ensuring Sheldon

had gone into his room as best he could without getting in the same lift, Larry soon extracted information from the hotel clerk that Sheldon had booked a wake-up call for 6am and a taxi to the airport for 6:30am.

Larry would be ready and waiting.

TWENTY-FIVE

Larry had seen it all in his years of pursuit, but this morning's task felt different. The moment his alarm buzzed at 5am, he was out of bed, ready to shadow Sheldon from a distance. Sitting in his car with the engine running to keep the AC on, it was already 25°C outside. He chewed on a breakfast burrito, black coffee coursing through his system as he waited. It was an early start, but patience had become Larry's greatest asset over the years. He'd wait for as long as it took.

At 6:30am, Sheldon finally emerged from the hotel, his black V-neck jumper snug over dark-blue jeans, tassels on his Italian loafers bouncing with every step. No hurry in his movement, yet there was something about his demeanour – a restlessness, a tension that Larry could sense even from twelve feet away. Sheldon wasted no time jumping into the back of a taxi, his small suitcase still in hand. The waiting was over.

Larry slid the car into gear. He was dressed in his own

version of camouflage – nondescript white linen shirt, and beige chinos – which allowed him to blend in with any crowd. He had followed worse men to worse places, and a taxi ride to the airport was as routine as it got. But routine never dulled his edge. In this line of work, one wrong step and you were out. He'd spent too long mastering his craft to make that mistake now.

The drive to the airport was uneventful, Larry following Sheldon's taxi without a hitch. Inside the terminal, Larry kept six feet behind as Sheldon queued at the American Airlines counter. When Sheldon uttered the words, "Grand Cayman at 8:45am", Larry's instincts flared. His pulse quickened, but he kept his pace slow, careful.

At the ticket counter, Larry blurted out his request for the same flight, cutting off the clerk before she could finish telling him the price. "I'll take it; charge this," he demanded, shoving his credit card over the counter; time was of the essence. A flash of panic surged when he briefly lost sight of Sheldon for five minutes, but he found him again, perched at a bar, casually sipping an early morning rum and coke the other side of security.

Larry relaxed slightly as he picked up his ticket and cleared security. He grabbed an orange juice from the airside bodega, and during the thirty-minute wait, he pretended to read an old *Economist* magazine he found lying around, keeping Sheldon in his peripheral vision at all times.

Suddenly, Sheldon picked up his mobile and started making a call, which spurred Larry into action as he launched himself in the direction of the bar to be within earshot just in time to hear Sheldon say, "Hill Copeland please, Gold Leaf Bank, fifteenth floor."

Larry wrote it down and listened in on the rest of the brief call. "Hill, it's Sheldon, I'm on my way to the Cayman Islands; I'll hit the banks as planned so watch out for the funds in Switzerland. Keep me posted." He hung up. Larry wrote most of the information down in his notebook and waited nearby for the flight to board, now knowing he was surely on to something. Possibly money laundering if the Cayman Islands and Switzerland were involved.

The flight itself was a short ninety minutes. Sheldon downed three beers, oblivious to the eyes watching him from five rows back. Larry let himself relax, catching a brief nap. The landing at Owen Roberts International Airport snapped him back into action. Sheldon wasted no time, and neither did Larry. Another cab ride; another tail to chase.

"Follow that car with the 052 licence plate and don't lose him," he instructed the driver, pointing at Sheldon's taxi.

"No problem," the driver replied, skilfully weaving through traffic.

When Sheldon entered the Loyalty Trust Bank, Larry positioned himself at Casey's coffee shop across the street, watching Sheldon grow more agitated with every passing minute. His hands gestured wildly as he argued with a bank official, flailing in frustration. After several phone calls and a tense wait, a brown holdall was passed across the table. Larry's gut told him everything he needed to know. Cash. Lots of it. The Cayman Islands were a notorious hub for dirty money, and Sheldon was in the thick of it.

"Check please," Larry called to the server, ready for the chase to resume.

His mind was racing. Money laundering, drug deals – it all fitted. But his focus remained sharp. With practised ease, he slipped a small tracking device under Sheldon's car before darting into the bank to gather more intel. The unattended phone on the desk yielded three numbers in the memory. Two were dead ends, but the third was a New York number. Larry's fingers itched with excitement as he scribbled down every detail.

"Can I help you, sir?" asked Viv, the ageing bank secretary.

"No thanks, I haven't got time to wait; I'll call back," Larry replied as he charged past her, not waiting for a reply, and jumped back into his waiting taxi.

Larry instructed the driver through the traffic, directed by the tracking device that was doing its job to perfection. After less than ten minutes, the target vehicle had come to a stop, which Larry's driver concluded was at the Ponderosa Hotel on the west coast of the island. "Take me there please," Larry instructed as he started to punch the New York number into his phone.

It rang three times. "Hill Copeland, Gold Leaf America Bank," the man answered.

"Sorry, did you say Gold Leaf America Bank?" Larry replied, scratching down the name in his pocket pad as the taxi made a sudden sharp left turn.

"Yes, correct, sir, how may I assist you?"

"I'm sorry, I didn't catch your name," Larry replied.

"It's Hill Copeland, to whom am I talking?" Hill asked.

He hung up – Larry had the information he needed – just as the car pulled into the Ponderosa Hotel compound on the island's west coast. As Larry arrived, much to his delight, Sheldon was finishing a cigarette outside the lobby, and as he discarded his butt, he entered and walked straight through without checking in.

The hotel was pristine but eerily empty, like it had only just opened.

Larry followed Sheldon through deserted hallways, past a tranquil pool, a deserted bar, and two seemingly disinterested security guards dressed all in white, with dark sunglasses on. Sheldon didn't check in, and Larry didn't need to either. He watched as Sheldon disappeared onto the beach, hauling the same brown bag onto a yellow kayak and paddling out towards the gleaming superyacht anchored offshore.

His breath caught as he pulled out his binoculars; he wiped the persistent sweat from his forehead with the back of his hand as the sun relentlessly beat down on his meagrely covered head. This was no ordinary exchange. The boat must have been over one hundred feet long, luxurious, elegant, and far too large for one man to operate alone. Sheldon disappeared behind the yacht, leaving Larry with a sinking feeling in his gut; he looked at his watch: 11:34am.

Something far bigger was in play.

Less than five minutes later, Sheldon reappeared and headed back to shore, which was Larry's cue to start moving again, back in the direction of the front lobby and his waiting taxi. But before he could move, he felt a heavy hand clap his shoulder. Larry's heart jumped, but he remained calm, turning to face a security guard. The sunglasses were as dark as the man's expression. Larry spun a quick lie, avoiding Sheldon's gaze as the kayak bobbed its way back to shore.

"Just leaving," he muttered, and the guard pointed to a side path. Larry didn't need another invitation; *what type of hotel doesn't want guests?* he thought to himself as he made a hasty exit.

He moved quickly, retracing his steps through the pristine, deserted grounds of the hotel. He avoided the expansive lobby and its polished marble floors, opting for the side paths through the lush gardens. As he reached the front of the hotel, he saw his taxi driver still waiting patiently by the curb.

He slipped into the back seat.

"Just wait," he instructed the driver.

Less than three minutes later, Sheldon was back at the front of the hotel, minus the bag, and waiting for a taxi, which soon arrived and pulled away.

Larry's taxi followed and blended back into the traffic in pursuit.

He was determined not to lose sight of Sheldon, aware that every move from here on was critical in uncovering the full extent of Sheldon's operations and passing the information to his employer.

The day drew longer and longer as Sheldon moved from place to place, with the relentless Larry observing his every move, making notes like any good cop should.

By the end of the day, Sheldon had criss-crossed the island, stopping at four different banks, delivering cash to various locations like it was just another day at the office. He went back a second time to the Ponderosa and back out to the boat to drop two further bags. Larry wasn't just following a man anymore; he was unravelling a web – a dangerous, international network of money and possibly drugs. And with every move Sheldon made, Larry was one step closer to understanding what was going on.

Eventually, Sheldon headed to the Bay Tree Hotel, giving Larry a much-needed rest before a similar routine of pick-ups and drop-offs continued the following day.

TWENTY-SIX

Jacob hired a hotel room a good ten-minute walk away from his dorm block back in Boston; he didn't want any interruptions and needed focus. The familiarity seemed to relax him; he preferred to stay in Massachusetts rather than back in New York, keeping up the pretence to Greg and Isabelle that he was back in college.

Contemplating his next move, showering and going out for the evening in pursuit of taking his mind off things quickly turned into ordering a pizza from Gino's across the street from the hotel, two cold bottles of Coke from room service, and a pay-per-view film. Nevertheless, before his night in began, his pay-as-you-go phone started to rattle on the table next to the bed as the vibrate alert kicked in.

He quickly walked over, picked up the phone, and flipped it open to reveal one of only two numbers stored in the phone; this call was from Larry, the other being Claire in London.

"Hello," he answered, sitting down in the large seat in the corner of the bedroom next to the window.

"Mr Williamson."

"Yes, hi, Larry, what have you got for me?" Jacob replied.

"I think we need to meet."

"I'd love to get together and shoot the breeze, Larry, but I really don't have the time. Plus, I'm several hours' flight from Florida."

"Okay," Larry responded.

"So, what did you find out?"

"Well, I followed Sheldon Vaughan as you instructed and ended up in the Cayman Islands after a one-night stop in Miami."

"What did he do in Miami?"

"Nothing really. He quietly kept to himself and acted like a tourist waiting to catch the next flight out."

By this stage, Jacob was starting to jot down notes on the hotel's notepaper parked on the table next to him. Larry proceeded to tell Jacob everything about the trip, from the visit to the bank, the holdalls of what he presumed was money, visiting the empty hotel, dropping off bags to the boat moored offshore and various other locations. He continued, telling Jacob how he followed Sheldon back to the bank the next day and watched him make more withdrawals and visit four different banks, collecting a bag at each.

"Four different banks?"

"Yes, that's right. All in the Cayman Islands but internationally known financial institutions, none of which are American." He also told him about Hill Copeland at the

Gold Leaf Bank in Manhattan, who they both presumed had wired the money to the banks for collection.

"It all looked to me like some type of money laundering or drug-running exercise, but I never saw cash or drugs, just the holdalls coming out of a bank and being left somewhere else," Larry surmised. "The Ponderosa Hotel was huge, immaculate, and empty, so I have no idea what Sheldon was doing there. It was literally like a ghost town, other than gardeners and waiting staff – no customers," he continued.

"Thank you, Larry; are you able to get back to the US and head to Manhattan tomorrow?"

"Yes, sir."

"Charge my credit card again for the travel expenses; we need to pay a visit to this Copeland, and I'll need your help."

"Sure thing, Mr Williamson, I'll call you tomorrow." Larry hung up, knowing damn well that wasn't his real name.

The twenty-minute conversation left Jacob with swirling thoughts and a notepad that read:

Sheldon
Miami –one night
Cayman Islands –one night/two days and counting
Four Banks in CI
Hill Copeland – Gold Leaf Bank Manhattan
Holdalls full of cash (possibly)
Ponderosa Hotel – empty
Superyacht moored offshore

A tap at the door interrupted his thoughts.

"Room service."

Jacob ate the pizza, drained the beers, and watched half the film before falling asleep on top of the covers without even managing to kick his shoes off. He woke at 3:31am, probably from the temperature in the room sending a chill over his skin. He kicked his shoes off, climbed inside the sheets, and pulled the covers over his shoulders. He instantly felt warmer as he reached for his phone to call Claire back in London. He checked his watch as he punched the speed dial.

"Hello," Claire said in her usual, soft way.

"Hi, Claire, how are you doing?" Jacob said, curling his body up to try and get warmer.

"I'm good, thanks. I've been to see your father, and he asked me to tell you to be careful; nobody knows if Greg is mixed up in drug running, money laundering, or racketeering, and there are all sorts of dubious characters that you could end up running into."

"Tell him not to worry; I'm okay, but he could be right. I think Greg is involved in some sort of money laundering scheme using banks in the Cayman Islands. Call Patrick and tell him I've discovered a friend of Greg's taking large amounts of money from accounts in the Cayman Islands, distributing it around several other banks and depositing a bag full of, presumably, high volumes of cash to a luxury yacht."

"What?"

"I know; it all sounds a bit crazy, but I hired a private investigator who tracked his closest friend down there, so

I can only assume they are both involved in something illegal and obviously very lucrative."

"That would explain a few things for sure. How do you think Greg is involved?"

"I don't know, but he must be. His friend sent him an email telling him of his movements, so he must know what's going on and be involved in some way from a distance."

"Okay, I'll plan to visit your dad again. I researched Fredrick Milne, and your dad was right – he is related to Charles Faulk as he married his younger sister Penny Faulk in 1976."

"Thanks for all your help, Claire; I couldn't do any of this without you. I need to send you some money."

"What for?"

"Just incidentals, call it expenses. What are your bank details?"

"Will I see you again?" Claire asked in anticipation, ignoring his offer of financial aid.

"I hope so, very soon."

"Me too; I'll just get my bank details now if you're sure you don't mind sending me a little, it would really help," she replied, relieved at his positive answer.

TWENTY-SEVEN

Sheldon was so consumed with himself since becoming a career criminal that he failed to notice his whole life caving in around him. He had quit his job a couple of years ago as he had so much money and no longer cared about keeping up the pretence of working for a living; he was now a career criminal.

He had blown over one million dollars on gambling and girls alone, not to mention the sports cars, private jets, and penthouse suites in hotels across the globe. Spending days sleeping, nights partying, gambling, and womanising with little time for anything else other than monitoring the black hole that was raking in the dough from The First Bank and Gold Leaf.

His passport was littered with stamps from London, Hong Kong, Tokyo, Prague, Amsterdam, Lima and Mexico City, to name a few destinations over the last few years alone, and each destination had a tale of drunken destruction, overindulgence, and debauchery.

In London, he was thrown out of a casino after heavily drinking all day and being obnoxious to the croupier after losing twenty-five grand in less than two hours. In Hong Kong, he almost came to blows with the Chinese triads after trying to get too affectionate with one of their women. Prague, Amsterdam, and Rio were all about the hookers, and if Sheldon sat down for five minutes, he would have been ashamed by some of the places he cruised looking for sex.

In Holland alone, he slept with over six women and paid countless thousands in euros for the pleasure. Peru, Rio, and Aruba were all about the sunshine, which was thirsty work and soon turned into a drink-fuelled orgy of more gambling, drinking, and taking drugs, sometimes all at the same time. The wealth he had accumulated through the black hole had turned him into a sleazy drug addict who had become so detached from reality that he would frequently be jailed overnight for being unconscious in a street or urinating on public monuments.

With little family who cared, and even fewer real friends, he had no one to support his struggles with drugs and alcohol, so he did little to pull himself together other than what the police would force on him after being arrested, which was a regular occurrence. Sheldon was a mess, and his days were numbered.

Not knowing how to spend his money wisely, he got caught up in conversations in Belize five years ago that led to him becoming a drug dealer in Boston for a cartel he regularly met at the Ponderosa Hotel in the Cayman Islands. They put him in contact with affiliates of the mafia in Boston, who used him as a soldier with the promise of moving him to Capo if he shifted enough product, which excited Sheldon as most of the films he loved had some interest in guns, drugs, and the mafia, but he was disorganised, never covered his tracks, and was amateurish at best. He was bored; despite all the fun, everything had become the norm, so the challenge of running drugs interested him. The problem was, taking the drugs interested him even more.

He hid everything from Greg, whom he had seen less and less since infiltrating Hill Copeland's world at Gold Leaf Bank. They talked regularly, but Greg had his own demons and had little desire these days to go on an all-night party with his partner in crime.

He never intended to become a drug dealer, but money, drugs, and other addictions have a way of changing people. He moved in large circles of so-called friends in some of the biggest cities in the US with their endless hidden corners and temptations at every turn. None of this mixed well with his inflated ego, massive bank roll, and entrepreneurial spirit.

After getting involved with the cartels, he was far beyond the point of no return, and what started as a small enterprise on weekends, soon turned into a much larger operation. The packages got bigger, the clients more dangerous and unknown; he started operating in the shadows but could never have expected what was about to happen.

Sheldon had a team of college kids, street vendors, pimps, fast-food waiters and low-level street dealers running his poor show, so, under pressure from the cartels, it was time for the mafia to clean up their act and eradicate their ill-thought-out liability.

He became known to club owners in both Boston and New York as someone who would regularly drop one hundred thousand dollars on a night out at a VIP lounge, often surrounded by as many as thirty people, magnums of champagne with fireworks spraying out of them, and a couple of heavies to stop more freeloaders entering the fray. As a result, he was now on the FBI watch list as a person of interest.

During a routine conversation with Benny from Miami about his upcoming visit to the Cayman Islands, Sheldon let slip that he had so much spare cash he was virtually giving the product away for free throughout the city. Benny fed this back to the dealers in the Cayman Islands and word eventually got back to the head of the cartel in Bogotá, who was incensed that Sheldon was basically purchasing the product himself, which was always going to end in disaster. The mafia underbosses soon became aware that Sheldon was fast becoming a liability and could no longer be trusted with the distribution.

With such competition on the East Coast, and investing heavily on paying off authorities in the multiple ports in several countries, purchasing private planes, submarine technology, and even drone technology that was fast improving, they couldn't have one of their distributors partying and getting high on his own supply.

Despite many warnings, their patience had run out; they were never going to conquer their distribution goals with such a weak foundation as Sheldon Vaughan. They had an excellent product supplied from the mountains of Colombia, but the distribution channel was diseased and needed to be cured quickly, and Sheldon wasn't the only one to take the fall; two or three other soldiers were not playing fairly and would also be taken out.

Their major competitors in the city left nothing to chance and ran their businesses like major corporations operating on Wall Street, with their professional players in all industries paying off judges and police chiefs if they ever ran into trouble.

This clearly was not going to be a lasting legacy, so with the decision to get rid of Sheldon having been given the green light, he was about to be fired the drug cartel way.

In the end, his own greed, laid-back style, and could-not-give-a-shit attitude contributed heavily to his demise as the cartel finally turned against him. He was frequently warned not to touch the product, but he didn't listen.

Sheldon thought he was invincible; little did he know he was being watched at every turn – silently, predatorily, and patiently – it wouldn't take much to eradicate the disease in their supply chain – a couple of Magtech slugs from a 9mm pistol with silencer to match would do it.

They sent in their regular predator.

As Sheldon jumped round his apartment listening to House of Pain full blast with complete disregard for his neighbours below, the assassin casually took up position for yet another payday.

Black leather gloves, head to toe in black in fact, with

a plain black baseball cap covering his blond locks and hiding his face from all cameras throughout the apartment building. As the music died down in between songs, the assailant rang the bell and banged on the door just in time to be heard before the next track bellowed out. Ten seconds later, the door flew open to the sounds of yet more hip-hop as two expertly aimed bullets hit Sheldon in the forehead before his corpse had time to hit the floor. His whole body flew violently to the right and bounced inside the doorframe, residing in a crumpled and bloody mess just inside his apartment. Dead before he hit the ground.

The police were soon surmising it was drug related as they found over two kilos of cocaine in his apartment. This quickly told the police everything they needed to know, including putting limited resources into ever finding his killer.

Another one ticked off the FBI watch list.

TWENTY-EIGHT

At 11:23am, Greg DeWitt's world began to crumble. After nearly two decades of slipping past auditors and dodging the authorities, living a life more suited to a Hollywood star than a financial executive, he had always known this day would eventually come. He'd built a fortune – nearly twenty million dollars siphoned through embezzlement – silencing anyone who got too curious with hush money. He'd prepared for every possible scenario: arrest, exile, escape. But when it finally began, it didn't come in the form of an indictment or an armed raid. It started with a simple knock at the door.

Rap. Rap. Rap.

"Mr DeWitt? NYPD. May we come in?"

Greg froze as the two officers stepped into his sleek corner office, their badges gleaming in the morning sunlight pouring through the windows. No SWAT team. No federal agents. Just two detectives, wearing cheap suits, in a room where Greg had overseen millions flow through his fingers for the last two years. The calm before the storm.

The game's over, Greg thought, standing as if in slow motion to greet them. His palms were already slick with sweat.

"Please, come in," he managed, his voice tight.

They moved in, eyeing the office, its minimalist luxury, and sat down across from him like wolves circling prey.

"I'm Detective Woods, and this is Detective James. Homicide division. We're here to ask you about a friend of yours, Sheldon Vaughan."

Greg's stomach dropped. Sheldon? He fought the instinct to roll his eyes but caught himself. Homicide division?

"What's happened?" Greg asked, dread creeping into his voice, his mind racing through the worst-case scenarios.

"Sheldon is dead, Mr DeWitt. Shot twice in the head in his penthouse last night."

The words hit Greg like a punch to the gut. He exhaled sharply, too surprised to hide his shock. The room seemed to close in around him, every sound amplifying, his heartbeat thudding in his ears.

"Oh... God," he muttered. But his concern wasn't for Sheldon. His thoughts were spinning. Did the police know? Did they find the offshore accounts, the Cayman Islands transactions? What the hell had Sheldon got mixed up in?

"We found some texts between you and Sheldon, discussing money. We're also combing through his emails,

personal records... a lot of which lead back to you."
Detective Woods leant in, watching Greg closely.

"Did you know Sheldon was a drug dealer?"

Greg blinked. "What?"

"There were substantial amounts of cocaine and cash in his apartment. Were you aware of his involvement in the drug trade?"

Greg's mouth went dry. "He liked to party. Everyone knew that. Cocaine, sure, but dealing? No. He wasn't that kind of guy."

Woods didn't flinch. "So, you knew he used drugs?"

"He enjoyed a line or two, yeah, but who didn't at a wild party? Sheldon was... flamboyant. He liked to gamble, liked women. But dealing drugs? Never."

"You're sure?" Detective James chimed in, narrowing his eyes.

Greg felt the sweat prickling along his collar. "Never. He wasn't a dealer."

The detectives traded glances. Greg's anxiety was rising by the second. The longer this dragged on, the more exposed he felt. Had Sheldon's death somehow connected the dots to their operation? Had someone discovered the offshore funds? Every second they sat there chipped away at his carefully constructed wall of lies. He needed to get out.

"You seem shaken, Mr DeWitt. When was the last time you spoke to Sheldon?" Woods pressed.

"Last week," Greg lied smoothly, leaning back in his chair, trying to feign nonchalance. His mind screamed for the exit. "We weren't that close."

The detectives stood, signalling the end of the

conversation, but Greg knew they weren't finished with him. As they neared the door, Woods paused, with a tight grip on the handle.

"One last thing, Mr DeWitt... do you take drugs?"

"No," Greg replied, his voice dry. The lie came out effortlessly, but his heart hammered in his chest. Woods nodded, and the door clicked shut behind them. Greg slumped back into his chair, exhaling sharply. He was sweating, his shirt clinging to his back.

Within a couple of minutes, he was up, shoving files into his briefcase, grabbing his phone and keys with trembling hands. He couldn't stay here. Not now. Not when everything was about to unravel.

As his secretary, Miriam, knocked lightly on the door and stepped in, her timid voice barely registering, Greg was already in motion.

"Everything alright, Greg?" she asked, her face creased with concern.

"No, Miriam. A friend was murdered last night. I'm taking a few days off." He didn't even glance up as he spoke, rifling through his desk drawers.

"Oh no, I'll clear your schedule..."

"Thanks," Greg muttered, already halfway out the door.

By the time the lift doors closed, Greg had flipped open his burner phone and dialled the number without even looking, his pulse racing.

"Hill Copeland."

"Hill, it's Greg. I'm leaving tonight. I'll contact you tomorrow. Be on alert. Sheldon is dead."

"What the hell…" Hill started, but Greg snapped the phone shut mid-sentence.

His heart pounded in his chest as he weaved through the crowded streets of Manhattan, heading to collect his car, every shadow now a potential threat. *They'll come for me next*, he thought. Sheldon's death wasn't random. It was connected – it had to be – *but why drugs?* They had never discussed it, not even once.

Pulling into the driveway of his sprawling suburban mansion, Greg didn't look back as he sprinted up the steps and inside the house. Isabelle was off at one of her endless social classes – yoga, coffee, whatever. None of it mattered now. He was leaving, and he wasn't coming back.

Racing up the stairs, Greg threw open the door to the master bedroom, his eyes locked on the painting above the bed. He yanked it down, sending a lamp crashing to the floor. Behind the canvas was the safe he'd installed years ago, hidden, packed full of cash, waiting for this moment.

His fingers spun the combination with practised precision. The bolts released with a satisfying *clunk*, and the door swung open to reveal stacks of neatly wrapped cash – dollars, euros, pounds – all waiting for him. He stuffed them into a black duffel bag, along with fake IDs, passports, and the essentials: clothes, toiletries, and a couple of his finest watches.

He picked up his phone and dialled a pre-stored number he had used on a few occasions.

"NYC Jet, this is Huck," a gruff voice answered.

Greg's grip tightened on the phone. Commercial airlines were out of the question – too many eyes, too many questions about the kind of cash he'd be carrying. While private jets had their own security checks, no one batted an eye at the rich carting bags of money.

He'd keep it low-key tonight – just enough cash to make his escape. The rest he could rely on Hill Copeland to wire to him later, no questions asked.

"I need a jet out tonight," Greg said, his voice clipped, urgent.

There was a pause on the other end, a rustle of papers. "Sure thing, sir. Where to?"

"Paris," Greg replied, his mind already racing ahead.

"Charles De Gaulle?"

"No, Paris Orly." He needed to avoid the busiest airport.

Another pause. "It's not gonna be cheap. We'll need six hours to file a flight plan."

"How much for one passenger?" Greg asked, not bothering to hide his impatience. Money was the least of his concerns.

"For one passenger and light luggage, you're looking at a Lear jet. Sixty-eight grand and some change."

"Fine. Book it," Greg snapped. "Name's Leo Macy. I'll be there by 7pm. I want wheels up no later than 9pm."

"That'll give us enough time to crew up and get the flight plan filed," Huck said, his voice steady. "What about the return?"

"This is one-way," Greg said. "I'll pay in cash when I arrive." His tone was final. He didn't wait for Huck's response before hanging up.

Before long, he was on the move again and back in his

car, speeding away from the house without a final glance.

Greg tossed the burner phone onto the passenger seat, his fingers tapping the steering wheel. Every nerve in his body was on edge. He was running now, and he had no illusions about what would happen if he didn't make that flight. Sheldon was dead – could he be next? *Surely Faulk's heavies haven't caught up with me nearly twenty years later?* he thought to himself.

He sped towards the hotel near the airport he would use to kill time for the afternoon.

TWENTY-NINE

The following wet and dreary morning, grey clouds hung over the city as Larry navigated through traffic across the Queensboro Bridge into Manhattan. He was on his way to meet Jacob for the first time. Greg had been on the run for nearly twenty-four hours and with Sheldon lying in the Bellevue Hospital morgue, the only hope of discovering why Greg had fled the United Kingdom so abruptly and never told Jacob the truth about his parents was Isabelle.

Jacob believed Isabelle held the answers about the illicit dealings that had significantly contributed to their privileged lifestyle since moving to the United States. He hoped that a surplus of dark secrets was burning away inside Isabelle and that she would finally crack, releasing nearly twenty years of guilt and anguish. She was in his sights, but first, Jacob needed Hill Copeland to start talking – and fast.

"Larry?" Jacob asked as the tall, retired cop from Florida, with his perm-tan, walked through the door of the coffee shop on Canal Street.

"Yes. Mr Williamson?" he replied, extending a handshake.

"You can call me Jake. Thanks for all your help; you've been great," Jacob gushed.

"That's what you pay me for. I'm glad I can help," he said as they both sat down opposite each other in a booth.

They quickly hatched a plan over two cups of coffee and double chocolate brownies, and it became clear something major was going on. Jacob told Larry about his father in the UK, and Larry researched stories from twenty years ago on his phone.

Jacob regaled stories of the good times he had shared with Sheldon – playing baseball in the park, basketball in the driveway, and watching films with the family in the garden. Sheldon's death filled them both with even more intrigue, though it didn't surprise Jacob. He was saddened by the loss of someone he had known his whole life and who had always been kind to him as he grew up.

"Sheldon and Greg would always take me and Matthew to various ball games in the city," Jacob told Larry. "I remember one game when the Knicks played the LA Lakers at Madison Square Garden; it was so much fun. I never had any reason to doubt them."

Soon, they were walking through the grand reception of Gold Leaf Bank. Jacob strutted with a confidence he didn't usually possess, while Larry scoped out the area like a true professional. Both were kitted out in NYPD jackets with highly realistic badges hanging round their necks, thanks to Larry's costume kit.

Jacob clocked the sharply dressed employees with their

attaché cases and aluminium coffee cups cruising through the shiny marble-floored hallways, glinting under the overindulgent chandelier dangling sixty feet above. Some were arriving with breakfast bagels; some looked like they had been up all night; and some were already leaving for meetings, while others were just hanging round gossiping.

As they approached the well-groomed receptionist behind a huge marble-topped counter, Jacob's heart started to race. He knew Hill Copeland was in the building and had no problem challenging him, but he also knew what he was about to do was highly illegal and could land him in jail. His heart pounded as he halted at the desk.

"Good morning, ma'am. I'm Detective Mason Nair, NYPD. Do you have a Hill Copeland working out of these offices?" Larry asked without showing any ID.

"I'll check for you now, Detective," replied the navy-with-silver-piping-uniformed employee. "Yes, we do. Would you like me to call him?"

"No," Jacob responded quickly, thinking on his feet. "We'll pay him a visit; can you sign us in, please?" He pointed to the visitor's book on the counter and flipped out a black ballpoint from his inside pocket.

"Sure, please fill in the top section, and I'll get you some visitors' badges."

After completing the necessary forms and being told to head for the fifteenth floor, Jacob took a few deep breaths as they waited for the lift.

"So far, so good," Jacob muttered to Larry.

"Just keep cool, Jake," Larry replied.

Jacob was wearing his best police outfit, designed to

make him look older than his years, consisting of one of Greg's jackets, a white Ralph Lauren shirt, a blue tie, khaki slacks, and brown loafers. Certainly not the everyday attire for a young college kid, but a purposely grown beard helped make him look considerably older.

Both wore NYPD jackets bought from a local souvenir shop that made them look more than plausible. Jacob looked like a cop, apart from appearing a little on the young side, while Larry looked the part of an ageing detective who had done this sort of thing numerous times before. *It's all in the act*, Jacob told himself, as he felt sweat start popping through his scalp while the lift ascended faster than expected.

If all else fails, Larry is definitely cop material, he thought to himself.

He mopped the beads of sweat from every angle as the bell pinged on fifteen, and the doors opened to reveal a smaller reception area, decked out with a large crest and the words "Gold Leaf America Bank" emblazoned on the wall in shiny metallic letters.

Following the signs to the right, Larry asked the woman behind the desk for directions to Hill Copeland's office. She pointed down the hallway to the fourth door on the right, and he took a few deep breaths.

The door to Hill's office was closed, so he peered through the long pane of glass running floor to ceiling along the edge of the doorframe. He saw a round-faced man with thinning hair and glasses seated behind a large wooden desk, peering into two brightly lit computer screens.

"It's go time," Larry said as he knocked on the door hard. Without waiting for an answer, he turned the handle and barged in like a bull, flashing his fake badge in Hill's face. Too late now – the act was underway.

"Hill Copeland?" Larry asked in a deep, rounded voice as Jacob carefully closed the door behind him.

Hill sprang to his feet, staring at the NYPD ID and nervously pushing up his shirtsleeves.

"I'm Detective Mason Nair, NYPD. This is my partner, Adam Bridges. I'd like to ask you a few questions," Larry said, snapping the wallet shut so Hill could not continue his lingering look at the fake ID.

Hill fell back into his chair, clearly reeling from the fact that the police were finally on his doorstep, as he had always feared.

"Hi, Officers. Do you want some coffee? I'm going to get a cup; how d'ya take it?" he rambled, grasping the phone nervously and punching various numbers with his chubby, unusually hairy, digits.

"Casandra, can I get three coffees in here right away?"

Jacob paused for a second to gather his thoughts as his target floundered with the phone in one hand and his Montblanc pen in the other. *If he isn't guilty, he sure looks it*, Jacob thought.

"Mr Copeland, I have reason to believe that you may have known a suspect I am trying to trace, named Sheldon Vaughan," Larry began, poker-faced.

"Let me think, Vaughan, eh?" Copeland said, scratching his left sideburn as if to buy time.

"We also believe you know another suspect we have

been tracking for over a year now, Greg DeWitt. Do you know either of these men?" Jacob asked in his best authoritarian voice.

"I have so many customers, I—"

"I understand, Mr Copeland. I can prove you know both Mr DeWitt and Mr Vaughan very well, so please choose your response carefully," Larry said, casually looking around the modest but adequately teak-fitted office decked out with a smattering of memorabilia from various sports.

"I'm sorry, I don't think I know either of these men. Do they work here?" Hill questioned, trying to stall while he thought up a plausible story.

"No, sir. Both are freelance computer analysts, one of whom called you from the Cayman Islands two days ago."

A knock at the door provided more breathing space for everyone to gather their thoughts as the coffee was delivered by the overly polite Casandra. Jacob sat down, acting as if he had done this many times before, sipping his coffee and looking out the window at the several smaller buildings nearby.

"Detectives, I do not recall that conversation. We deal with many IT companies in this bank; I cannot remember individuals' names," Hill responded with a nonchalant brush of his hair and a nervous sip of the piping hot black coffee.

"I didn't mention anything about an IT company, Mr Copeland," Larry replied.

The room fell silent, and a look of panic crept across Hill's face once more.

"Let me help you, Mr Copeland," Jacob spoke up, about to drop his first set of aces on the table. "Sheldon Vaughan was murdered a couple of nights ago, and we have reason to believe Greg DeWitt was somehow involved, so start talking."

"What?" Hill said, now looking seriously perturbed.

"That's right, Hill. Murdered. He took two to the head in his apartment in Boston, so we are exhausting every avenue available to us until we find Greg DeWitt. So I suggest you tell me the truth," he paused, "hell, I don't care if you and Mr DeWitt are robbing this bank; I'm on homicide, not bank fraud." He chuckled.

With that, Hill Copeland appeared to resign himself to being rumbled and collapsed into a withering mess of lengthy confessions about how he had been taking money from frozen bank accounts for the past two years, facilitated by a unique program given to him by Greg DeWitt.

Jacob's heart skipped a beat as the story unravelled right in front of his eyes. Hill knew Sheldon Vaughan but claimed to have only met him once.

"Tell us in your own time, sir," Larry asked in a more calm and comforting voice.

"I met them several years ago. They coerced me into exploiting my position at the bank. They had this foolproof scheme they had used for years at some bank in the UK," he whimpered without putting up a fight.

"Go on," Jacob said in a state of shock and confusion.

"I'm innocent, you have to believe me, this is not my fault," Hill pleaded.

Jacob knew he was onto something but never expected it on this grand scale as he glanced at Larry, who didn't return the look. His heart bounced so hard it felt like a ball on a string pounding in his ears.

"Mr Copeland… Hill, I'm not interested in your petty cash crimes. I want to know where the money has been going so I can track down Greg DeWitt and arrest him for the murder of Sheldon Vaughan," Larry said calmly, trying to mask his excitement at unearthing such a juicy scam.

"Paris."

"Paris?" Jacob replied.

"He told me just a few days ago that he was leaving the country, and now I know why."

"We are not saying he is involved at this stage. Go on," Jacob said, sitting back in his chair and crossing his left leg over his right knee.

"I deal with all of Greg's finances, and I noticed a payment made for a private jet a few days ago. I tracked the tail number of the flight to France."

"Anything else?"

"Yes, I think I need a lawyer."

The first and inevitable roadblock was presented, but Larry was well prepared.

"I'll tell you something for free, Mr Copeland. You're in deep shit right now, so why not cut me a deal and help me find DeWitt, and I'll make my recommendation that you don't see the inside of a jail cell. Now, where in Paris?"

"I don't know, but I'm sure I could find out. Greg is going to contact me at some point today," Hill said, now looking seriously grey and even sweatier.

"Well then, I'll be pulling up a chair and waiting," Larry said, sitting down across the desk from the mess that was once Hill Copeland.

"What are you going to do?" Hill asked in a timid voice, rubbing his expensive fountain pen for comfort.

"Wait for you to deliver DeWitt, and if you don't, I'll have the FBI trawl through your personal, professional, and financial life. I guarantee you will see a jail cell for a long time." Jacob didn't think for one minute that Greg had killed Sheldon, but this was his only strategy.

"I understand, Officer."

As Hill and Larry sat in silence, Jacob pulled his phone from his left trouser pocket and texted Claire: *With private investigator at Gold Leaf America Bank, Manhattan. Think we might be onto something. Looks like Greg might have been laundering stolen money. Sheldon has been murdered. If anything happens to me, remember the name Hill Copeland. Call you ASAP.*

Hill sat nervously watching Jacob texting away, wondering if he was calling the cavalry in.

"Oh, sorry to interrupt," a visitor said as she tapped lightly on Hill's door before letting herself in.

"No problem," Hill replied, glad to see a friendly face from the office even though she looked startled as she read the large white NYPD letters on the back of Larry's jacket.

Hill answered Sarah from Accounting's series of questions before returning to his stubborn visitors.

"Are you guys just going to sit and wait here all day?" Hill asked.

"Well, Mr Copeland," Larry said. "If he doesn't call

soon, we are going to have to take you into custody for aiding a potential felon, so why don't you hand over your driver's license and wallet?"

"What for?" Hill said, starting to look panicked.

"You are now my witness and informer, and if you get startled, contact Mr DeWitt, or attempt to flee the city, you will be hunted down by every agency in the country."

Hill started to fidget again and fiddle with his ghastly yellow and purple tie.

"Secondly, for your information, we have all methods of communication tapped, so my operators will know who you talk to, for how long, and at what time, regardless of whether it's a voice call, email, page, or text message. Understand?"

Following a shallow nod, Jacob asked to use the bathroom and was given directions before making his exit. As he walked down the corridor, his phone vibrated in his pocket to reveal a message from Claire: *OMG, stay safe and hopefully I'll hear from you soon.*

By the time he had relieved himself and returned to the office, Larry was in full investigator mode once again.

"Fire away," he heard Hill saying as he opened the door.

"When was the last time you saw Greg DeWitt in person?"

"We went to Chicago a while ago. I swear I have only met him on a handful of occasions. Listen, I want to talk to one of your superiors before I tell you anything else," Hill mustered.

Luckily for Larry and Jacob, they were ready for this

and had someone on standby to help. Jacob dialled the number of his friend Parker, stored under Precinct, and handed the phone to Hill.

"Hello, who is this please?" Hill asked.

"Lieutenant O'Malley. Who the hell is this?" Parker said, quickly stuffing gum into his mouth to help his act.

"Oh, hello, I am Hill Copeland. I was just checking on your Detective Mason Nair and his colleague. Do they work with you?"

"Yep, our homicide guys. If you're calling me, they should be with you at Gold Leaf Bank downtown. Anything you need, Mr Copeland?"

"No, thank you," Hill said, passing the phone back to Jacob, seemingly happy things were genuine.

Looking dejected, Hill was about to use the bathroom himself when the phone on his desk rang, startling everyone.

"Act normal, no code words or funny business, understand?" Larry asked.

Hill nodded and picked up.

"Speakerphone, straight away," Jacob insisted.

"Hill, it's Greg. Is everything okay your end?"

"Yes, everything is fine, thanks, Greg. What about you?" Hill mustered.

"I'm okay. I'll be glad to get this over and done with."

"Me too. What's the plan?"

"Gimme a second," Greg said, before sounding as if he was rummaging through a stack of papers at the other end.

Larry pressed his finger to his lips and pointed at the

phone with his other hand. Hill did as he was told and pressed a button on the phone.

"Find out where he is; I need details," Larry instructed.

"I told you – he's in Paris."

"But where in Paris? Find out what is going on," Jacob implored.

"Jake, what are you doing there?" Greg's voice suddenly boomed through the phone speaker.

Jacob sat motionless, with his hands gripped in terror to the arms of the chair; the game was up.

Hill stared at Jacob as Greg spoke again, "Jake, is that you? What the hell is going on over there?"

"You little bastard, you set us up," Larry whispered in a venomous tone, realising the phone wasn't on mute after all.

"I thought it was your son playing the police, Greg. I recognised him the second he walked through the door. Even brought some washed-up grey-haired guy with him for backup. Stupid kid, your picture is all over those social networking sites. I knew I'd seen you before, which is why I just played along with your silly little game."

"Damn it, Jake, what the hell are you playing at?" Greg shouted down the phone.

"Hi, Dad, Greg," Jacob said, briefly leaning into the phone on the desk. "Where are you?"

"I've left the country for a while. What are you playing at? Why are you calling me Greg and not Dad?"

"Yeah, what the hell do you want?" Hill said in a very annoying manner as he smirked at Jacob on the other side of the desk.

"Sheldon mentioned the name Hill Copeland to me once. I thought he might have some idea why he was murdered, so I thought I would do some investigating," Jacob lied.

"Bullshit," Hill said, looking more relaxed by the second.

"Sheldon being murdered was just a random street killing," Greg lied back, assuming he met his demise because of the daylight bank robbery they had been benefiting from.

"Where are you?"

"I'm in Paris," he replied.

"Why?"

"I needed to get away for some time to gather my thoughts after hearing the awful news about Sheldon," Greg lied once again.

"When are you coming back?" Jacob quizzed, desperate to find out more information.

"I don't know, but not for a while."

"Right, you guys, enough of your messing, get outta my fucking office," Hill said with a new sense of purpose.

"I was only trying to help, Dad," Jacob lied further as he started to exit the office.

"Okay, Jake, I'll speak to you later. I think you better leave."

As they both left the office, Larry, thinking quickly on his feet, went straight back to Hill's secretary.

"Hi, Miriam, wasn't it?" he asked.

"Yes, that's right. Can I help you with anything?"

"You probably wonder what is going on," he said,

flashing the fake identification. "Hill is helping us with some inquiries as it would appear he is managing some accounts for a well-known money laundering criminal gang we have been tracking for the past few years."

"Oh, I see," Miriam said, clearly looking shocked.

"I need to listen in on this phone call Hill is currently having with the suspect now. Can you get me on the line without them knowing?"

"I..."

"We need to move quickly. The call could be over very soon, and we could miss our chance to nail this outfit."

"Okay," she conceded, rising from her seat, briefly adjusting her skirt, picking up the phone, and punching a few buttons.

Jacob stood still, not knowing what to do, still reeling from Greg knowing he was there, but Larry took charge and quickly sat in Miriam's seat, grabbing a pen and pad before taking the handset from her and listening in.

He pressed mute, which clearly displayed a red light on the base unit of the phone, something Hill clearly did not do earlier.

"...So, are they going to be after me too?" Hill asked.

"I have no idea, but the second I found out about Sheldon's death, I didn't wait to find out. I suggest you take off for a few weeks too," Greg replied.

"For sure."

"And who was that guy with Jake?"

"No idea, but don't worry, they don't know shit," Hill replied.

"Before you go, I need you to make a transfer from

each of the sub-accounts in the Cayman Islands, evenly split for the full amounts, and then send to multiple accounts in Napoli."

"Napoli, Italy?"

"Yes, you fool. If we don't get pinched after all this, you need to start travelling more. Of course, it's bloody Italy," Greg quipped.

Larry was busy writing on the pad the valuable information from the call as the conversation continued.

"I want ten million in US dollars transferred. Don't forget, spread evenly across the following accounts over the next week." Larry's heart raced; *damn, ten million dollars!* he thought to himself.

"National Bank of Italy account numbers 34967423, 45986613, 87635194, 61579856, 25879315, and 00351984. They are all my accounts held at the main Naples Bay branch in the name of Arthur Fielding. Got it?" Greg asked.

"Yes, but you won't be able to withdraw that amount of cash without giving them at least forty-eight hours' notice. When shall I start sending it?" Hill replied, busily scribbling on the pad in front of him.

"Send it now, with specific instructions to have three million ready in cash in two days' time and a certified bank cheque made payable to Naples Marine for €1.75 million exactly. I have bought myself a boat and called it *Hidden Treasures*. Like it? Somewhat ironic, hey?"

"Sure is," Hill replied.

"I will pick the cash up from the Naples branch, so make sure they are expecting me, two days from now."

"I will; I will process the instruction now and then call them to confirm the detail again."

"Good. Get it done."

"What about your son?"

"I'll sort him out. If he comes back again, tell him to piss off," Greg instructed.

The line went dead as Larry ripped the notes from the pad, put the phone down, and raced from his seated position, not fully digesting the detail he had just gleaned. Miriam was nowhere to be seen, and he had little time to wait around.

"Come on, Jake, we have what we need."

They raced into the open lift, and as the doors closed, Larry began to talk.

"Ten million dollars. They have stolen ten mil! I have all the bank account information for the National Bank of Italy: account numbers 34967423, 45986613, 87635194, 61579856, 25879315, and 00351984, Naples Bay branch, under the name of Arthur Fielding. I hope I've written these down correctly."

"Holy shit," was all Jacob could reply.

"Looks like he is heading for a place called Naples Marine, possibly to pick up a boat called *Hidden Treasures* worth €1.7 million."

"I can't quite get my head around all of this," Jacob replied as they walked hastily through the bank's lobby.

"How else can I help you?" Larry asked, placing his hand on Jacob's shoulder.

"I'll keep you on standby for the next two days. Can you stay in town just in case I need you?"

"Sure thing. What's your plan?"

"Looks like I'm going to Naples. I can't thank you enough for your help, Larry, please send me your final invoice; I couldn't have done this without you."

"Yes, sir, good luck," he replied as they shook hands and headed in different directions.

THIRTY

As Jacob pulled into traffic, he called Claire to share the news.

After less than three rings, she picked up. "How's it going?"

"Looks like they've been draining money from Gold Leaf Bank in New York for the last two years and have probably done the same elsewhere for many years prior. I know Greg first met Sheldon when he worked at The First Bank of London; this could have been going on for almost twenty years."

"Oh my God, Jacob, your dad was right – something *is* going on," Claire said, letting out a squeal.

"Feed this all back to Patrick. Are you still picking him up tomorrow?"

"Yes, he's being released at 9:30am."

"Okay, tell him to get to Naples in Italy immediately; don't forget he hasn't had a passport in twenty years, so you'll need to get an emergency one – you'll figure it out…

and a phone too, and let me know the number. Use the money I sent you."

"Okay, why Naples?" Claire asked, writing down passport, tickets, and phone on a scrap piece of paper as she stood behind the bar at Cavendish Square.

"Greg is currently in Paris but believed to be on his way to Naples, so we need to intercept him. Can you travel with Patrick?"

"I guess so," she replied hesitantly.

"Thank you so much, Claire, I will never forget how much you have helped. I'm on my way to talk to my mum now; depending on what happens, I will fly to Europe tonight to meet you."

They agreed to text later in the day, and Jacob rang off.

Could these illegal dealings have been going on for over twenty years and somehow contributed to the death of my mother? Could this now help to prove that Patrick is, in fact, innocent? he thought to himself as he continued the drive home for the last time.

Claire immediately called the prison and arranged a brief call with Patrick, who was allowed increased access to phone calls now that he was in his last twenty-four hours of incarceration. She congratulated him on the success so far, as it appeared Jacob was making satisfactory progress and his hunch that Greg was up to no good was right.

"I'll be out of here in less than twenty-four hours; I always knew something wasn't right, and now we are closer than ever to finding out why Charlotte was killed. I'll need a passport," Patrick said with excitement seldom seen in him during his eighteen years of pain and ruin as he clutched the phone close to his ear.

"No problem. Jacob mentioned that too and he has given me some money, so I'll get a passport form and tickets to Naples."

"I need your help on this, Claire. I cannot do it all on my own, especially with Jacob still in the States. Book two plane tickets – we need to get there as fast as possible. I knew Greg would go on the run, but at least he's in Europe and easy for us to get to."

"Okay."

"How much cash did Jacob send you?"

"Four thousand pounds."

"Bloody hell, someone's got deep pockets. Book two rooms at a hotel in the middle of Naples, and please don't forget the passport. Can you arrange?"

"Will do," she replied.

"Can you please pick me up a few items? I'm going to need some toiletries and clothes when I get outta here. I wouldn't normally ask a young lady I hardly know, but I don't have anyone else who can help."

"Of course, what do you need?"

Jacob didn't have time to waste and was soon back in his car heading to the DeWitt family home for what he would later realise was the last time. Driving through the usual heavy traffic north out of Manhattan, his stomach churned just as fast as the thoughts and questions in his head. The heavy dose of caffeine running through his veins made him edgy and alert as he navigated his way back to the house, cocooned in near silence in his sixty-thousand-dollar prestige car he seldom used.

Sat at a traffic light on the corner of Worth and Lane, Jacob took his mobile from the centre console and rapidly tapped a text message to Isabelle that read: *On my way to the house. Please meet me there, need to talk. J*

Jacob didn't want to be sitting and waiting for her; he just needed to get the necessary answers before packing up his things and following Greg wherever he may have gone.

He finally got home to an empty house and sat in silence in the large leather and teak-clad sitting room at the front right of the house with its impressive, oversized windows looking out over the sweeping, well-manicured lawns. While he waited for Isabelle to come home and the inevitably difficult conversation that was about to ensue, he could not help thinking back on all the happy memories he had experienced growing up as a DeWitt in this house.

He could vaguely remember moving into the house and the sheer excitement at the size of the place; he had never been in such a grand house. Jacob and Matthew, just a few years apart, played in every nook and cranny and spent hours climbing trees in the large gardens that surrounded the house. He fondly remembered the many barbecues and summer parties thrown by his parents to impress their wealthy friends and associates, to which he was always invited to join in with the children's entertainer or fun activities. The pool parties for his birthdays and the sleepovers with ten friends at a time watching films and eating pizza and ice cream.

As the sunlight dimmed and the crisp evening air wafted in through the crack in the window, he heard the faint hum of Isabelle's Range Rover pulling into the drive and the hard thud of the driver's door closing in the garage. He braced himself for a confrontation as he heard the front door open and the firm, fast steps of his mother heading towards him.

Isabelle sailed in, unaware that Jacob's request for her to come home was about to erupt into a long and emotional confrontation. She walked into the kitchen, dressed in a burgundy Nike tracksuit with black trousers and a red zip-up top, complemented by black Nike trainers.

"Hi, Jake, I picked up your message. I was at my yoga class. You okay?" Isabelle said breezily, holding her car keys and an undoubtedly expensive Prada bag.

"Do you know that Sheldon is dead?" Jacob replied with a coldness she had never heard from him before.

"Yes. Who told you?"

"It doesn't matter. You didn't think to tell me?"

"I've hardly seen you, Jake. You don't answer your phone."

"There was always something shady about Sheldon, wasn't there? Something he always tried to hide behind that larger-than-life blasé facade."

"Yes, dear, I know what you mean."

"When was the last time you saw Greg?"

"Your father? About three days ago. He's out of town in Dallas." Little did she know he was no longer in the US.

"He's not my father, Isabelle. My father is in jail in England. It's time to drop the act," he said, staring straight at her across the large central island in the kitchen.

Isabelle froze, leaning slowly against the twin sinks that overlooked the gravel driveway and sweeping lawns at the front of the house. Neither said a word. They didn't need to; both knew the truth but had to confirm it.

Isabelle went first. "What do you mean, Jake?" she mustered, trying not to make eye contact.

"Why did you lie to me for all these years?" Jacob replied, now seated with his chest deflated and arms crossed.

"I don't know what to say, Jake."

"All my life, I was led to believe that both my parents were dead. As their closest friends, you adopted me and brought me to the States for a new and better life. Now I find out my father is in jail for killing my mother. What the hell were you thinking?" He sighed.

Isabelle stared at Jacob in utter disbelief, always petrified that this day would darken her door. She had a well-rehearsed speech planned, but it had deserted her as tears of regret and relief began to drip down her face.

"With the internet so easy to search, did you really think I wouldn't find out eventually?"

"Is that how you found out?" she finally muttered through her tears.

"It doesn't matter how I found out. I just want to know why you kept this from me."

"You were young and—"

"Bullshit, Isabelle!" Jacob shouted as he sprang to his feet. "I've been old enough to understand for years now; you should have told me."

Isabelle, still shocked by Jacob calling her Isabelle instead of Mum, was hunched over the central island, her head hanging low like a defeated boxer.

"It was Greg's idea, and the older you became, I wanted to talk to you, but he always prevented me," she said, her voice trembling. "He told me it was better that you didn't know the truth and that you'd be happier if we didn't tell you. I wanted to tell you the truth, but I fear him, you know I do."

"Don't you think my father could have used some support over the past eighteen years?" Jacob said, animated, throwing his right hand in the air like he was hailing a cab.

"Support? He killed your mother," she yelped in an unusually high-pitched voice.

"Allegedly. What happens if he is innocent? Some other guy has now admitted to murdering my mother," Jacob replied.

"What, who?"

"Some shady guy in London who was related to the big boss at the bank Greg once worked at."

The weak and timid Isabelle didn't respond as Jacob sat back down. Both remained silent for well over two minutes, though it felt like thirty.

"Do you think he did it?" Jacob finally asked, continuing to look away from Isabelle.

"I don't know, Jake, Patrick always seemed such a kind man; I was shocked when he was convicted and assumed he was guilty. I still do."

"You knew him. Was he capable?"

"In my opinion," she paused, looking across the lawns outside, "no, he was a soft and gentle man, your father."

"Then why didn't you and Greg try to help him clear his name, hire him a good lawyer? You clearly have the money."

"Greg always said it wasn't our place to help, that we should leave it to the courts and not get involved. After all, we did enough by agreeing to look after you."

A few more minutes passed in tearful silence before Jacob turned his attention to the lifestyle they had enjoyed over the years.

"How much money does Greg make a year?"

Isabelle, unsure how to reply, now looked directly at Jacob, her eyes still moist. Clutching a tissue, she replied, "A lot. Why?"

"How much? A mil, two mil, five million, what?"

"I really wouldn't know, Jake, and it's really none of our business. Why do you want to know?"

"Knowing how much your husband makes a year is really none of your business? Give me a break."

"Clearly, he did well when he was working for the banks, and when he got the opportunity to work here, the money increased again. But I never asked."

"You never asked?"

"No, I was always told money was no problem for us."

"How much did you buy this house for?"

"About one point six million."

"At the time of the purchase, Greg's boss at the bank made three hundred thousand dollars. So Greg would have earned less than him. I looked it up on the internet. So how can say two hundred thousand dollars a year buy you a house worth over one and a half million dollars, along with all the other expensive stuff and you not working? Is he connected to the mob?"

"Don't be stupid, Jake. This isn't some gangster film."

"You could have fooled me sometimes."

"You have to remember, Greg is a very well-paid and talented analyst and—"

"Not when he bought this house," Jacob said, cutting her off.

"I know how it seems, but—"

"Didn't you ever question where the money was coming from when it suddenly seemed like you'd won the lottery?" he continued, gesturing wildly.

"Of course, I did, but I was always told to keep out of the finances. I just think Greg is traditional like that."

"So, as long as you had your fancy cars, holidays, and your country club membership to show off your latest designer handbag, you didn't care, right?"

"How dare you!" Isabelle retorted through squinted eyes.

"Sorry," he said, opening the large silver fridge and pulling out two bottles of water. "That was too much."

"What do you know, Jake?" Isabelle asked, trepidation written all over her face as he passed her a bottle.

"That expensive car, the Prada handbag, your ten-thousand-dollar memberships may all be real in your world, and the money probably did come from Greg's 'work', but I doubt the bank paid it to him. So, what type of work is he in?"

Isabelle started to sob into her tissue as she sat down, a broken woman, four feet across the table from Jacob. He was still seething at both of them for not telling him the truth about his parents but also knew all too well what Greg could be like in a fit of rage. He felt sorry for her. Clearly, she was in the process of losing her husband and was about to lose him for good one way or another. As soon as the web was untangled, she would be lucky to still be living in the States, let alone in a luxurious mansion in a private gated community in the suburbs.

Jacob stood up and walked round the table as Isabelle stood up.

"I'm sorry we didn't tell you sooner, Jake. I really am," she pleaded.

In a genuine sign of love, Jacob wrapped his arms tightly round Isabelle and held her for a few seconds before whispering to her that she needed to clear out all her bank accounts and hide the money, preferably in cash. The FBI would soon be freezing all assets as part of an investigation.

Looking dazed and confused, she wiped her face. "What is going on, Jake?"

"That's what I'm trying to find out," he replied, before kissing her on the cheek.

He picked up his bag and walked out of the family home for the very last time, without looking back. Isabelle sat in shock, sobbing endlessly into a handful of tissues.

THIRTY-ONE

After his last breakfast and first solo shower in nearly twenty years, Patrick sat in the dimly lit cell, the weight of anticipation heavy upon him. Freedom beckoned like a distant light at the end of a long, dark tunnel. Yet, as the minutes ticked by, a whirlwind of emotions churned within him.

He had longed for this day, yearned for it with every fibre of his being during his time behind bars. But now that it was here, it felt surreal, almost unreal. The prospect of stepping out into the world once more, of reclaiming his life, filled him with a strange mix of hope and apprehension.

His mind wandered back to the past, to the events that had led him to this moment. The memory of Charlotte, his beloved wife, haunted him still. Her death, shrouded in mystery and suspicion, had ruined his life, leaving him branded as a murderer in the eyes of the world, something he would always struggle to cope with.

And then there was Greg, his former friend and confidant, the man he held responsible for tearing his life apart. Patrick's heart burnt with a fierce desire for revenge, for retribution against the one he believed had betrayed him.

But amidst the turmoil of his emotions, there lingered a glimmer of uncertainty. Would his new-found freedom bring him the closure he sought? Or would it only serve to reopen old wounds, to reignite the flames of his inner turmoil?

As the clock inched closer to 10:30am, Patrick's heart quickened with anticipation. The moment of his release loomed before him like a beacon of hope in the darkness. And though he knew that the road ahead would be fraught with challenges and obstacles, he also knew that he was ready to face them head-on.

For Patrick, the journey towards redemption seemed like it had only just begun. And as he prepared to step out into the world once more, he vowed to leave behind the shadows of his past and embrace the light of a new beginning.

Since Milne's confession to murdering Charlotte, Patrick had been consumed by a fierce determination to clear his name and exact revenge on those he believed had wronged him.

His release, attributed to good behaviour rather than the revelation of the truth, only intensified his thirst for justice. The label of "murderer" had weighed heavily on him for too long, staining his reputation and haunting his every waking moment. Now, as he stood on the brink of freedom, he vowed to shed that tag once and for all, but the odds were stacked against him, and time was running out.

Greg, his supposed friend, was strongly in his thoughts more than ever as he harboured an unshakeable conviction that he was somehow linked to Charlotte's demise. The betrayal of their friendship fuelled Patrick's desire for revenge, igniting a fire within him that burnt brighter with each passing moment.

"Patrick James Reade, today is your lucky day," said the release clerk as he walked into the cell. "Sign these forms to get your belongings back."

"Keep the belongings; just give me my watch. It belonged to my father."

"I don't want your rubbish, Reade. Take it all with you. You have a package here too, which you cannot have until you are officially released. We opened it and found some trousers, a checked shirt, a navy V-neck sweater, new brown leather shoes, cotton briefs, navy socks, deodorant, aftershave, and a brand-new mobile phone. It looks like you'll be leaving here smelling and looking fresh as a daisy. Somebody must still care about you."

He smiled, thinking about feeling like a man again with a slap of cologne to complete his new shave. *Well done, Claire*, he thought, staring out of the window as the doctor entered the room to complete one final medical.

As Patrick stood on the brink of freedom, he couldn't help but notice the physical changes he had undergone during his time behind bars. The weight loss was evident, a testament to the harsh conditions he had endured. His once vibrant hair now bore streaks of grey, a stark reminder of the passage of time. And his complexion, once bronzed by the sun, now appeared pale and sallow from the lack of sunlight.

But perhaps the most noticeable change was the hardened look in his eyes, a reflection of the countless scuffles and confrontations he had faced during his incarceration. Each encounter had left its mark, shaping him into a tougher, more resilient version of himself.

Despite the hardships he had endured, Patrick found solace in the camaraderie he had forged with his fellow inmates and prison staff. In his final days behind bars, he took the time to bid farewell to those who had become like family to him. Their well-wishes and warnings served as a reminder of the journey that lay ahead.

As he prepared to step back into the world beyond the prison walls, Patrick couldn't help but feel a sense of gratitude for the experiences that had shaped him. Armed with his new-found strength and resolve, he faced the future with determination, ready to embrace the challenges that awaited him.

Claire's heart pounded as she raced towards Pentonville Prison, and with each passing moment, her anxiety mounted, her mind consumed by thoughts of Patrick's imminent release, doubts over why the hell she was getting herself involved and the daunting task that lay ahead for everyone. *What would they do if they caught up with Greg?* she asked herself. She was scared and exited in equal measure.

The cramp sensation in her stomach only intensified as she pushed her ageing Honda Accord to its limits, breaking every speed limit in her haste. Despite her best efforts to focus solely on the road ahead, her thoughts wandered across the Atlantic, where Jacob's mission hung in the balance.

Suddenly, the wail of sirens pierced the air, causing Claire's heart to leap into her throat. For a moment, panic threatened to overwhelm her as she glanced in her rear-view mirror, only to see the flashing lights of a police car bearing down on her.

She tried to reassure herself they weren't after her, though the guilt of her speeding offence gnawed at her conscience. With trembling hands, she pulled into the middle lane of the motorway, bracing herself for what seemed like an inevitable confrontation.

But to her relief, the police car swept past her with ease, its lights and sirens blazing as it pursued another vehicle down the busy road ahead. As Claire watched it disappear into the distance, a wave of gratitude washed over her. She had narrowly escaped detection, allowing her to continue her race against time to reach Pentonville Prison before Patrick's release.

Claire's pulse quickened as she mentally calculated the remaining distance and time. With just over forty minutes left until Patrick's scheduled release, every second was precious. She stole a glance at her watch, noting the ticking minutes with growing unease. 9:49am; *tick-tock, not long to go*, she thought to herself as the deadline loomed large in her mind.

The pressure weighed heavily on her shoulders as she considered the tasks that lay ahead. First, she needed to make it to Pentonville Prison in time to pick up Patrick. From there, they had to navigate through the maze of London's streets to reach the passport office, all before embarking on the journey north to Stansted Airport.

The thought of missing their flight to Naples sent a shiver down Claire's spine. Time was of the essence, and any delay could jeopardise their chances of catching up with Greg, and as she gripped the steering wheel tighter than ever, she couldn't shake the nagging worry that plagued her mind constantly. Despite all of the protests of innocence, was she actually helping a convicted murderer leave the country? Was all this searching for answers just a convict grasping at straws?

They didn't have much to go on either – they were wholly reliant on Jacob's ability to extract information from Hill Copeland, their only tangible lead in the hunt for Greg.

She pushed aside her doubts and focused on the task at hand; her gut was telling her something was not right, and she wanted to find the answers and be part of something potentially amazing.

"What's the plan then, Reade?" the release clerk asked.

"Get myself a passport and a plane outta here," he replied, slinging his old jacket over his left shoulder and carrying a small transparent plastic bag of pointless keepsakes from his previous life.

"All right for some, Patrick. You take care and, for what it's worth, I'm glad you are out. Don't come back," he shouted, as he always did to departing inmates, turning to walk back into the prison.

"No intention," Patrick shouted without looking back.

Patrick fumbled with the phone in his hand, marvelling at its compact size and advanced features. Mobile phones had been a novelty when he was first incarcerated, and he had never had the opportunity to familiarise himself with them. But now, as he navigated through the menus, he couldn't help but feel a sense of wonder at the technology in his grasp.

As he selected Claire's contact from the directory list, he felt a rush of anticipation. The phone began to ring, and when Claire's voice greeted him on the other end, he couldn't help but smile.

"Claire?" he said, relief evident in his voice as he heard her familiar tone.

"Yes, Patrick," she replied, the sound of her voice bringing him comfort in his new-found freedom.

With their brief exchange confirming their plans, Patrick's heart swelled with gratitude. Claire had been there for him when he needed her most, and he was eager to repay her kindness.

As Claire sped round the corner into Ship End Lane, Patrick's pulse quickened with anticipation. Seeing her for the second time filled him with relief and joy, a tangible reminder that he was no longer alone in his journey.

With a quick exchange of greetings and a brief and very awkward embrace, Patrick and Claire wasted no time in setting off towards the passport office. As they raced towards their destination, their focus turned to the task at hand: securing Patrick's new passport in time for their flight.

"I've got you an appointment at midday," Claire explained, her voice steady and reassuring. "We may encounter some hurdles, given your recent release, but all of your paperwork is in order."

Patrick nodded, grateful for Claire's foresight and meticulous planning. With their sights set on their 4:30pm flight from London's lesser known airport, Stansted, they had little time to spare. But with Claire by his side, Patrick felt a renewed sense of hope and determination. Together, they would navigate the challenges ahead and embark on the next chapter of their journey, united in their quest for justice and redemption.

"That is going to be tight. Worst-case scenario we fly out later or tomorrow instead, but let's hope we make this flight," Patrick announced as he pulled his seat belt on.

Patrick marvelled at the size of the cars, which had increased in the last twenty years, everything seemed so much bigger, busier, and with more garish advertising banners than before he went to jail.

It felt good to be out, and he would have loved to take the wheel himself, but now was not the time for renewing life skills. They had a passport to collect, a plane in waiting, and an old friend to catch up with.

THIRTY-TWO

The following morning, Jacob was up early and getting ready to head to the airport; he had stayed the night before at an airport hotel to prevent any further confrontation with Isabelle. He was unable to decide where to fly to, so after discussing with Claire and Patrick, he decided to hang tight and make a last-minute decision on which early morning flight to catch.

He glanced at his buzzing phone, the screen illuminating with Claire's message. With a mix of anticipation and anxiety, he unlocked his phone and read her text: *Your dad and I made it to Naples last night. Not sure where to go from here? Keep me posted and be careful. Claire x*

His heart swelled with relief knowing that his father and Claire had arrived safely in Naples. Despite the uncertainty of their situation, knowing they were together brought him a sense of comfort.

With Claire's message serving as a reminder to stay vigilant, Jacob pocketed his phone and took a sip of his coffee, steeling himself for the day ahead. Whatever challenges lay in store, he was prepared to face them head-on, believing he was doing the right thing and now seemingly having a new English girlfriend who was only too eager to help.

"Claire, how are you?"

"Jacob, hi. Let me put your dad on – we are having some lunch," she replied.

"Jacob, are you okay?" Patrick said, sitting with his legs crossed opposite Claire outside a quaint but expensive coffee shop in the foothills of Mount Vesuvius.

"I think so," Jacob whispered urgently into his phone. "We intercepted a call from Greg yesterday about withdrawing millions of dollars, or maybe euros, from a bank in Naples, and he recently purchased a boat for another €1.7 million."

Patrick's voice crackled with excitement on the other end. "I knew that bastard was up to no good! Millions for a guy who used to have a middle management job at a bank. Do you believe me now, Jacob?"

"Yes, I'm convinced something fishy is going on, but I'm still unsure how any of this links back to my mother, but thanks for trusting me," Jacob replied.

"Jacob, you were my only shot at unravelling what happened to your mother; I don't care about his shady pilfering – all I care about is finding the truth about what happened to Charlotte and clearing my name once and for all. With all these loose ends leading back to Greg, he is the common denominator, so he must be involved somehow. Why else would he snatch you away and keep me in the dark about it? At least now we know his dirty dealings have made him filthy rich."

"What if this is all just an elaborate ruse?" Jacob's voice wavered with uncertainty for perhaps the first time.

"We have no way of knowing for sure. We'll just have to roll with it, unless you've got a better plan," Patrick said, casting a glance at Claire.

"No, you and Claire need to stay in Naples, keep an eye out just in case you can find him, and I'll fly out today. Get a pen?" Jacob instructed.

"Claire, pen," Patrick called, reaching for a napkin. "Okay, Jacob, shoot."

"The boatyard is called Naples Marine Boatyard, and the boat Greg is buying is called *Hidden Treasures*," Jacob stated, eliciting a scoff from Patrick.

"Okay, got it. What are you going to do now?" Patrick asked.

"I'm heading out to JFK; I'll be on the next available flight to Rome, and I'll meet you both in Italy either later today or tomorrow. What are you going to do if you find him?"

Patrick gazed into the void as the question reverberated in his mind. It had haunted him ever since Greg and Isabelle's sudden departure to America. "I've mulled over that question for almost two decades, and honestly, I still don't have an answer. I suppose my reaction will be instinctive if we ever come face to face," he replied solemnly.

"Just don't do anything rash. Maybe just try to locate the boat, the money, and find out where he is staying," Jacob pressed.

"This was never about money, Jake; it's about seeking justice for eighteen years of torment, for your mother's death, and for you being torn away from both of us. I'm convinced he played a part in it somehow, and I won't rest until I uncover the truth," Patrick declared, a glint of tears shimmering in his eyes.

"We both need to know the truth; I'll see you soon. Can you put Claire back on?" Jacob said, reaching for his keys as his taxi to the airport arrived.

"Claire, thanks for all your help on this; you've really been a huge support. I'm sorry for dragging you into all of this," Jacob said, his tone sincere.

"No problem; I needed some excitement in my life. This is great. Did I hear something about three million dollars?" Claire asked, her curiosity piqued.

"Ten million is being wired to an account in Naples, and in two days' time, Greg is going to purchase a boat for €1.7 million and withdraw three million dollars in cash. I need you to stay vigilant," Jacob explained.

"Wow, okay. What are you going to do?" Claire enquired.

"I'm heading to the airport now; I'll try to catch a flight today. Hopefully to Rome, possibly Milan, and then I'll make my way to Naples to meet you straight away," Jacob replied.

"Great, I'm looking forward to seeing you again," Claire said coyly.

"Me too, Claire, I cannot thank you enough for your help, and I'm looking forward to putting this behind us and moving on with our lives. You need to identify which branch in the centre of Naples Bay is considered the main or central bank of the National Bank of Italy, as that is where Greg is supposed to be heading," Jacob instructed.

"No problem, speak to you later today; call me when you get in," Claire said as she ended the call and put the phone inside her backpack.

"No time for sightseeing," Patrick said as they hastily finished their coffees and decided on their next move.

Claire and Patrick were weary, their energy sustained by overpriced coffee. Yet, it was adrenaline that fuelled their focus the most.

"Jacob should be landing around 10pm, probably into Rome first. What's our plan now?" Claire enquired, her voice reflecting their exhaustion.

"The banks will be closed until around 2pm, so we have time to locate the boatyard and take a quick look," Patrick replied, his tone resolute despite their fatigue.

They headed to the boatyard but weren't able to gain access or a peak as the perimeter fence was closed and a large sign stated "*Chiuso*", which, after a quick internet search, confirmed they would have to come back tomorrow. The plot was surrounded by CCTV, so they decided against scaling the fences for a better look and instead headed to the harbour to see if the boat was there.

As Jacob arrived at JFK, a sinking feeling settled in his stomach when he realised he had no luggage, or even a change of clothes, all he had was his wallet and passport. With a sense of urgency, he sprinted into the terminal building, and, amidst the bustling chaos of the airport, he navigated through the throngs of travellers until he spotted the row of ticket desks, each adorned with familiar brand logos and less familiar taglines.

Opting for a US carrier, he swiftly secured a business-class flight one-way for eighteen hundred dollars, departing at 1pm to Rome, giving him enough time to head to a local discount shopping centre in Queens, where he hastily gathered a few sets of clothes, a holdall, and half a dozen toiletries. Time was of the essence, and he couldn't afford to waste a single moment.

THIRTY-THREE

Greg DeWitt was many things, but a fool was not one of them. As he lounged in his hotel room in the heart of Naples, he waited patiently for the bank to reopen after lunch. He had orchestrated his journey to Italy meticulously, flying on the first commercial flight of the day and manoeuvring across Europe in an effort to shake off anyone who might be tracking him. And as soon as he had his boat, he would be off, having secured his competence certificate online in preparation for this day. Now he just had to hope his sea legs would hold out, having never really spent much time on the open waters before.

Relaxed on the hotel bed, Greg leisurely flipped through the brochure showcasing his new, nearly seventy-five-feet Sunseeker power cruiser. Every detail had been carefully planned, from the sleek black-and-white paint finish to the luxurious oak tables, pristine white leather sofas, and state-of-the-art flat-screen televisions designed to entertain up to twelve guests in unparalleled comfort.

The main helm of the vessel had a Marex 3D joystick system, which included three joysticks, a marine propulsion controller, and a three-axis joystick to help manoeuvre the boat even in the tightest of places. The boat was powered by two 1,300bhp engines, amply fuelled by the five thousand-litre onboard tank and came equipped with two multifunction touchscreen chart plotter displays, GPS, and autopilot, making it as easy as possible for one person to control everything.

Amidst the allure of Italian sports cars, Swiss watches, and French wine, this yacht was Greg's ultimate desire. Its delivery date couldn't have been more perfect, coinciding with his departure from the United States, following Sheldon's demise and his own wavering resolve.

While the black hole operation would continue under Hill's vigilant oversight, Greg knew that with vast sums of money soon to be scattered across the globe, it would be a long time before the fuel tank of his new acquisition ran dry, even with the hefty price tag of twenty thousand dollars to refill it each time.

Greg had originally christened the boat *Immortal*, but after Sheldon's murder, he felt it wise not to tempt fate so instead, he settled on the more tongue-in-cheek moniker of *Hidden Treasures*. The vessel boasted luxurious touches, including the finest pre-chilled champagnes and a small cellar stocked with French wines he was looking forward to indulging in.

To maintain a low profile, Greg opted for the Italian flag to fly from the impressive array of aerials above the upper cockpit canopy. It offered a level of privacy and attracted less attention compared to the more conspicuous Union Jack or Stars and Stripes, both of which could raise unwanted questions.

As the clock struck 2pm, Greg approached the final hurdle towards his freedom in international waters. He had recently obtained his skipper's license and took the operation of his €1.7 million craft seriously. Despite the boat's state-of-the-art navigation system and autopilot, which could handle most tasks, Greg remained the captain of the ship, and his inner belief was he could handle the boat by himself. With an array of electronic equipment onboard, the vessel could sail, navigate, calculate depths, and avoid adverse weather patterns and busy shipping lanes across the globe. Yet, Greg understood the importance of his role at the helm.

His plan was meticulous, honed over years of careful calculation and patient execution. Vanishing would be the easy part. He would slip away unnoticed, aboard the sleek yacht, a ghost ready to disappear into the azure waves of the Mediterranean. In the hidden compartments below deck, his treasure would lay stashed: ten million dollars in untraceable notes and money orders, each one painstakingly acquired, each one a lifeline to the new identity he would craft far from the reach of anyone who might come looking.

There was uncertainty gnawing away at him – he was deeply unsettled about Sheldon's demise and concerned he would be the next target for some reason unknown to him, an unsettling whisper in the back of his mind he tried to ignore. He had trusted no one, yet betrayal had a way of creeping in through cracks he hadn't seen. Was someone on to him? Were they already watching him?

His route would wind across the Ionian Sea towards Athens, then possibly veer towards Cyprus, Turkey, and even Egypt. His boat was capable, but was he? Another doubt he tried to ignore. Worst-case scenario, he would use the money to hire experienced hands to help him cruise the high waters.

He always wanted to return to Dubai where he and Isabelle had enjoyed a fabulous stay many years before, so the Dubai Marina near to the Palm was on his stop-off list too. Greg relished the prospect of exploring upscale ports throughout the Mediterranean, where he could flaunt his wealth and charm any willing females to a trip on his ill-gotten boat.

Aware of the need to carry his ill-gotten gains in sizeable amounts of cash, Greg had a custom-built deep vault installed in the hull of his new boat, specifically designed to conceal his loot. The safe was attached to the inside of the hull and to forcibly remove it would rip the boat apart and sink it in a matter of minutes. With this seemingly bottomless reservoir of money at his disposal, and Isabelle no longer in his life, he envisioned a future as an international multimillionaire bachelor – or so he thought.

Meanwhile, in his hotel room in Rome, Jacob groggily unpacked his new shiny laptop, picked up in Queens before boarding the flight from New York. Equipped with a plug adapter, he was poised to exact revenge on Greg and safeguard the interests of Isabelle, whom he still regarded with the deepest affection despite his distress at her hiding so many secrets from him. She had raised him as her own, and he cherished her as any son loves his mother. Jacob held no resentment towards Isabelle.

With Greg seemingly on the run and his whereabouts likely to become more difficult to pin down should Patrick uncover any harrowing secrets of the past and the true origin of the amassed wealth, Jacob realised he needed to act swiftly to protect the only mother he had ever known before it was too late.

Next to the laptop's keyboard lay a haphazard stack of handwritten notes, bank statements, interest letters, passwords, PIN mailers, social security numbers, and copies of passports and driver's licenses for both Greg and Isabelle. Jacob had accumulated these during his last few visits to the DeWitt family home. Through self-teaching from an online discount bookshop's self-help book, he had learnt how to access bank accounts and reset passwords with the help of all their personal information. Now, he intended to infiltrate a series of bank accounts under Greg's alias, Arthur Fielding. His goal: redirect everything to Isabelle and Matthew's accounts, with a portion left for himself depending on his findings.

Seated before the PC, Jacob drew a deep breath through his nose as he began tapping away at the keyboard.

The clock was ticking, and he could feel the weight of every passing second pressing down on him. With only a couple of hours left until his departure and a short train ride to Naples ahead of him, the window for action was closing fast.

Doubts lingered in his mind about the success of his endeavour – to find out what happened to Charlotte – but for now he was on a mission to ruin Greg financially. Armed with a secure and encrypted internet connection, he plunged into the heist. It was akin to a classic bank robbery, albeit without guns and balaclavas; this was twenty-first-century bank heist tactics at their most sophisticated.

Opening one account was a breeze with the right pieces of information: account details, Greg's date of birth, and a numerical password unearthed from one of his emails from Hill and he was in. Despite the account's recent dormancy, Jacob wasted no time in initiating a transaction. With deft keystrokes, he transferred the entire sum of $947,000 to himself, leaving a symbolic one cent as a final fuck you.

"Payback's a bitch," he muttered, satisfaction evident in his tone as he pressed the enter key with his thumb. Almost immediately, he instructed his own bank to forward half of the sum to Mrs Isabelle Reade upon receipt.

The second and third accounts proved more challenging as these accounts based in Italy were in the names of Arthur Fielding and Leo Macy, and despite his efforts, Jacob couldn't replicate the success of the first. With time slipping away, he was left with just two more chances to siphon any remaining funds from two other known accounts, one in Belize and one in Geneva.

He'd given up on the Belize bank account after being locked out too many times, and after numerous failed attempts, he finally struck gold with a series of successfully answered security questions for the account in Geneva

– it led him to a coveted password reset email being sent to one of Greg's accounts. Intercepting the email and immediately deleting it, he promptly changed the password to "Naples12$!" before accessing the account.

He was astonished upon discovering the remaining balance: a cool $3.5 million, steadily increasing with daily interest.

Jacob's bank account was poised to swell once more, with one million redirected to Isabelle and another million to Matthew, both accompanied by the reference "Love from Jacob".

Upon completion, he texted them both to advise them to withdraw as much cash as possible and hide it in untraceable safety deposit boxes before the authorities seized all assets.

He quickly finished the final transaction before gathering his belongings and heading to the train station for the ninety-minute journey to destiny.

Dressed impeccably in a navy pinstriped Saville Row tailored suit, complemented by tan leather accessories and Italian lace-up shoes, Greg exuded the aura of an Italian businessman as he made his way to the last bank to collect his fortune in banker's draft and cash. Nerves fluttered in his stomach as he pressed the button for the lift, which soon arrived at the ninth floor of the Intercontinental in the heart of Naples.

Having successfully collected his illicit gains from several other locations the day before, he wasn't expecting any hiccups.

Exiting through the grand, darkened glass doors adorned with gold-trimmed handles, he indulged in a deep breath of the fresh, early-afternoon breeze, though it did little to calm his nerves. His audacious scheme had flown under the radar of finance managers, auditors, bank managers, and chairmen – except for one man who had stumbled upon the steady stream of disappearing money: Charles Faulk.

On occasion, other low-level bankers had come close – a few were paid off; a few uncovered nothing and went on with their lives.

Still unfamiliar with Naples, Greg took no chances. A chauffeur-driven black Mercedes provided by the hotel awaited him at the curb, glistening in the afternoon sun, ready to whisk him away to any destination of his choice.

Meanwhile, Claire and Patrick were en route to the largest number of banks in a single street from the opposite side of the city in the hope of spotting Greg. The hunt was underway, but both harboured doubts that their plan of even finding Greg, let alone unearthing what happened to Charlotte, would succeed.

Their fears loomed large that Greg would slip away forever, along with a fortune presumably obtained through illicit means. More crucially, they yearned to uncover the long-hidden secrets surrounding Charlotte's fate.

THIRTY-FOUR

So far, the stakeout near to the collection of banks had not proven fruitful, and the frustration was beginning to show. Greg managed to successfully elude everyone the day before, and with the afternoon sun casting its golden hues over their rented grey Alfa Romeo, Claire and Patrick's tense expressions were illuminated as they parked across the bustling street from the National Bank of Italy. Amidst the frenetic energy of Naples, their silent vigil stood in stark contrast.

Each person entering or exiting the historic banks along the main strip, all with their large swinging doors, fell under their scrutiny, their eyes darting to the latest photo of Greg sent by Jacob and then back to the doors. Patrick couldn't rely on his memory of his old friend, knowing well that time could change a person, and Claire had never laid eyes on Greg before. They took it in turns to watch cars pulling up and bank entrances, swapping every five minutes or so.

As they waited, Jacob was closing in fast on Naples' central station, and his incessant calls to Claire's mobile kept interrupting her focus.

"Nothing has changed since you last called less than five minutes ago," she responded tersely after the third call in what felt like as many minutes. "I'll notify you the moment we spot him, if we spot him at all," she assured him before disconnecting the call.

Patrick sat, his grip tight round the cold plastic cup of coffee, his gaze fixed unwaveringly on one of the bank's front doors.

"Come on, DeWitt, where are you, you scumbag?" he muttered under his breath.

"What do we do if he doesn't show?" Claire asked, her expression softened by the large-rimmed sunglasses she wore.

"I was just thinking the same thing. I have no clue," Patrick replied, his eyes briefly flickering over his shoulder.

"Let's just hope he shows, keep positive," Claire said, offering reassurance.

Ten minutes passed, then fifteen, twenty. Still nothing.

"Where is Jacob? He should be here by now," Patrick grumbled, his gaze still fixed on the bank's entrance.

Ten more agonising minutes passed before Jacob finally appeared, clumsily tossing his luggage into the back seat of the car, startling Claire.

"Sorry, sorry to startle you guys. What's up?" he asked, a hint of concern in his voice.

"Nothing yet. Great to see you, Jacob," Patrick replied, reaching out to touch Jacob's shoulder as a gesture of greeting. Claire beamed at Jacob, who returned her smile with a wink, a shared moment of camaraderie in the midst of tension.

"My heart is pounding," Claire confessed.

They all agreed as they sat together, their disappointment growing palpable by each passing minute.

As the clock approached lunchtime, they knew the banks would soon be closed as it became increasingly clear that Greg had likely slipped through their grasp. None of them were willing to admit defeat until the security shutters descended over the bank's front entrances, signalling the end of their stakeout for now. As each bank closed, it was like a swift kick to the stomach, but Jacob was already brainstorming plan B, the boatyard.

Claire, Jacob, and Patrick were weary, frustrated, and increasingly furious at the prospect of not finding Greg as Claire drove them through the rush-hour streets of Naples.

"Two fucking decades and we are so close," Patrick expelled. "Excuse my language, Claire."

He sheltered a bitterness that threatened to linger indefinitely if he couldn't exact some form of revenge, while Jacob grappled with the unanswered questions about his real parents and the fate of his mother, leaving him to wonder for a lifetime.

"The more I think about him, the more I want to kill him," Patrick muttered almost to himself, sat in the passenger seat of the car.

Claire's grip on the steering wheel tightened as

Patrick's chilling words hung in the air. She glanced at him briefly, her mind reeling at the intensity of his statement. Picking up a former inmate and finding herself entangled in a potential vendetta was not what she had signed up for.

"He either didn't show up, or he managed to slip in and out without you noticing. Disguise maybe?" Jacob's voice broke the tense silence from the back seat.

"Anything's possible," Patrick replied tersely, his gaze fixed on the passing scenery outside the car window.

"We know he just dropped almost two million euros on a boat. Let's head to Naples Marina and find out where it's moored, right?" Jacob suggested, his voice tinged with urgency.

Claire nodded, a sense of determination replacing her earlier uncertainty. "We tried to find it yesterday but no luck so far," she said, her voice steady despite Patrick's killing comment. With renewed purpose, she manoeuvred the car towards the coast.

"I'll get the address on the internet, and we'll head there now," Jacob said, pulling his new smartphone from his jacket pocket.

"Wait, you can access the internet from a phone?" Patrick quipped in a bid to break the tension. Both Claire and Jacob burst out laughing at his wit in such stressful times.

"Cool, hey?" Jacob replied, breaking the tension with a hint of levity.

"Very," Claire agreed, a small smile playing at the corners of her lips.

"I'm just kidding – I've seen lots of stuff online over the years," Patrick said with a faint smirk across his face.

"When this is all over, we need to reintegrate you into the twenty-first century," Jacob joked.

"Were mobiles a thing years ago, Patrick?" Claire teased, her sarcasm evident.

"Yeah, but they were much bigger back then, and all you could do was text and make calls. I never had one though; too expensive for me. This phone you gave me is so thin, and the screen is like a TV. I bet payphones no longer exist." Patrick chuckled.

"I don't think I've ever used a payphone," Jacob said, focusing on navigating to their destination. "Got it, continue heading west for the coast."

"So the phone now navigates for you?" Patrick asked, bemused.

"We seriously need to talk," Jacob said, patting Patrick on the shoulder, eliciting more chuckles from his younger, tech-savvy companions.

After what felt like an eternity in the car but was actually less than thirty minutes, they finally arrived at the boatyard.

They sat with the windows open, out of sight from the main entrance, for over five hours. The tension was palpable as each of them leant towards their open windows for fresh air.

Floodlights suddenly came on across the yard as the sun began to set over the Tyrrhenian Sea.

"What are you thinking, Jacob?" Patrick enquired.

"I'm not sure. We've waited so long and not seen him," Claire added.

"I'll go in on my own and take a look," Jacob said, pointing over Claire's shoulder.

"Shall I come with you?" Claire asked, glancing round.

"There are some lights on over there; I think you should stay here," Patrick pointed out, indicating the small office at the far end of the yard.

"You guys stay here and keep quiet. I'll see what's going on and tell them my dad asked me to meet him here or something if anyone asks," Jacob instructed, forgetting who he was talking to.

"Watch yourself, Jacob," Patrick cautioned.

Followed by a heartfelt "be safe" from Claire.

As Jacob climbed out of the car, Patrick couldn't help but feel a pang at Jacob referring to Greg as his "dad".

With a click, the door closed, and Jacob walked away slowly, hands tucked into his navy jeans. Patrick's gaze followed him until he disappeared into the shadows of the shipyard.

Jacob approached cautiously, his unease growing as he spotted figures inside the main boatyard's office.

As Claire and Patrick watched from afar, a black Mercedes approached the boatyard and, in a blind moment of panic, Claire pressed the horn to alert Jacob.

"Shit," he muttered under his breath, ducking behind a fence for cover. He sat motionless for a few minutes and heard voices in the distance but not clear enough to make out what was being said.

Eventually he heard a door close, and the yard's parking area fell quiet once again.

Peering round the corner, he recognised Greg among

the men inside, clenching his fists in excitement and self-praise.

He watched for a couple of minutes as the sky grew darker, beads of sweat making their way down either side of his face as if they were in a race to reach his chin.

Undecided on his next move, he quickly made his way back to the car, his eyes never leaving the figures inside the boatyard shop.

"He's here, Claire. Get ready to move," Jacob announced as he flung open the car door and jumped into the back seat once more. "Go, go, go, he's inside," Jacob urged, his urgency palpable.

"What, where?" Claire exclaimed, her heart racing.

"It's definitely him. He's in the shop. Now get round the corner quickly," Jacob instructed, pointing past Claire.

"Yes!" Patrick exclaimed, his fist connecting with the car's ceiling in triumph. "We got him."

Claire swiftly raced the car round the corner and parked behind a haulage truck on the main road, but with a clear view of the boatyard's gates and, this time, sight of the main office.

"What now?" Claire asked, her voice tinged with anticipation and a hint of fear.

"We sit and wait," Patrick replied, his tone determined.

"And when he comes out, then what?" Claire pressed.

"Then we follow him to his hotel, or wherever he's going," Jacob answered.

"Could be his new boat," Patrick added with a hint of satisfaction.

As the sun finally disappeared, the three of them sat

in near silence, waiting for Greg to make his move. The air was thick with anticipation, each heartbeat echoing the urgency of their mission.

As Jacob sat lost in thought, memories of his years as a DeWitt flooded his mind. He searched desperately for any clues or hints of a different life, a life left behind in England. He squeezed his eyes shut, straining to recall his mother or Patrick from his childhood, but the memories remained elusive, locked away in the recesses of his adolescent mind.

Meanwhile, Claire grappled with fear and uncertainty, questioning the wisdom of her involvement in this dangerous game. Was her budding romance with a man she barely knew worth the risks they were taking? Despite her apprehension, she couldn't deny the thrill of the unexpected twists and turns unfolding before her. The crisp sea air wafting through the window stirred conflicting emotions within her, tempting her to abandon her mundane existence in London and embrace the excitement of life in Naples.

Patrick's mind churned with thoughts of his years in solitary confinement as he listened to the waves lap at the harbour walls. Pondering why he never once considered giving up on his quest for revenge against Greg; perhaps he was entirely innocent, and he was not involved directly or indirectly with Charlotte's murder.

The toll it had taken on him was immense – losing the love of his life, only to be replaced by the bleak existence of prison walls. He reflected on the dreams that had been shattered, the life that had been stolen from him, and the fleeting hope of reclaiming some semblance of normalcy.

Another hour dragged by, and Patrick found himself on the verge of falling asleep, exhaustion weighing heavily on him. He wasn't used to moving round so much, and the sea air was making him tired. But then, Jacob and Claire suddenly jolted upright in unison as someone emerged from the offices, but they couldn't make out who it was as the bright floodlights shone in their direction, darkening the face of the man as he strode towards a white BMW parked at the front of the shop.

Suddenly, they were on the move again.

"Here come some headlights from the yard – could this be him?" Claire asked, peering through the darkness.

"I've no idea, good question," Patrick replied, studying the car pulling out onto the road.

"Damn, it's going in the opposite direction, and he arrived in that black Mercedes," Claire said, her excitement notching up a gear.

"Follow that car, find out where he's going, and then call me. We need to know if it's Greg," Jacob instructed, jumping unexpectedly from the car.

"Wait, what?" Patrick called out, but it was too late. Jacob was already darting across the street, taking cover behind stacked crates directly opposite the boatyard entrance.

Meanwhile, Claire and Patrick hurried to catch up with the BMW that had moments before exited the boatyard. Jacob remained concealed in the shadows, no longer visible from the main road.

For a tense couple of minutes, the only sound was the noise of the engine in the distance and the waves lapping away to his left, occasionally drowned out by Jacob's heavy breathing and pounding heart. After a period of stillness, he cautiously crossed the road and crept along the railings past the remaining silver car parked to the side of the boatyard's collection of buildings.

Suddenly, the Mercedes' locks disengaged, causing Jacob's heart to almost stop. The lights flashed twice with a steady clunk at the same time as the door of the boatyard offices swinging open, and Jacob found himself less than twenty feet away from someone, who he could now clearly see was Greg. Thinking swiftly, his heart pounding heavier with each passing second and with no means of following him if he drove off, Jacob quietly opened the back left-hand-side door of the car and slipped into the darkness.

"Thank you, Mr Fielding, enjoy your new boat," came a heavily accented send-off from the Italian marine architect.

"Thanks again," Greg replied before climbing inside the Mercedes. Jacob curled up inside the rear passenger footwell as best he could, covering his face with his dark jacket, hopeful he would not be spotted.

"Ciao."

"Ciao."

Jacob's heart pounded so hard he was certain Greg would hear it. After the near miss in Hill Copeland's office, this would surely be impossible to talk his way out of. Keeping himself as small as possible, Jacob hugged his knees tightly, trying to breathe slowly and shallowly. Every bone in his body prayed he was out of sight from the driver's seat, well hidden by the large front seats and shrouded in the darkness of the night, but his situation was not helped by the damn floodlights.

The sudden intrusion of music from the radio made the hair on the back of his neck stand on end as the satellite navigation engaged, guiding Greg through the near-empty streets towards his prized asset. Jacob seized the opportunity to pull his mobile from his pocket and power it off, just in case of an incoming call from Claire.

Hidden from view and accompanied by the intermittent voice of the satellite navigation, Jacob's heart gradually began to settle as the car continued its journey under sporadic street lights. Brief glimpses from under his jacket revealed illuminated buildings, the occasional darkened house, and an empty wood-panelled white church.

What felt like an eternity passed, though it was in fact only fifteen minutes, as Greg drove himself to the exclusive Martino Marina and Resorts. The marina, well lit and signposted, finally provided Jacob with a clue as to their whereabouts, and with an abrupt halt, Greg exited the vehicle, removed some items from the boot, before leaving Jacob enveloped in silence once more as the car locked itself.

Waiting a few minutes, Jacob cautiously powered on his mobile phone with minimal hand movements, eager not to trigger any internal alarm systems the luxurious car likely possessed. After what felt like an eternity, the welcome screen appeared. He pressed the green button and dialled the last and only number called.

"Hello, Jacob, where are you? It wasn't Greg," Claire answered.

"I'm in Greg's car," he whispered.

"What! Is Greg with you, what's going on? He's in Greg's car," Claire relayed the information to Patrick in the background.

"Oh my God!" both voices exclaimed on the other end of the phone.

"I'll explain later. I know where he is. Get directions to the Martino Marina and Resorts and look out for the black Mercedes he arrived in earlier, or the boat called *Hidden Treasures*. I'll be nearby, but don't call me back again as I don't want you giving my position away, okay?"

"Got it, now stay out of sight until we get there," Claire ordered.

Jacob silenced his phone and returned it to his pocket, peering out at the row of boats from behind the driver's seat, pondering his next move. Would the alarm sound? Could he open the car from the inside? He could either wait or act now.

With only the marina lights to guide him, Greg located his boat in bay thirty-two, as confirmed by the boatyard. He busily inspected his new purchase as best as he could in the dim light, excitedly toggling switches and pushing buttons that illuminated lights inside and outside the boat, activating the state-of-the-art navigation system he had paid an extra thirty thousand for.

He stood marvelling at the large LED display screens as he ran his eyes over every gadget available on the market, including a built-in humidifier for his vast collection of expensive cigars.

As he looked round the quiet boatyard, he settled into

the large L-shaped sofa after pouring himself a generous glass of pre-stocked cognac. Fresh food and an assortment of alcoholic beverages, added earlier at his request, awaited his indulgence.

As he sipped the cognac, he watched a small fishing boat heading out for the night and finally felt relaxed and proud of his accomplishment. He surveyed his new pride and joy, surrounded by sheer luxury. Alongside him on the supple leather sofa sat two large black holdalls brimming with three million euros in used notes, his cruising-around money for the next few years.

Glancing out of the window at the immediate neighbouring boats, both smaller than his vessel, Greg observed their dark, motionless forms, occasionally stirred by passing ripples of water. Though distant lights flickered in the distance, Greg felt a sense of solitude as the water gently lapped against the hull of his new prized possession. Exactly as he desired.

With his feet propped up, he took another slurp of his drink, fizzing the potent liquid through his teeth, reminiscent of an old, wily sailor from years gone by, and after a few more swigs, he carelessly drifted into sleep, his head supported by the bag of cash.

The folding gangway, adorned with chrome poles and white rope, remained down.

THIRTY-FIVE

Early the next morning, just as the first rays of sunlight pierced the horizon, Greg was sprawled awkwardly across the main sofas inside the yacht, his bags haphazardly piled beside him. The chill of the night had driven him here from the deck, but he hadn't made it far, his body too drained to even reach the plush cabins below. The warmth of the rising sun kissed his face through the wide glass windows, yet he remained oblivious, lulled in a half-conscious daze.

Then, the sound. A woman's voice – faint but clear – echoed from outside, shattering the silence.

"Hello? Is there anyone there?" the voice called out, each word sharp against the stillness.

Greg jerked awake, disoriented, the remnants of sleep clinging to him like fog. He stumbled to his feet, his leg knocking over an empty glass that crashed to the floor, shattering the fragile peace of the morning. His heart pounded, the abruptness of the voice triggering an instinctive wave of unease. He glanced at his bags – untouched, thankfully – but the suddenness of the situation kept his pulse racing.

Rubbing his face, trying to shake off the grogginess, he moved towards the sleek, smoked glass doors that opened onto the deck. He squinted into the blinding sun, feeling a knot of irritation twist in his gut.

"Hello," he greeted warily, shielding his eyes with a hand. The last thing he needed was company, especially this early. Despite the youthful charm of the woman standing on the jetty, Greg's instincts screamed caution.

"I'm so sorry to bother you," she said, her voice sweet but tinged with desperation. "I'm in a bit of a bind. I managed to lock myself out of my father's boat. Do you think you could help me get back on board?"

Greg's gaze sharpened, subtly scanning the jetty left and right. "Are you alone?" he asked, his voice flat, his suspicion barely masked.

"Yes, just me. I thought my father would be here, but…" she glanced round nervously, "he's not."

Greg hesitated, his brain firing off warnings he couldn't quite place. Something felt off, but he couldn't put his finger on it. He forced a smile. "Alright, let's see what we can do."

They stepped off his boat, walking down the jetty towards her father's vessel. The girl made polite conversation, complimenting Greg's boat, but he barely registered her words. His mind was elsewhere, scanning for threats, for shadows that didn't belong.

Then, without warning, a crushing blow struck the back of his head.

Pain exploded through his skull as darkness swallowed him. His body crumpled to the ground with a sickening thud, the world around him dissolving into nothing.

"Well done, Claire," a man's voice, thick with approval, cut through the silence. Jacob stood behind, his eyes glinting in the early morning light. Behind him, Patrick discarded the heavy wooden plank he had used to render Greg unconscious.

Claire's face paled as the reality of what she had been involved in began to sink in. "I don't want to get into trouble, guys," she whispered, her voice shaky. "You're not going to... hurt him, are you?"

Patrick shot her a cold look. "Claire, you've been in this from the start. No one's getting killed, but we need answers."

Jacob, his face tight with urgency, moved quickly. "Help me get him back on the boat before anyone sees."

Together, they dragged Greg's limp body back to the yacht, hauling him onto a chair bolted to the floor. Ropes tightened around him, securing him in place. For a moment, they stood there, breathless, tension hanging heavy in the air as they watched Greg's chest rise and fall, confirming he was still alive.

Inside the boat, Patrick and Jacob conferred in hushed tones, their expressions grim, discussing what to do next. The idea of dumping Greg into the sea had surfaced more than once, but neither had the stomach to follow through. Claire sat outside, staring blankly at the now-busy marina, her hands trembling.

Thirty agonising minutes passed before Greg began

to stir. His eyelids fluttered, and a deep groan escaped his lips as the throb in his head returned with a vengeance. He blinked rapidly, trying to focus, and when his vision cleared, he was met with the sight of two familiar faces staring back at him.

"Jesus Christ," Greg muttered, his heart slamming against his ribs as fear gripped him. "What the fuck are you doing here, Pat?"

Patrick's face twisted into a snarl, a look Greg had never seen before. "You son of a bitch."

Greg's pulse quickened; he shifted uncomfortably in his restraints, struggling against the ropes. "Why am I tied up? What the hell is going on?"

Patrick's voice was low, menacing. "I want answers, Greg. And until I get them, you're not going anywhere."

"What the fuck are you talking about?" Greg demanded, panic setting in.

Patrick leant in close, his breath hot against Greg's skin. "What happened to my wife? Why did you run off with my son? And what the hell does Fredrick Milne have to do with all of this?"

The colour drained from Greg's face. Fredrick Milne – his mind raced, trying to suppress the dread crawling up his spine. He opened his mouth, but no sound came out.

"Tell me!" Patrick roared, his patience snapping as he threw the remains of a bottle against the wall, the glass shattering in a violent burst. Greg flinched, the cut on his head throbbing harder now.

"I… I don't know," Greg stammered, but the fear in his eyes betrayed him. He did know but tried to hide it as much as possible. "What is going on, Patrick? When did you get out?"

"A couple of days ago."

"Why am I tied up, and why did you have to take me down like that?" Greg demanded, his confusion evident.

"Wasn't sure how you'd react," Patrick responded cryptically.

"To what?" Greg pressed for answers.

"Seeing a ghost from your past."

"I must admit I didn't expect to see you ever again."

"Wishful thinking on your behalf, I think," Patrick said, surprisingly calm.

"What do you want, Patrick? Why are you here? Untie me now," Greg screamed.

"I want answers, and until I get them, you remain tied up," Patrick replied, taking a seat on the other side of the cabin.

"I—"

"Why did you take Jacob to the States and cut him off from me?" Patrick questioned.

"I thought it was best for both of you," Greg lied.

"You thought it was best for both of us? That's bullshit, Greg, and you know it," Patrick snapped, his anger simmering.

"I had a job offer in the States and couldn't turn it down," Greg explained.

"Fair enough, but why cut Jacob off from me and not tell him the truth about what happened? That killed me inside, Greg, not seeing my son. I thought I could trust you; you were my friend." Patrick's tone grew more accusatory.

"I'm truly sorry. Now take these ropes off me," Greg requested, clearly uncomfortable with his restraints.

"No chance. Continue," Patrick demanded.

"Then how about a slug of something?" Greg asked, gesturing towards the bottle still open from the night before.

Patrick walked to the table, grabbed an open bottle of thirty-year-old cognac, and, without breaking eye contact with Greg, took a long swig. The tension was suffocating, thick with years of unresolved fury and buried truths. Greg, bound to the chair, squirmed uncomfortably, sensing the storm that was about to erupt.

Then, with a sudden, violent motion, Patrick smashed the heavy bottle against the steel handrail. The impact sent glass exploding outwards in a spray of sharp shards, the remaining cognac splattering across the wooden floor. Greg flinched, instinctively jerking his head away, but not fast enough. A shard of glass struck his forehead, leaving a deep cut that began to bleed almost immediately.

"Fucking hell!" Greg shouted, his voice betraying the fear he'd been trying to suppress. He could feel the warm blood trickling down his neck, soaking into his collar. His head pounded from the wound, but the look in Patrick's eyes terrified him even more.

Claire's hand tightened in Jacob's grip as she flinched at the bottle smashing. They both hid out of sight on the side of the boat, listening intently. Her view obscured, she panicked about the broken bottle neck that Patrick presumably still held. Looking at Jacob, who appeared equally pale and frightened, did little to calm her down.

"Does the name Fredrick Milne mean anything to you?" Patrick's voice rose.

The blood ran down Greg's face as he started to sweat profusely.

"No," he replied, his voice barely above a whisper.

"Stop playing," Patrick said, kicking a large section of broken glass away from him.

"No, I don't know who he is; should I?" Greg asked, clearly starting to get agitated and unnerved about how his first morning of his supposed new life was panning out.

"Are you sure? One last chance."

"I'm sure, I'm bloody sure, why?" Greg spat.

"I'll remind you then, shall I?" Patrick shouted, pacing up and down the spacious cabin like a legal professional addressing the jury in court. "Do you think I killed Charlotte?" he boomed.

"No, I always told you I believed you were innocent, and I still do," Greg replied.

"Why is that, Greg? Because you *know* I didn't do it?"

"Because you were my friend, and I knew you weren't capable of such a thing. What do you want from me?" he replied, clearly showing the signs of a guilty man.

"I'll tell you," Patrick began, his voice tight as he paced back and forth, the heels of his shoes tapping rhythmically on the polished hardwood floor. "For the past twenty years, you've been involved in something very profitable. And I'd bet my life it's illegal. Somehow, that led to Charlotte being killed by Fredrick Milne. Maybe you didn't know, but Milne happens to be the cousin of your old boss, Charles Faulk."

Greg sat frozen, his posture slumped, like a balloon

slowly losing air. Patrick's words cut deeper with every passing second. "Because of whatever shady business you've been mixed up in, Charlotte got caught in the crossfire. She's dead because of you." His tone grew colder, the accusation hanging heavy in the air. "And after you agreed to adopt Jacob, you bolted. Left the country to escape the chaos you caused."

"I—"

"Shut up, you piece of shit!" Patrick screamed as he threw the remains of the bottle in the direction of Greg, just missing the right side of his head. Jacob and Claire stood rigid with fear, not knowing what Patrick was capable of or what he was going to do next.

Continuing to pace from Greg's right to left, but with much more aggression, Patrick was not finished; after all, he had waited a long time for this.

"So I'm guessing that after your move to the States, you decided it was best for you to keep Jacob away from me. Once he got older, he could help me prove my innocence and get you convicted of murder at the same time."

"Murder? Wait a second here. Whose murder?"

"My wife's!" he shouted back.

"That wasn't me, Patrick. I swear to God, that wasn't me."

"Well, I think the authorities will be looking at you very closely when I tell them all about your fancy life and seedy connections to the London underworld."

"I swear, Pat, it wasn't me," Greg muttered, his voice barely holding together. He knew there was no easy way out of this.

"Was it Milne?" Patrick's question sliced through the air like a blade.

Greg flinched, his eyes darting to the floor, every inch of him radiating guilt. He was unravelling, and Patrick knew it.

"Answer me, damn it, before I *do* kill someone this time!" Patrick's shout reverberated through the small cabin.

Greg's head dropped, the silence between them stretching agonisingly. The weight of what he was about to confess pulled him down further. Finally, after what felt like an eternity, he lifted his eyes and locked onto Patrick's, his voice barely more than a whisper. "Yes. Milne killed her as a warning shot to me because I refused his demands for money."

Patrick's breath caught in his throat. "I fucking knew it," he roared, his voice cracking as rage and grief collided. "You evil son of a bitch!" The words left his mouth like a tidal wave, before his legs gave out, and he collapsed into a heap on the cold floor. "My wife is dead; my son doesn't know me; and I've lost twenty goddamn years of my life!" His voice broke, and he buried his face in his hands, sobbing uncontrollably.

Greg sat there, paralysed, shame twisting his features, his hands trembling as panic coursed through him. He could feel Patrick's grief like a suffocating weight in the room. He glanced up occasionally, watching helplessly as his body shook with sobs.

A soft sound came from behind. Jacob stood at the edge of the hallway, tears silently streaming down his face. His eyes were hollow yet burning with emotion. He stepped towards Patrick without a single glance at Greg, as though he no longer existed in his world. Claire followed close behind, her grip tight on Jacob's arm, as if seeking some kind of anchor.

But there was an undeniable strength in their silent approach. Kneeling in front of Patrick, they enveloped him in a quiet embrace, arms encircling the broken man. In that moment, Patrick's sobs quieted, though the weight of his loss remained. Both Jacob and Claire held him tightly, their touch a lifeline, unaware of the love they'd soon offer to a man shattered by his past.

Now in total shock himself, Greg's head sprung up. "Jake, what the hell are you doing here?"

"You sick bastard, I trusted you like a brother!" Patrick shouted at the top of his voice, spraying saliva and tears into the morning air.

"My mother was murdered; you knew who did it, and you let my father rot in jail for more than eighteen years?" Jacob's voice trembled with anger as he stood over Patrick, who was still collapsed on the floor, Claire's arms wrapped around him in a desperate attempt at comfort.

Jacob's steps were deliberate as he moved towards Greg, bending down to meet him at eye level. His eyes burnt with fury, the tears flowing faster now, unstoppable. He jabbed Greg hard in the chest with his finger, again and again, as Patrick and Claire looked on in silence, their expressions frozen.

"What kind of heartless bastard are you?" Jacob muttered through clenched teeth. "These were your friends. They *trusted* you."

Greg's voice started to tremble. "Jake, I raised you like my own son. I gave you everything you ever wanted. The best schools, the best holidays. Money, comfort – I gave you everything."

Jacob's response was bitter, cutting like glass. "But none of it was yours to give in the first place, was it?"

Greg blinked in confusion. "What do you mean?"

"I'm not your son; that large pile of cash over there isn't yours; you couldn't afford this boat without stealing," Jacob pointed out.

Greg's voice was small, defensive. "What do you want me to say?"

"We just want the fucking truth!" Jacob exploded, his voice shaking the walls. His face flushed from pale to crimson in an instant, fury radiating from every inch of him. The deck was silent, broken only by the sound of Patrick's sobs and Jacob's heavy footsteps. Claire's breath quickened as she watched the confrontation unfold, her heart pounding.

Jacob turned to Patrick, voice low, calm now but loaded with finality. "You were right. He's never going to tell us. We'll just have to turn him in to the police. Let them figure it out."

Patrick's voice came back in a low growl. "Or we could take this boat out a few miles, tie a weight round his neck, and dump him in the sea." He said it without blinking.

"Now wait a second," Greg stammered, with more panic creeping into his voice. "Let's not get crazy here. I've done bad shit, I know, but we can work this out. What do you want – money?"

Patrick wiped the tears from his face, and a dark energy surged through him as he stood, towering over Greg. His voice dripped with venom. "Do you have any idea what it was like for me? I lose my wife – that pain was enough to rip me apart – then I'm told I'm being jailed for her murder, and my so-called *best friend* runs off with my only child, without a word, without an explanation. Do you know what that did to me? No money can ever replace that."

Greg's head hung low, his own sobs mingling with Patrick's rage. "I'm sorry, I swear… I'm so sorry…"

Patrick's expression hardened, his hands balling into fists. "You're not sorry. You're just sorry you got caught. You didn't care about anyone but yourself. You were gonna live out the rest of your days on this boat, never once thinking about me, or Jacob, or Charlotte, or even your own family. You're only sorry because it's all crashing down on you now."

"Did you kill Sheldon?" Jacob asked, his voice chilling in its calmness.

"I may be a lot of things, but I'm no murderer. He got himself killed."

"You're as good as in my book," Patrick responded, pointing directly at the crumpled mess sat in the chair.

"Are you going to tell us what *really* happened?" Claire said.

Greg sighed and kept his head low as he started to explain how he had been taking money from static bank accounts through a software program Sheldon had written. Charles Faulk, the chairman of the bank, had discovered his pilfering and began extorting him.

He detailed how he had initially gone along with it, thinking he was invincible, but as the demands and risks grew higher, he pushed back with fatal consequences. He had no idea Faulk had connections to the London gangs and could order the killing of an innocent young woman.

"Why Charlotte?" Patrick asked.

"Faulk found out that Charlotte and Isabelle were very close. He decided that if he killed Isabelle, he'd never get a penny out of me again, so he chose Charlotte, close enough to hurt me and keep me toeing the line, but not close enough for me to stop what I was doing."

"You bastard. So because of *your* greed, *her* blood is on *your* hands, and I was the one who suffered for it while you lived the high life with my son," Patrick shouted, lunging at Greg and repeatedly striking him in the face with his tightly clenched fist.

Jacob jumped between them both and pushed Patrick away before surprisingly taking a shot himself, which caught Greg cleanly on the nose, sending blood spiralling across his cheek. Patrick stood at the kitchen area that adjoined the lounge, wiping the blood from his knuckles and staring out at the peaceful sea amid all the stationary boats.

Greg shook his head and continued his ramblings.

"Then, when you asked me to adopt Jake, I thought I could help put right a wrong and try to give him a good life. I swear at that stage I didn't think once about moving abroad at all. But after adopting Jake, I started to become paranoid and couldn't live my life in constant fear of what might come next, so I bolted," he said, with tears running down his face.

He continued, "I had every intention of telling you about your father when you were old enough, Jake, but I was too engrossed in stealing money from the US banks. I didn't want Faulk or Milne to find us, which would have happened if you two were in contact with each other. I did it to protect you, Jake."

"You're all heart, DeWitt," Patrick said, still with his back to the proceedings and with a notably lower tone to his voice, which sounded like defeat.

"How did you figure out Faulk was involved?" Greg asked.

"I didn't figure it out. I was told about a confession Milne made on his deathbed, so I researched him constantly until I came across his connection to Faulk. I recalled the name so researched him and found out he was the chief of your bank so put two and two together. When you are sat on your bed in a cell for twenty-two hours a day, you have a lot of time to cover every last scenario… and the betrayal of your so-called *friends*."

"So what now?" Greg said, trying to brush the dripping blood from his nose against his shoulder.

With the only look of cheer on his face all morning, Patrick replied, "Now, Greg, it's payback time. You're going to jail for the rest of your life."

"Huh, for what? You can't touch me, Reade, and I've got the best lawyers in my corner," Greg replied with a show of arrogance.

"That's where you are wrong," Claire said, walking towards him, "I've recorded your conversation and confession, which I'm sure the police will take great interest in as I've just called them," she said, handing Jacob's phone back to him before bending down to pick up her mobile from underneath his chair that had been recording the whole time.

"You stupid bitch," Greg stated, spitting blood onto the floor in front of her.

"What a charming man you are," Claire remarked.

"And as for your little friend in New York, Hill Copeland, he'll be getting a knock at his door in the next twenty-four hours and is certain to do some jail time when they start searching through his penthouse and his bank accounts," Jacob added.

"Surely we can come to some arrangement. I have millions and millions in cash. Here, take this boat and the three million in that bag," Greg tried to negotiate.

"Not a chance; you didn't allow any of us to do a deal with you when you trampled through our lives," Patrick said, knowing he was about to finally win the war.

Patrick picked up the ownership papers for the boat and passed them to Claire, who placed them inside the holdall full of cash. Jacob started to untie the straps round Greg's legs as Patrick watched on vigilantly, almost willing there to be a struggle.

With his arms still strapped tightly behind his back, Patrick shoved him out of the boat as Claire followed behind, struggling to carry the three million in cash and several banker's drafts in different currencies stuffed in the overweight holdalls.

Walking towards the end of the private jetty, surrounded by water and with his arms tied behind his back, Greg knew he was doomed as he could hear the sirens getting closer and closer to the marina, ready to deal him his fate.

"You and your buddy are going away for a long time, and I'll remind them of the confession from that scumbag Milne. I'd hate to see you go down *just* for fraud," Patrick said, gripping the back of Greg's sweaty neck as hard as he could.

"Get off me, Pat. Faulk is probably in his late seventies by now."

"Doesn't matter how old he is, he's guilty, so he's going to jail too. Feels good to know you'll probably end up in my old cell at Pentonville," Patrick whispered in disgust as three police cars suddenly swarmed the area at the end of the jetty.

Claire handed over her mobile phone, which held the entire conversation, as Jacob and Patrick embraced for the first time in eighteen years.

"I just hope Isabelle can be left out of this terrible mess," Jacob said, his voice heavy with concern.

Patrick started to feel anxious, worrying about the Italian authorities making a complete mess of their investigations. He feared what they would pin on Greg and where he would stand trial. In both the US and the UK, he could be charged with manslaughter, embezzlement, fraud, identity theft, and much more; surely he would be extradited to face trial.

THIRTY-SIX

After a lengthy discussion with the Italian police and an agreement to provide follow-up statements once the Metropolitan Police arrived in Italy, Jacob, Patrick, and Claire walked back to the boat for a final reflection.

The police hadn't mentioned the boat, and neither had the trio, so for the time being, it was not part of the investigation.

They sat and took an hour to calm their nerves and rest before Claire broke the silence.

"At one stage, I really thought you were going to *kill* him, Patrick," she said half-jokingly, lounging on a two-seater sofa on the main deck where most of the drama had unfolded an hour before.

Patrick remained silent, but Jacob replied, "He's not that type of guy." Turning to Patrick, he continued, "Although most people won't believe you after spending all those years in jail, I hope you get to finally clear your name now."

Knowing Sheldon had paid the ultimate price for his stupidity and Greg was finally on his way to where he belonged, Patrick sat on the outdoor deck at the back of the boat, clutching a cold beer from the fridge. With the sun beaming on his face, this moment couldn't have been any further from his years of torture on the inside.

He thought back on the many years, faces, sleepless nights in jail, and the days, months, and years plotting his revenge. His arch-enemy of eighteen years was finally defeated, and soon to follow would be Charles Faulk, who would likely be arrested at his holiday home in the south of France within the next forty-eight hours, facing charges of conspiracy to murder, embezzlement, and fraud.

Senior detectives of the New York Police Department had arrested Hill Copeland within hours of Greg being escorted into the central police station in Naples. The FBI would soon hold meetings with senior executives at the Gold Leaf Bank of Manhattan to explain the elaborate and technologically clever extortion that had been going on for years, urging them to get rid of Verick's systems as soon as possible. Knowing how weak-minded Copeland was, Jacob was certain he would collapse, confess all, and end up in an orange jumpsuit behind bars for at least twelve to fifteen years.

As the water lapped the bow of the boat, Claire walked out onto the deck to join the boys, who were deep in conversation, relief and happiness on their faces. She brought more ice-cold beers and several small bowls of fresh olives and some bread she had rustled up from the fully stocked kitchen on board.

"Might as well enjoy some free hospitality," she quipped, starting to relax.

"I like this girl, Jacob. Where did you find her?" Patrick asked, grinning at Claire as she handed him a beer.

"She served me a beer one evening on my visit to London, would you believe," Jacob replied, admiring her once again as she walked back inside the boat.

"She's a nice girl, Jacob, and to get caught up in all this mess, she must really like you. We couldn't have done it without her," Patrick said.

"I know, she really is something special," he said as Claire walked back towards them.

"You guys are going to need to come and look at this," Claire said, beckoning them both from just inside the boat.

"What is it, Claire?" Jacob said with a slightly concerned look on his face.

She gestured towards a large cupboard nestled at the far end of the lounge, just beneath a grand window that framed a perfect view of the boat's prow cutting through the water.

"I was just looking through the cupboard and found something you're not going to believe. Go and look in there," she said, pushing them both towards the cupboard.

"Is it a dead body?" Patrick said, not sure whether he was joking or not.

Patrick walked towards the cupboard and slowly opened it with a quick, inquisitive glance back towards Claire and Jacob, who was shielding her with his arms round her shoulders.

"Bloody hell." Patrick gasped.

"What is it?" Jacob said, walking towards Patrick.

"Take a look for yourself," he replied with a puzzled look on his face. "That is some serious cash."

Jacob opened the long cupboard door to reveal four shelves packed tightly with big blocks of cash, all shrink-wrapped and bearing the marks of various banks throughout Europe.

"Wow, I thought all the money was in the duffle bag," Jacob said.

"How much do you reckon is there?" Claire asked.

"About the same as the stash Greg had, and that was three million apparently, so easily the same if not more, I reckon," Patrick replied.

"There's a big block of US dollars, all in hundreds, which must be at least a million." Then, glancing into the cupboard further, Jacob noted, "Then we have a big stack of pounds, followed by more dollars and on the bottom shelf, and a huge stack of euros."

"Nice." Claire breathed out quickly.

"What are we going to do with it?" Jacob asked, turning to Patrick.

"Well, we did the right thing and turned in over three million with Greg, and no doubt the police will be back very soon to impound this boat, so I guess it will all go as evidence," Patrick surmised, looking at Jacob and Claire's seemingly disappointed faces.

"Or… we could keep some of it for ourselves." Jacob shrugged, pushing his hands into his pockets with a slightly uncomfortable look on his face.

"True," Claire said, trying not to look too greedy as the thought of paying off all her university debts popped into her mind.

"Well, I reckon I am owed some compensation for the last eighteen years, so it saves me taking on the UK government for getting my case so wrong, doesn't it?" Patrick asked.

"I like your thinking," Jacob said. "Shame we can't keep this nice boat too," he joked.

"Now that would be pushing our luck, and I wouldn't know where to untie the thing, let alone how to drive it," Patrick asked.

"Let's keep half the cash," Jacob responded.

"Yep, okay, but we should give some to charity," Patrick agreed.

"Let's get moving before the cops come back and ruin our little party," Claire instructed.

"Before we go, I would like to firstly thank Jacob for believing in me. I know it couldn't have been easy for you to leave everything based on someone you didn't know even existed, but you did, so thank you, son," Patrick said, shaking Jacob's hand and embracing him.

"You're welcome," Jacob said, raising his bottle of beer half in the air.

"It is going to take some getting used to for both of us, but I hope we can become father and son again in the future."

"Me too," Jacob said as they continued their embrace.

"And to Claire, for all your help over the past few weeks. We really needed a third person to help us out, and

I'm really glad it was you, so thank you," he said, kissing her on the right cheek.

"I needed some excitement in my life, so thank *you*," she replied.

They all slugged down their respective drinks and gazed out at the opulence surrounding them one final time.

Having experienced a life-changing turn of events over the last few months, Jacob sat on the back of the boat, trying to come to terms with the dramatic changes. Not only was he seemingly no longer a university student, but for the time being, it now appeared he would be relaxing for a few months in Europe with his new girlfriend, and a new father too.

"So, Jacob, are you going back to college to finish that degree?" Patrick asked, interrupting his train of thought.

Claire looked at him eagerly, waiting for his answer with a pang in the depths of her stomach that told her she wanted him to stay this side of the Atlantic and start a new life.

Jacob paused for a minute, glaring out at the turquoise horizon, contemplating his response with no real desire to face Isabelle or Matthew back in the US and keen to watch Greg squirm in the courtroom and learn more about his real mother from Patrick.

"I don't think so; I figure I could work my butt off for the next two years and life still wouldn't be this good. Especially with all that cash." Jacob chuckled, pulling on the final dregs of his beer. "Maybe I'll complete my education next year."

"You're damned right there, son; we can't take the boat, so the money will come in handy," Patrick replied.

"Unbelievable, I still can't believe all that cash," Jacob said with amazement, glancing round.

Claire smiled while ensuring the morning sun wasn't burning the pale skin on her exposed arms by moving into the shade.

"What about you, Patrick… Dad, what's next for you?" Jacob asked.

Patrick's face lit up as he heard the word "Dad" come from Jacob's lips for the very first time. It seemed so surreal, but he liked it very much.

"I could get used to you calling me that, Jacob. I finally have the three most important things in my life: freedom, revenge, and you," he replied, rubbing Jacob's left shoulder. "So I don't know, trying to get used to no longer being in jail, taking long walks on the beach, and exploring a bit of Italy would be a nice start. And of course, getting to know my son and his new girlfriend." He smiled.

"Sounds good to me," Jacob replied.

"Me too," Claire added.

"I just wish your mother was here. She loved you with all of her heart and was such a wonderful woman," Patrick said, looking at Jacob, which brought a tear to his eye. He continued, "But I know that if she was here now and this was our boat, there is no way she would have called it *Hidden Treasures*." He laughed.

"What do you think she would have called it then, Dad?" Jacob asked.

Patrick paused for a second, before replying, "*Free Spirit*."

"Nice, very nice." Jacob grinned.

ABOUT THE AUTHOR

Richard C Morgan, a British crime fiction author, is celebrated for his gripping, unconventional plots and fast-paced thrillers. Known for crafting complex scenarios and sharp suspense, his distinctive voice captivates fans of the genre, offering fresh twists and relentless excitement.